P9-DNA-237

Also by JILL CONNER BROWNE

The Sweet Potato Queens' Wedding Planner/Divorce Guide

The Sweet Potato Queens' Field Guide to Men: Every Man I Love Is Either Married, Gay, or Dead

The Sweet Potato Queens' Big-Ass Cookbook (and Financial Planner)

God Save the Sweet Potato Queens

The Sweet Potato Queens' Book of Love

Also by KARIN GILLESPIE

Dollar Daze: The Bottom Dollar Girls in Love

A Dollar Short: The Bottom Dollar Girls Go Hollywood

Bet Your Bottom Dollar: A Bottom Dollar Girls Novel

THE *Sweet Potato Queens'* First Big-Ass Novel

Stuff We Didn't Actually Do, but Could Have, and May Yet

Jill Conner Browne

WITH *Karin Gillespie*

Simon & Schuster

NEW YORK LONDON TORONTO SYDNEY

SIMON & SCHUSTER
Rockefeller Center
1230 Avenue of the Americas
New York, NY 10020

This book is a work of fiction. Names, characters, places, and incidents either are products of the author's imagination or are used fictitiously. Any resemblance to actual events or locales or persons, living or dead, is entirely coincidental.

Copyright © 2007 by SPQ, Inc.
All rights reserved,
including the right of reproduction
in whole or in part in any form.

SIMON & SCHUSTER and colophon are registered trademarks of Simon & Schuster, Inc.

Sweet Potato Queens® is a registered trademark of Jill Conner Browne.

The Sweet Potato Queens® characters, names, titles, logos, and all related indicia are trademarks of Jill Conner Browne and/or SPQ, Inc. All trademarks, trade names, trade dress, logos, or other discriminating marks, and indicia associated with Jill Conner Browne, the Sweet Potato Queens®, SPQ, Inc., and The Sweet Potato Queens' Website, LLC, are owned by Jill Conner Browne and/or SPQ, Inc. and may not be used without expressed prior written permission from Jill Conner Browne and/or SPQ, Inc.

For information about special discounts for bulk purchases, please contact Simon & Schuster Special Sales: 1-800-456-6798 or business@simonandschuster.com.

Designed by Jaime Putorti

Manufactured in the United States of America

10 9 8 7 6 5 4 3 2 1

Library of Congress Cataloging-in-Publication Data
Browne, Jill Conner.
The Sweet Potato Queens' first big-ass novel : stuff we didn't actually do, but could have, and may yet / Jill Conner Browne with Karin Gillespie.
p. cm.
I. Gillespie, Karin. II. Title.
PS3602.R736S94 2007
813'.54—dc22 2006050742
ISBN-13: 978-0-7432-7827-0
ISBN-10: 0-7432-7827-5

ACKNOWLEDGMENTS

First of all, you MUST KNOW that this whole entire book is completely made up. Not a word of it is true and none of the characters exist in real life—except for a couple of 'em. Now, if you've read all my other (totally TRUE) books—and I certainly hope that you have or will now—then you know that I do, in fact, exist and I really am the Boss Queen of the Sweet Potato Queens (real but nothing like the ones in this book)—and so does Malcolm White—founder of Mal's St. Paddy's parade—which also really does exist—co-owner of Hal & Mal's—really and truly our favorite bar/restaurant—in Jackson, Mississippi (also real). And y'all really are invited to come to Jackson the third weekend of each and every March—to be in the parade as The Queen of Whatever You Choose. (For true details, go to www.sweetpotatoqueens.com or e-mail the real me at hrhjill@sweetpotatoqueens.com. I answer all of 'em myowntrueself.) Other than that—it's all utter fiction and my mama is just tickled to death about that.

This book would not have been possible without the talent and willing spirit of Karin Gillespie, for which I am grateful. Y'all need to read all her books—you'll love 'em, I promise.

Nothing in my professional life—and very little in my personal life—would be possible without the talent and maybe not quite so willing spirits (but ultimately willing enough, thank God) of Alycia Jones and Sara Jean Babin.

Jay Sones has gone so far as to move off to Noo York City in his effort to get out of doing stuff for me, but thankfully he has been unsuccessful at this attempt and so I still have him to thank for the fact that the website not only shows up but actually functions properly.

The Cutest Boy in the World—Kyle Jennings—continues to carry me around on a little pillow, night and day, and I am the luckiest woman alive that it apparently pleases him to do this.

Bad Dog Management continues to guard, fetch, beg, wag, bark, and bite as necessary on my behalf—for which I am ever grateful.

Thanks to Damon Lee Fowler—for loving support and the use of his fabulous recipes! His cookbooks are as charming as the man himself.

I have a certain set of friends who read my books mainly to see how I've managed to work their names into the pages. Since this is a work of fiction—it was difficult to impossible—but I want to make sure that they read it anyway so here are their names IN NO PARTICULAR ORDER: Allen Payne, Jeffrey Gross, Cynthia Speetjens, Joe Speetjens, Judy Palmer (who is actually my real-life seester and author of *Southern Fried Divorce*), Melanie Clement, Michael Rubenstein, Elizabeth Jackson, Allison Church, Carol Puckett, Randy Wallace, Katie Dezember, Ellyn Weeks, Joanie Bailey, George Ewing, Smokey Davis, Larry Bouchea, Annelle Primos, John Cartwright, Wilson Wong, Jim Sumner, Laura Lynn, and Angie Gray. My daughter, Bailey, is just praying that she is NOT mentioned.

This is the first of what I hope will be many books with the fine and very attractive folks at Simon & Schuster. They have not only given me a fair-sized sack of money (for which my plastic surgeon adds his thanks to mine), but they have treated me like the Queen I Yam. So far, these are my favorite people there: David Rosenthal, Aileen Boyle, Deb Darrock, Victoria Meyer, Elizabeth Hayes, Deirdre Mueller, Leah Wasielewski, Jackie Seow, Sybil Pincus, Jaime Putorti, Annie Orr, and, of course, my editor—the beautiful, gifted, and glorious Denise Roy. Our future is so bright, we gotta wear rhinestone cat's-eye sunglasses!

With love and thanks to the cutest and best agent in the world—Jenny Bent of Trident Media Group—who had the idea for this book and then nagged me relentlessly to do it.

THE

Sweet Potato Queens' First Big-Ass Novel

Prologue

Is a queen created or is she born that way, making her entrance into the world with her hand curled into a fist as if grasping a teeny-tiny scepter? I can only speak for my ownself, but I think my queenly tendencies began in the womb, where I lolled around, fat and happy, the result of the swiftest, strongest, and cutest sperm to swim upstream and my mama's most excellent eggs.

Before I was a year old, I learned to wave bye-bye but did it in such a way as to be a precursor to The Wave, the gentle, regal hand motion I've perfected after over twenty years of being Boss Queen of the Sweet Potato Queens.

In family photographs there's a self-assured twinkle in my eye. It's the gleam of a queen. If you study baby pictures of Queen Elizabeth, Cher, and RuPaul, you'll see the very same sparkle.

In first grade, the teacher gathered all the little girls in a circle and told us to close our eyes, so she could crown a Valentine Queen.

My body tensed in anticipation. That cardboard crown was mine! I knew it before I squeezed my eyes shut and felt the slight whoosh of air as the teacher placed it on my head.

"Open your eyes!" she said. "Greet your new queen."

Fifteen pairs of eyes stared at me.

"Jill, you look bee-you-ti-ful!" said a classmate, obviously sensing the advantages to basking and cavorting in the golden light surrounding a queen.

"Pleeze let me wear your crown, Jill!" said another. "I'll be your best-est friend in the whole world."

One little girl, a moon-faced child nicknamed Poot for her remarkable talent for emitting genuine pants-rippers at will, making her the envy and idol of all the boys, said, "That's my crown, Jill Conner! I deserve it."

"Now, Poot . . . I mean Patsy," the teacher said. "Be a good sport, ya hear?"

But Poot wasn't having any of it, and the next thing I knew, she'd snatched that crown clean off my head and tore out of the classroom before the teacher could stop her, her little bottom bleating staccato-fashion with every step.

"I'm sorry, Jill," my teacher said. "But don't you worry. We'll get your crown back for you."

"That's okay, Mizz Peabody," I said, with all the noblesse oblige I could muster. "If Poot wants the crown so bad, she can have it."

It *was* a sight to behold, gold-leafed and glittering with sequins and all manner of fake jewels. And I *did* want that crown—bad. I'd like to tell you that even at that tender age, I understood a crown was only a *symbol* of my inner queenliness, but back then the sparklies were all that mattered, and presently, Poot slunk back in and handed it back to me with a muffled apology and a downcast look. I was happy and relieved to have the crown—and attention—returned to me. My time in the spotlight was short-lived, as Poot lowered herself into her desk chair with a blast worthy of a full-grown beer-bellied bean-eating MAN and once again captivated the audience. (No other girl in the first grade could—or aspired to—compete with her in her own game, but we did despair of ever being noticed by the boys as long as Poot was around.)

My first reign as queen officially ended when the dismissal bell rang, but throughout my remaining years in elementary school I continued to be treated like royalty, and as the years passed, Poot came to be more of a Patsy and our friendship grew. Girls clustered around us during recess, and the boys now tried valiantly to get *our* attention as we sashayed across the playground.

"Jill! Patsy! Watch this!" a little boyfriend-in-training would shout out as he attempted a lopsided cartwheel. Then several boys would commence to somersault and walk on their hands. Such show-offs! Since Patsy-formerly-known-as-Poot had evolved, it was the first time I noticed the striking difference between "us" (meaning us girls) and "them."

"You're the type of girl who is going to grow up to be homecoming queen," a plumpish babysitter once said to me, an envious edge in her voice, as I sat on the floor blithely trying to cut out paper dolls.

"Oh, I don't know about that," I said coyly. But inside, I was smugger than a hound with a ham bone.

I did expect my life to be one endless ticker-tape parade, and truly thought it was not an unreasonable aspiration—with me riding in a long, white Cadillac convertible as people cheered and threw roses.

Until I was twelve, I lived in a wood-shingled shotgun house in McComb, about ninety miles away from the not-quite-teeming metropolis of Jackson, Mississippi. During the summer before I turned thirteen, Daddy found a new job as a plant foreman and told the family we'd be moving to the big town.

Mama said that it was a good thing Daddy would be making more money, 'cause I was growing faster than kudzu. Her sewing machine smoked day and night as she tried to keep up with my growth spurt that summer.

We moved to Jackson a week before Labor Day, and we were thrilled to pieces about our new house.

"It's a split-level with a sunken living room," Mama bragged to her friends back in McComb. There was even a wood-paneled rumpus room where Daddy would go to sneak a cigar. I've yet to learn what it really means to Rumpus, but if making out with boys and gossiping with your girlfriends counts, then we Rumpussed pretty good in there over the years.

"Who lives in those big ol' houses?" I asked Daddy when we'd first seen a whole bunch of mansions across Yazoo Road.

"Your brand-new buddies," he said in his teasing way. "You'll be going to school with all kinds of fancy-pants. The children of doctors and lawyers. Maybe even a few Indian chiefs."

At the breakfast table my nose had been deep in my satchel, inhaling the heady smell of spanking-new school supplies.

"You're going to be late for the first day of school," Mama said, snatching dishes off the table. She shooed me out into a sunny and already steamy morning.

I reached the end of our block, and my junior high was to the left. My heart started beating faster when I saw all the kids in the schoolyard, buzzing around like bees. I strutted in the direction of the school, my chin held high.

I don't remember exactly what I was thinking at that moment, but it was probably something like this:

Hello, my darling subjects! Welcome your new queen.

I walked faster (not too fast: Queens don't run unless they're playing kickball, and I certainly didn't want to sweat and mess up my hair, such as it was). I reached the schoolyard just after the first bell rang.

"Hey, you," came a voice from behind me. "Hey you, Beanpole."

I looked over my shoulder to see a short blonde with a freckle-sprinkled nose and a smirk on her face. I later learned her name was Marcy Stevens. I knew she couldn't *possibly* be talking to me.

"Yes, you," she said, pointing a painted pink fingernail in my direction, making no mistake about which beanpole she was addressing. Two other girls were tee-heeing behind their hands.

"Is that dress homemade? Did your mama make it?"

"Yes," I said, protectively touching the collar of my forest-green dress. "My mama made it."

"Is she trying to dress you like the Jolly Green Giant?" Marcy asked. Then she pointed at me and shouted. "Ho! Ho! Ho! Green Giant!"

All the kids within earshot brayed like donkeys. That chin of mine, which only minutes earlier had been pointing heavenward, now dragged the ground.

When I plodded home that afternoon—my shoulders hunched forward so I wouldn't seem so tall—there wasn't a single molecule of queenliness left in my entire soul.

Things went downhill from that day. Hormones started coursing through my blood, wreaking their peculiar havoc.

Nature, it seems, is much kinder to caterpillars than to thirteen-year-old girls. When a caterpillar is busy turning into a butterfly, are other caterpillars allowed to watch, point, and snicker? Nosiree Bob. The caterpillar is locked up tight in its cocoon, and if anyone should come knocking, the caterpillar says, "Go away! Can'tcha see I'm in here metamorphosing?"

But a thirteen-year-old girl is forced to change in plain sight of the whole world. All during junior high, I scuttled around the halls with my hair hanging in my face, hoping nobody would notice how hard I'd been hit with the ugly stick. Whatever glasses I had were always at least two years out of style. I was so skinny, The Titless Wonder, that when I ran I looked like an eggbeater coming down the road. If I turned sideways and stuck out my tongue, I looked like a zipper.

Which brings me back to that question I've been contemplating my entire life: Are queens born, or are they created?

I've come to this conclusion: I think God sprinkles baby girls with queen dust before their big debut in this old world. That magic dust allows them to sparkle for a while, like rays of sunlight bouncing off a lake, until something or someone comes along to dull their sheens. Queen dust is only meant to give a baby girl a little boost in this world. Then she must build on it, until one day she's so strong, she's churning out her very own queen dust and nobody and nothing can stop her.

What follows is the story of the long—and not altogether pretty—road the very first Sweet Potato Queens and I took to learn how to make our very own queen dust.

Me and the other Queens were often slow learners. We made mistakes along the way. We learned slow—but we learned GOOD. It wasn't always pretty, easy, or fun, but I will tell you this: If you come to Jackson, Mississippi, the third weekend in March and see us on parade for St. Paddy, you will know that we finally learned how to sparkle again—and then some. And we can help you sparkle, too.

PART ONE

1968

Chapter 1

In Jackson, the "beautiful people" were separated from the great unwashed by a short strip of blacktop called Yazoo Road. If you lived north of Yazoo, like Marcy Stevens did, you peed champagne and blew your nose in silk. If you lived south—as I did—you peed Dixie Beer and blew your nose in burlap. We were shit. They were Shinola.

By my junior year at Peebles High, I had finished metamorphosing and was looking just fine, pretty even, when I was stopped in my tracks by a veritable vision. There, in the halls of my humble high school, stood the woman who, if God had loved me just a little bit better, would have been reflected in my mirror every morning. The tiny creature had a massive mane of red hair and big breasts. I still covet it all—the tits, the tininess, and oh, mercy, that fabulous hair. All of her wondrous voluptuousness was supported by the most precious little feet you could ever imagine. She was so pretty and delicate I figured she likely hailed from the snooty part of town.

Red hadn't noticed me gaping at her, because she was struggling mightily with her locker. She gave the combination lock one last turn and when she couldn't open it, a not-so-nice word spewed from her Cupid's-bow lips.

"Durn" and "heckfire" were two acceptable cusswords for all but the overly Baptist kids. There was also the frequently used "shoot," which Southerners drawl into the longest word in the English language (shoooooooooooooooooooooooooooot!). And even though most folks knew that "shoot" was just "shit" with eyeglasses on, you could get away with saying it during those innocent times as long as your granny wasn't in the same room.

But little Miss Tiny Feet wasn't "durning," "heckfiring," or even "shooting," she was using the granddaddy of all curse words. (The one we solemnly referred to as the "fire truck" word because it started and ended with the same letters.)

Even a potty-mouth like myself respected the F-word as cussing's fine china: I only drug it out for very special occasions. But Little Miss Redhead was saying it over and over. Maybe she wasn't quite the rich-girl-china-doll she appeared to be at first glance.

As I got closer, I also noticed her clothes were completely wrong. She wore the snob-city uniform of a twin set and skirt, but her sweater was a bit too tight and there were picks and pulls—signs of repeated wearings—in the Banlon knit. The silver-spooners wore perfectly smooth Breck girl flips and pageboys, but her hair was big—too big, and teased up like a red space helmet—and her blush and powder was a half inch thick.

"You new here?" I asked her. "Seems like you're having some trouble."

"I can't get in my fuckin' locker," she said with a sigh when she saw it was just big ol' me. "I tried, and now I'm fucking late for home ec."

"Why don't you let me give it a spin?" I offered, marveling at the fire trucks flying out of her lacquered lips.

She gratefully handed me her combination, and I took to twirling the dial until the locker popped open. Inside was a photo of the Beatles, a smiley-face sticker, and a textbook called *Adventures in Home Living.*

"Thank you so much!" she said. "My name's Tammy."

"I'm Jill."

"Nice to meet you, Jill. I just moved here from Killeen, Texas, and don't know a fuckin' soul." She pointed to a poster on the wall that read "Key Club Information Meeting at 2 p.m. today in the gym. Open to All Interested High School Girls." "I was thinking I'd join this. Are you going?" she asked with what would have been a beautifully executed hair toss except that not a single one of her heavily Aqua-Netted hairs moved from its appointed spot in her coiffure.

"No," I said, quickly.

"Why not?"

"I wouldn't fit in. It's mostly for girls who live north of Yazoo Road," I said, hoping she'd take the hint.

"It says it's 'open to all high school girls,'" Tammy said.

"They have to say that 'cause the first meeting is held on school property, but they're very particular in their membership. Their favorite activity is listing all the people who they WON'T let join."

"Well, lucky for me I *do* live north of Yazoo Road," she said with a smile. "Guess I better get to class. Thanks so much for helping me, Jill."

I'd heard they had some mighty big hair out in Texas, but a

style like Tammy's wouldn't get her into the Key Club. And the first time she let fly with a fire truck, they'd fall over in a faint—or pretend to, anyway.

•

Our lunch group was no Key Club. We ate outside on the steps of the vocational building. I settled beside Mary Bennett, who had a pronounced Southern accent. Where one syllable would do, she used three, saying my name so it came out like "Ji-ay-all." Bennett wasn't Mary's last name. It was part of her first name, kinda like Billie Sue or Betty Lou.

Unlike the rest of our lunchmates, Mary Bennett lived north of Yazoo Road in a sprawling English Tudor, and if it weren't for a *tiny* little problem of hers, she'd be having her pimento cheese sandwich (or "sammich," as we say in the South) and bottle of grape Nehi under the cool shade of a large magnolia tree with the other silver-spooners instead of shuffling around in the red dirt with us.

Back then, when people talked about Mary Bennett—and Lord knows they did—they would say (with an appropriately breathless whisper) that she had a rep-u-tay-shun: She was Fast—which, by the litmus test for Whoredom at Peebles, meant she'd made out with more than five boys and not only KNEW what all the Bases were, it was rumored that she'd been to some of them. Plus, she had pierced ears, and our mamas assured us that "only whores had pierced ears." We all wanted them, naturally.

"Can I help it if I have a strong sex-shu-al appetite?" she'd say, hand pressed against her chest in an aggrieved manner.

I was unwrapping my sandwich when Mary Bennett sniffed her armpits.

"I think I need to have me a little whore's bath."

"Every bath you take's a whore's bath, Mary Bennett," Gerald said, nibbling primly on the last bit of his PB&J on white bread. Gerald had unruly, wiry hair, which he slathered with a combination of hair relaxer and Brylcreem; his attempt at a "hairstyle" looked sorta like Buckwheat's—with a side of scented Crisco.

Mary Bennett grinned. She had one of those lazy, sexy smiles, which opened slowly like a bud blooming in slow-motion photography.

"Aren't you sharp on the uptake this afternoon, Geraldine," she said with a low chuckle. "Maybe you'd like to give me that bath?"

"I'd be honored," Gerald said, blowing her a kiss. He had the longest eyelashes I'd ever seen on a boy.

That was part of their routine. Mary Bennett propositioned Gerald, and Gerald acted as if he were happy to oblige her. Nothing ever came of it.

Mary Bennett opened her sandwich and poked her nose inside. "I'm so tired of pimento cheese. Whatcha got, Jill?"

"BLT," I said, holding my bag close to my body. "But you'll have to kill me for my bacon."

She jerked her head in Patsy's direction. "Hey, Swiss Miss! You got anything edible in that sack?"

"Sardines," Patsy said with a nod. Patsy still possessed the same round face she'd had since we were in first grade, with porcelain skin, enormous blue eyes, and genuine natural-blond hair, courtesy of her Scandinavian mama.

"That ain't nothin' to be braggin' about," Mary Bennett said.

"By the way," Patsy said. "Have you guys—"

"How many times do I have to tell you? It's *y'all.*" Mary Bennett stretched out the last word so it lasted several seconds on her tongue. She cupped her smallish breasts. "Do I look like a guy to you? What in the hell is going on up there in Montana? They think everyone is a guy?"

"My daddy's a guy and he's from Hot Coffee, Mississippi," said Patsy, in a huff. "My MAMA is from MINNESOTA."

"Same damn thing," Mary Bennett said.

"Would you just let the poor girl talk?" Gerald said.

"Chirp away," Mary Bennett said with a bored wave of her hand.

"I was wondering if you guys . . . I mean, *y'all,* have met that new girl, Tammy," Patsy said. "I was going to ask her to have lunch with us tomorrow."

Her "y'all" came out as "yuall," a mispronunciation Mary Bennett acknowledged with an aggravated eye roll.

"I talked to her for a minute," I said, brushing crumbs from my skirt. "Says she just moved here from Texas, and that she lives north of Yazoo Road, but she didn't seem the type."

Gerald rolled up his brown paper sack into a small, neat package and gently placed it in a nearby wire trash can. "Oh, she lives north of Yazoo Road, all right," he said, his lips pursed as if holding in a delicious piece of gossip. "I overheard Marcy talking about it in study hall. I sit right next to her, and get to eavesdrop on all her conversations."

That wasn't hard to believe. Marcy and her friends wouldn't pay any attention to a skinny Jewish boy like Gerald.

"It just so happens that Tammy lives with her mother, who is the new housekeeper for the Peterson family on Marcy's street," Gerald said, in a low, secretive voice. "She lives in the converted carriage house behind the main house."

Tammy was the daughter of a maid? There was no lower ranking in our school's social strata.

"Oh Lord," I said, biting my bottom lip. "She mentioned she

was going to try and join the Key Club today. I tried to discourage her, but she insisted."

My news stunned us into silence, as we all imagined Tammy's dreadful fate.

"She was such a pretty girl," Gerald said solemnly, as if delivering her eulogy.

Mary Bennett fanned her face with a napkin and said, "Those monsters will eat her alive. Her ass is grass."

•

The next day I nearly fell out when I spotted Marcy and Tammy in the hall, walking arm in arm like sisters.

"Hey there, Jill," Tammy said. I noticed she was wearing the same skirt as yesterday, which is a fashion felony with Marcy's crowd. "I wanted to thank you again for opening my locker for me. You saved my life." She turned to Marcy. "Do you and Jill know each other?"

"Of course we do," Marcy said. Her smile was blinding, her hair gleamed platinum, and even the whites of her eyes seemed brighter than the average person's. "Jill and I go back a *long* time, don't we, hunny? We're like this." Marcy crossed her fingers together.

She sounded so sweetly sincere that I was momentarily caught off guard. But when I looked at her face, her blue eyes held a reptilian coldness that seemed to say, "Go ahead and contradict me, little missy. I dare you."

I felt my shoulders slumping, an automatic reaction to being in Marcy's presence.

"Hey, Marcy. Good to see ya," I mumbled.

"I better get to class," Marcy said. She reached out to squeeze Tammy's wrist. "See you at lunch?"

"I'll be there," Tammy said.

I winced at her familiarity with Marcy.

"Everyone is so friendly here," she said to me after Marcy left.

"It does appear that way," I said, not meeting Tammy's eyes.

"And you were wrong about the Key Club. They welcomed me with open arms. If you're interested I could put in a good word for you. There's supposed to be a reception at Marcy's house tomorrow night. Maybe you could come?"

"I have to wash my hair, but thanks."

"Too bad," Tammy said with a pout. "I bet it's going to be a blast."

•

"Now, let me get this straight, y'all only use the first few books of the Bible?" Mary Bennett said, propping her elbows on the Formica table and cocking her head quizzically at Gerald, who was sitting across from her.

"You're not supposed to talk about religion or money or politics in polite company," I said, sliding across the high-backed vinyl booth. Most days after school the four of us gathered at the lunch counter at Brent's Drugstore about three blocks from the school.

"Who says we're in polite company?" Mary Bennett said. She pointed to Patsy, who was sitting next to Gerald. "Look at Swiss Miss over there picking her teeth."

"Oh, sorry," Patsy said, dipping her blond head in embarrassment.

"Anyhoo," Mary Bennett said. "What do y'all do? Read the Bible and ignore the parts you don't like? Does the preacher say, y'all don't read ahead 'cause we don't believe in that mess coming up?"

"It's called the Torah, Mary Bennett," Gerald said patiently. "And it has only the first five books of the Bible. And Jews have rabbis, not preachers."

"You *do* realize that y'all are missing out on the best parts?" Mary Bennett said, wagging a finger at him. "The Christmas story, Sermon on the Mount, and getting saved."

"Jews don't get saved," Gerald said, bemusedly shaking his head. "We don't believe in an afterlife."

Mary Bennett's mouth dropped wide open. "How does your rabbi get y'all to do anything without threatening you with eternal damnation? I bet the collection plate is flat-out empty come Sunday morning."

"Friday night. That's when we have our services."

"Crazy," Mary Bennett said, twirling a finger beside her temple. "What kind of church was it your mama went to up there in Michigan, Swiss Miss?"

"Minnesota," Patsy corrected. "And Mama was Lutheran. They didn't have a Lutheran church in Hot Coffee and Daddy was brought up Baptist, but the only church within walking distance of their first house was Presbyterian, so apparently we were predestined to be the Frozen Chosen."

Mary Bennett's brow bunched. "Lutheran—is that the one with snakes?"

A weary-looking waitress with a messy topknot of hair sidled up to us, pencil poised over a pad. "What'll y'all have?"

"A Big Orange for me," Patsy said, handing the waitress the plastic menu.

"We're out of orange," the waitress said.

"Oh," Patsy said in a disappointed voice. "What other kind of pop do you have?"

"Did you just say *pot*, missy?" the waitress said, raising an accusing eyebrow.

"Oh for pity sakes, just bring her a Co-Cola," Mary Bennett said. She pointed at Patsy and whispered to the waitress. "Her mama's a Yankee. 'Pop' is what they call Co-Cola up there in Milwaukee. God only knows why."

The rest of us gave our orders for homemade lemonade or milk shakes and burgers; then I told them about how Tammy had been invited to a Key Club reception at Marcy's house.

"What do you suppose is going on?" I said, directing my question to Gerald. If anyone knew the dirt, he would.

"Nothing good, that's for sure," Gerald said, shaking his head. "They were all gathered around Marcy's locker, whispering and giggling before study hall. I was only able to catch a snippet. Marcy said something like, 'Don't worry, I made sure Mother would be out of the house tomorrow night.'"

"I'll bet she's talking about the reception," I said. "And obviously, she doesn't want her mama to know about the horrible things they've got planned for Tammy."

"I don't know why we're all worked up about this Tammy person," Mary Bennett said. "Who is she to us, anyway?"

"I like her," Patsy said, her normally placid forehead rumpled. "It frosts my butt that those girls want to be mean to her."

Mary Bennett's nostrils quivered at the blatantly Yankee "frost my butt" expression. In Mississippi, one's hindquarters would get "chapped"—it's rare we get a frost on the punkins, let alone our asses.

The waitress plunked our drinks down on the table.

"She *is* really nice," I said. "Our kind of people, if you know what I mean."

"Well, good gravy, if you're so wound up over her, just tell her not to go to that stupid reception," Mary Bennett said, throwing her hands out, palms up. "What could be simpler?"

"Yeah, Jill." Gerald shook his straw loose from its paper wrapper. "You're the closest to her, why don't *you* explain to her the social food chain around here?"

Three pairs of eyes looked at me expectantly.

"Me?" I said, pointing at my chest. "What if she doesn't listen to me?"

"Then get strong with the girl," Mary Bennett said, leaning forward. "Have a come-to-Jesus meeting with her. Tell her Marcy and the rest of them never hang out with the hired help unless they want someone to clean up their messes."

"I just hate to hurt her feelings," I said, a knot of dread forming in my throat.

"Just remember," Gerald said. "Whatever you say to her will feel like a mosquito bite compared to what Marcy and those other haints will do to her if she goes to that reception."

All of them were staring me down so hard I knew I couldn't refuse. The trouble was, I wasn't yet accustomed to shifting the direction of my own life, much less anybody else's. (This would, of course, change, and now I'm quite comfortable directing others' lives.)

"Okay," I said, with a sigh. "I'll talk to her before tomorrow night."

•

The next day I tried to catch Tammy, but she was like a new cult inductee constantly surrounded by its members. Finally, I saw her dart into the girls' restroom just before last period. I followed her and was hit in the face by a blue shelf of smoke. Three sophomore girls were passing around a Marlboro Red. Tammy was at the mirror, her mouth a round O as she applied pink lipstick.

"You hot-boxed the hell out of this thing," said a girl with hair the color of bright brass from an overdose of Summer Blonde as she pinched the burning cigarette between her fingers.

The bell rang and she tossed the butt into the sink, where it made a *sssss* sound. The smokers all scattered, and Tammy smacked her lips together and turned away from the mirror.

"Hey, Jill," she said. "Whatcha doing?"

I snuck a glance behind me to make sure none of the Key Club bitches were around and whispered, "I have to talk to you."

"I'm going to be late for P.E.," she said, pointing to her wristwatch.

"This is your first week here. You can pretend you got lost. Coach Ryan won't mark you tardy." I head-gestured to a corner of the restroom near a broken Kotex dispenser. "This is important."

"If you say so," Tammy said, a questioning look in her eye. She stood under a scrawl of graffiti that said "Mary Bennett is easy." The handwriting on the pale green cinder block looked suspiciously like Mary Bennett's.

"Look," I said nervously, pushing my glasses up on my nose. "You shouldn't go to that reception tonight."

"Why?" Tammy said, with mild curiosity.

"You shouldn't go is all," I said. "You gotta trust me on this."

She paused a moment, a look of disappointment in her eyes. "Marcy warned me you might say something like that. She said the two of you had a falling-out in fifth grade, and although she's apologized to you profusely, you've continued to hold a grudge."

"Tammy," I said, measuring my words carefully, "she's lying."

"She said you'd say that, too," Tammy said, a pained expression on her face.

Danged if that Marcy hadn't covered all the bases. I didn't think there was a thing I could say to stop Tammy from going to that reception.

"Does 'Hang on, Sloopy' mean *nothing* to you?" I said, bumping my hip on the sink as I awkwardly turned away from her. "You know—how she lived on the very bad side of town and everybody, yeah, tried to put her down?" Willfully blank, she looked at me. I gave up. "Okay. Fine. Have a good time."

"I could speak to Marcy. She and I are getting to be good buddies," she said, taking a step toward me. "Maybe the two of you can patch things up?"

Her expression was so earnest I had to look away. I weakly shook my head and then hitched my purse higher on my shoulder. Just before I pushed open the door I heard her call out, "I hope one day all of us can be friends."

Chapter 2

Friday was pep-rally day. I spotted Mary Bennett at the top of the bleachers—our usual spot, underneath the scoreboard. She held a pen and a notebook, and kept staring into the crowd of students. She'd scribble something, and then gaze out again.

"What are you doing?" I asked as I planted my behind beside hers.

"Just keeping a little tally," she said, brightly. I looked over her shoulder and saw a series of two-digit numbers on her pad. There were stars beside some of the numbers and frowny faces beside others.

"Ooooh! Thirty-eight," she said, pointing at a player with a thirty-eight on his jersey. "Although *sixty-nine* would have been a better number for him," she said with a wink.

"So it's that kind of list," I said, playing along, although the discussion of Mary Bennett's "extracurricular" activities always made me uncomfortable, mainly because I was a total virgin and therefore didn't have a whole lot to say about sex.

"All in the name of school spirit," she said with a cackle. "If there is anything sexier than a football player's butt, I'd like to see it."

Patsy was ascending the bleachers, wearing a Minnesota Vikings sweater.

"Good Lawd," Mary Bennett said. "Remind me to get that girl a sweater from Ole Miss."

"At least she got the school colors right," I remarked.

"Uff dah," Patsy said as she sat next to me. "What a climb, eh?"

"Someone is going to 'uff' your 'dah' if you don't quit talking like that," Mary Bennett said, looking up from her notebook. "Repeat after me. Say, 'I swanee that was a haul.' "

"Swanee?" Patsy said.

"It means 'I swear.' You say it a few times, and no one will ever guess you're a damn Yankee."

"You know, Mary Bennett, I am *not* a Yankee," Patsy said, raising her voice to be heard over the crowd. "I may have been born up there but that's ALL, and besides, Minnesota wasn't even a state during the Civil War."

"It wasn't? You sure about that?" Mary Bennett said, a puzzled look on her face. " 'Cause I coulda swore Massachusetts was right in the thick of things."

"It's not Massachusetts," Patsy said. "It's—"

"Looky, there's Geraldine," Mary Bennett interrupted. "Come on up here, darlin'!"

Gerald stood at the foot of the bleachers and shook his head. "Y'all get down here!" he mouthed. "It's an emergency."

The three of us rose from our seats and zigzagged our way

down until we reached Gerald, standing with arms crossed and his weight on his left leg.

"What's wrong?" Mary Bennett said as she reached him. "You want to sit somewhere else?"

"No," Gerald said. His mouth was a thin, serious line, and he was tapping his right foot rapidly as if bursting with pent-up energy. "We need to talk. Let's sneak out different exits and meet at the usual spot."

"Done," Mary Bennett said immediately, obviously alarmed by Gerald's uncharacteristically agitated state. She tucked her notebook under her arm and sauntered to the south exit. Patsy headed to the east exit and Gerald went west. That left the north exit for me, which unfortunately was guarded by Mr. Blalock, the school principal.

"Jill, where do you think you're going?" Mr. Blalock asked, blocking my way as I tried to slink past him.

I arranged my features into an expression of acute embarrassment. "Omigawd, Mr. Blalock, I'm so embarrassed!"

"What is it, Jill? What's wrong?" he said. He was dark and intense-looking, like Raymond Burr playing Perry Mason.

"I can't begin to say it." I covered my face with my hands. "It's *mortifying*."

"Just tell me," he said, making an effort to be patient.

"Female troubles," I mouthed, and then squeezed my eyes shut as if I couldn't bear to see the impact my words would have upon him.

"Well, then, you just . . . uh . . . go right ahead and . . . uh . . . take care of that."

"Okay, Mr. Blalock," I said meekly as I slipped into the hall outside the gym. At my high school, "female troubles" was a magic password. If used judiciously, it could get you out of any activity and most trouble.

I scurried out a side entrance and headed to the vocational building. It was still warm, but there was a whisper of fall in the air.

My friends were situated in their usual places on the steps. Mary Bennett was smoking a cigarette, blowing fluffy doughnuts of white that drifted across the sky. Gerald was pacing in front of her, hands on his hips, thumbs forward, and Patsy was knotting her pale, wispy hair into a skinny single braid, thin as a ribbon.

"Finally," Gerald said when he spotted me, stopping his pacing. "Have you seen Tammy today?" There was a note of accusation in his voice.

"No," I said, swallowing nervously. I'd failed to save her from the Key Club massacre, and now I was going to have to admit it. I glanced at Patsy. "Was she in your English class?"

"A no-show," she said. "And we had a big assignment due today."

Gerald snapped his fingers at Mary Bennett until she surrendered her cigarette to him, and then he took a long, deep drag.

"Well," he said, blowing out a great cloud of smoke. "After what Marcy did to her, I'm not at all surprised."

The air crackled with electricity. Mary Bennett, Patsy, and I swapped a charged look and Mary Bennett's arms shot out, her fingers grabbing at Gerald's plaid pants legs, which were paired with a white patent leather belt. Very unfortunate fashion statement.

"You know what happened?" I demanded.

Gerald nodded slowly, like a man carrying an unbearable burden. "The whole horrifying story. Every nasty detail."

Mary Bennett's eyebrows arched ever so slowly upward. In a low, languorous voice, she said, "Do tell."

"It's all they could talk about during study hall," Gerald said, his eyes narrowing as he looked at me.

"I *tried* to talk to her," I said helplessly. "I really did. She refused to listen."

Gerald sighed deeply. "I guess she was just doomed from the get-go."

"Could we skip the previews and get to the main attraction?" Mary Bennett said, jiggling her knees with impatience.

Gerald said, "Well . . . it's not the easiest tale to tell. Y'all are just gonna DIE when you hear it." He took a deep breath and began. "Tammy showed up at the Key Club meeting, wearing that very same skirt she'd worn for the last few days. Marcy took one look at her and said, 'Servants enter through the rear.'"

We all gasped. None of us had expected the guillotine to fall so fast.

"That ain't the half of it," Gerald said, holding up his index finger. "Tammy laughed, thinking Marcy was making some kind of joke, but when she tried to take a step into the house, Marcy blocked her path and said, 'Didn't you hear me?' Tammy stood there for a moment, confused, until Marcy winked at her. 'Oh, I see,' Tammy said. 'This must be part of my initiation,' which, of course, is exactly what Marcy wanted her to think, because it would drag out the 'fun' for everyone."

"Assholes," Patsy breathed. Gerald acknowledged the interruption with a sharp look.

"So our poor little Tammy went through the servant's door and was ordered to change into a maid's uniform. They immediately put her through the rich-bitch wringer, making her fetch their drinks, clear away empty plates, and wash the dishes. Finally, after a couple of hours, Marcy rang a silver bell and called the Key Club meeting to order—first piece of business, the admittance of new members, specifically Tammy Myers."

"We can all guess what happened next," Mary Bennett said, stretching out her long legs.

"Do you want to hear this story or not?" Gerald said sternly.

"Sorry, hunny," Mary Bennett said, making a motion of locking her lips and tossing an imaginary key over her shoulder.

"As I was saying," Gerald continued. "Tammy was told to leave the room, so that voting could commence. The members were going to vote by putting poker chips in a bowl. A white chip was a yes, black was no. Several girls yelled out 'good luck' and a few gave Tammy a hug before she left. After a few minutes, they called her back into the room. 'The vote was unanimous,' Marcy announced. They were all beaming at Tammy, so *of course* she thought she'd passed her initiation with flying colors.

"'Tammy Myers,' Marcy said to her. 'After observing you very carefully this evening, and seeing how helpful you were at our party, faithfully completing the lowliest task without complaint, we have come to our decision—Sergeant at Arms, may I have the bowl?' Then Marcy paused a moment for dramatic effect, and looked Tammy directly in the eye. 'Unfortunately, you were a little *too* good at your tasks. You demonstrated a familiarity with menial labor that we found quite disturbing and certainly not the type of quality we're looking for in a Key Club member.' She then lifted the cloth to reveal a glass bowl brimming with black chips. 'Therefore, your application for membership has been unanimously declined.'"

Patsy moaned and clutched her face.

"It gets worse," Gerald said, ominously. "According to Marcy, Tammy was so wigged out, you'da thought it was a bowlful of spiders. Then, and this is the most unbearable part, Tammy looked at Marcy and said, 'I thought you liked me. How could you fake that?' Marcy, of course, didn't skip a beat. She smiled and said, 'I *do* like you, Tammy. You're one of the best maids I've ever had. But that's no surprise, since you come by it naturally.'

Tammy's face turned white and she hightailed it out the front door without another word."

We fell silent. Gerald took a handkerchief out of his back pocket and swabbed his shiny forehead. Then he crouched down and collapsed against the steps as if completely spent.

"Shi-it," I whispered, idly cracking the knuckles of my right hand. "I wish I'd done more to stop her."

"Well, boo-hoo-hoo—that's a real sad story." Mary Bennett brushed off the back of her skirt as she got up. "But I don't know what the hell we're supposed to do about it."

"What about starting our own club?" Patsy asked, her "about" sounding like "aboot." "We could ask Tammy to join. It might make her feel better."

"Club?" Mary Bennett said, with a frown. "What? Are we going to build a fort out of a refrigerator box, and put a homemade sign on the door that says 'No rich bitches allowed'?"

Gerald and I laughed.

"Go on and laugh, but all we ever do is sit around here or Brent's, complaining about our situations," Patsy said, her brow knitted together. "Marcy and her friends might be terrible people, but at least they're making things happen in their lives. They're creating memories. Why shouldn't we?"

All three of us stared at Patsy in surprise. We weren't used to her saying much, prolly because when she did talk, she stuck out like a turd in a punch bowl.

"What sort of things did you have in mind?" I asked cautiously. "I mean, it looks like to me the only 'memories' they're creating are horrible ones for other people—I don't wanna do THAT. I don't WANT to be like THEM."

"Our own parties. Trips. Why don't we forget that we're not the In Crowd and just make our own fun together?" Patsy said.

"Come to think of it," Gerald said, "we *don't* do too many things together like other kids. Why is that, I wonder."

Maybe because we don't really think of each other as friends, I almost said but didn't. It was our outsider status that had brought us together, not common interests or mutual respect.

"Maybe a club isn't such a bad idea," I said. "It could be fun."

"Hold the phone," Mary Bennett said. "The reason we started talking about a club was because we wanted to ask Tammy to join. Who's to say she'll want to fool with us bottom-feeders? She was aiming pretty high with the Key Club."

"Yeah," Patsy said, with a resolute lilt to her chin. "But after her 'initiation' story gets around, she'll have nowhere else to go."

"Except to be a loner," Gerald said. "Let's see, if being a loner is a fate worse than death, would hanging out with US be an even WORSE fate? I mean, look at us—we're not THAT bad, are we?"

"We'll just have to figure out a way to make ourselves and our club irresistible to her," I said.

"How are we going to do that?" Mary Bennett said, her arms crossed in front of her chest. "Give away money at the meetings?"

A germ of a scheme was forming in my mind.

"I've got an idea," I said with a sly little smile. "But I gotta warn you. It's pretty damn crazy."

Chapter 3

"You look so FINE, baby, fine as WINE!" yelled a young man leaning out the window of a passing Camaro.

"I've never felt so adorable," Gerald said, dangling his hand outside Mary Bennett's Chevrolet Impala convertible. Gerald waved and blew a kiss in his direction. "Did you hear that?" he said, waving his hand in front of his face as if he were swooning. "I'm 'fine as wine'!"

"Damn straight you are! But he was talking to ME," Mary Bennett said, peering over the tops of her black cat's-eye sunglasses with rhinestone detailing. We were all wearing them. Mary Bennett had bought each of us a pair at Brent's Drugstore and charged to it her daddy's account. "He never questions the bill," she said. "I don't think he even looks at it. Just writes the check."

"Hey, Red! Wanta go to my place?" someone shouted as he streaked by in a banana-yellow GTO.

"Get the tag number of that car!" Mary Bennett shouted. Then she lovingly patted her long, curly red locks. "Who says 'blondes have more fun'?"

We were all wearing matching long fiery red wigs (from the Ann-Margret collection) newly purchased from Sassy Styles in downtown Jackson.

"I've never had so much hair," Patsy said, tossing it all around her shoulders. We were all fine-haired people (except for Gerald, whose abundant mane was too frizzy and uncontrollable to do him much good). Naturally, we couldn't stop touching, flipping, and bouncing our luscious locks.

The Beach Boys' "Good Vibrations" was playing on the radio, and we were all singing along and blowing kisses and waving to passersby.

"It's that house," Gerald said, pointing to a white Greek Revival mansion set back on a hill. "The little road to the left goes to the cottage in back."

"I hope this works," Patsy said, checking her reflection in a compact mirror as Mary Bennett made the turn.

"How can it not?" I said, taking a swig from my bottle of Coke.

Mary Bennett parked in the gravel patch in front of a white structure that wasn't much bigger than a band's tour bus. It was small but welcoming, with shrubs and flowers that repeated the grand landscaping of the mansion, yet situated as it was in back of Jackson's equivalent of a castle—well, one couldn't help but feel the disparity, which I suppose was the point.

"I hope she's home," Gerald said, staring intently at the house, looking for signs of life.

"Somebody's in there," Mary Bennett said. "I saw a curtain twitch."

None of us made a move to get out of the car.

"I'll go," I said, my voice thin and uncertain, even to my own ears. I glanced in the visor mirror, expecting to see my familiar timid self, but the sunglasses and red hair made me look like another person entirely.

"Here goes nothing," I said, exiting the car and swinging my hips as I strutted. Mary Bennett yelled out, "Shake it, baby! Don't break it!" which prompted me to exaggerate my walk even more.

I knocked on the screen door, straining to hear anything inside.

"Come on out, Tammy," I coaxed. "We know you're in there."

Still no response. I was about to knock again, when I heard a slight rustling. Then the door cracked open.

"Can I help you?" said a faint voice.

"Tammy?"

"Yes?" The door opened a little wider.

"It's me—Jill." I lowered my sunglasses. "From school."

"Jill?" Tammy said. Her face was bare of cosmetics and her eyes were puffy, but she still looked very pretty. "Why are you here? Wearing *that* thing?" She pointed to my wig.

My plan, skimpy as it was, had been to flatter her into joining our little group, hence the wigs. They were meant to resemble her own big, beautiful tresses. It seemed like a fun (although somewhat silly) plan when I'd concocted it, but now, standing in front of her, I wasn't so sure.

"I'm here to invite you to join a very exclusive society," I said, trying to make my voice sound as confident as possible. "It's called the Tammy Club."

"What?" Tammy said. She opened the door all the way and stepped outside, blinking like a mole just emerging from its hole.

The others had gotten out of the car and were now standing behind me.

"We're all charter members," I said. "It's called the Tammy Club because all of its members are named Tammy. That's Tammy Gerald and Tammy Patsy from your English class and Tammy Mary Bennett. And I'm Tammy Jill."

The others waved, flipped their hair, blew kisses, and pranced around like show ponies. They were truly getting into the spirit of things.

"Oh, and that's the Tammymobile," I said, pointing to Mary Bennett's car, which had a banner affixed to the side that said OFFICIAL TAMMY CLUB VEHICLE.

"I don't understand," Tammy said, shaking her head in confusion. "Why would anyone have a group called the Tammy Club?"

"Because you're fabulous and it's named after you!" I said.

"I'm not fabulous," she said softly, shaking her head.

"Yes, you are," I insisted. "First of all, you have big, fat, beautiful hair. I, personally, would murder my own mother for such hair!"

"You're kidding me, right?" Tammy said, looking even more perplexed.

"And it's also because your name is Tammy," Gerald chimed in. "Tammy is the *best* name in the universe. Everyone knows God didn't make any ugly Tammys. They all have pert noses, small feet, and tiny waists."

"That's right, hunny," Mary Bennett drawled. "And ever since we've been wearing this big hair and calling ourselves Tammy, we've been as happy as pigs in the sunshine. Nobody should be more giddy than you, because you, lucky girl, get to be Tammy and have this amazing hair all the time!"

"I love being Tammy," Patsy said, with such a vigorous hair toss I was surprised she didn't get whiplash. "Tammy isn't just a name, and it's not a wig and sunglasses, it's a state of mind."

I decided Patsy's simple statement would define our group from that moment on.

"So, how about it, Tammy?" I said, brushing some excess bangs from my face. My entire head was sweating profusely from the wig. "You wanna come play with us?"

Chapter 4

"Don't get me wrong," Mary Bennett said. "I like driving around getting honked at by total strangers, but there needs to be more to our organization than that."

We were all plopped down in beanbags in Mary Bennett's enormous rec room discussing the purpose of the Tammy Club. They had a Ping-Pong table, bumper pool, and a lit-up Elvis pinball machine. The pine-paneled walls were covered with posters of Tom Jones, who was Mary Bennett's current heartthrob.

"Are you saying the Tammys should plan to be more civic-minded?" Patsy asked, sliding out a pencil from behind her ear. She'd taken on the role of club secretary. "Maybe we should raise money for charity by holding bake sales or car washes."

"No!" was the very vocal and very unanimous answer from the rest of us.

"I think Mary Bennett means we should come up with other stuff we'd like to do together—you know—'activities,'" I said.

"Right," Mary Bennett said. "So long as those 'activities' are fun. That should be our official club motto: 'If it ain't fun, we ain't doin' it.' Sound good to you?"

"Perfect!" Gerald said, and the rest of us murmured our agreement. Patsy recorded the motto in her spiral notebook.

"Suggestions, anyone?" I asked.

"Well, I can think of *one* thing in particular, but we'd have to ship in a few extra fellows," Mary Bennett said with a grin. "Unless Geraldine thinks he's up to the job."

"I'd have to eat my Wheaties before the meetings," Gerald giggled.

"Polka's fun," Patsy offered.

"Good suggestion, Swiss Miss," Mary Bennett said. "I'm particularly fond of strip poker."

Patsy frowned. "I didn't say poker, I said—"

"Food," Tammy said softly.

"That's the best idea yet," Mary Bennett said, lighting a cigarette. "We should open and close all meetings with the appropriate snack foods."

"Do your parents let you smoke?" Tammy asked with wide eyes.

"*Parent,*" Mary Bennett said, tapping an ash. "All I have is my daddy, and he's hardly ever home. That's why we should have all our meetings here. The housekeeper's off on Saturdays, and we'll have the whole joint to ourselves."

"Far out," Gerald said.

"I was thinking out loud when I mentioned food," Tammy said, rubbing her stomach. "Y'all picked me up before I had lunch."

"Well, food is a helluva thought," I said, feeling my own

stomach rumble. "We should each bring something to eat at our meetings. I'm partial to anything fried."

"I'll bring something sweet," Tammy said, licking her lips.

"I'll do salty," Mary Bennett said, and then she pointed a finger at Patsy. "Don't you be coming 'round here with those smelly little fish, Swiss Miss. Now, lemme think. We've got sweet, salty, and fried. Why do I feel like an important food group is missing?"

"Au gratin," I said.

"Egg-zactly!" Mary Bennett said. "Patsy, that is perfect for you—you are now in charge of all cheese-related foods."

"And I'll bring kosher," Gerald said with a nod.

"I hope that's some kind of sausage," Mary Bennett said.

"Kosher refers to Jewish dietary laws," Patsy explained. "That means Gerald can't eat anything with pork."

"Oh, hunny," Mary Bennett said, patting his leg sympathetically. "You really ought to convert to Baptist. We don't allow drinkin' or dancin', but we sho'nuff do like to eat us some pig."

•

Our Tammy Club meetings fell into familiar patterns. First we'd eat, and then we'd loll about planning what we were going to do the rest of the day. Shopping, swimming (in Mary Bennett's heated pool), gossiping, watching old movies, and cruising around town were some of our favorite pastimes. A Pageant Party was a must whenever a beauty pageant was on TV—Miss America, Miss Mississippi, or our favorite, Miss Hospitality. This was our favorite because instead of the fairly degrading "talent" competition in the other pageants, aspiring Miss Hospitalities had to dress as something representing the major industry in the county they were representing. So it was not unusual to see nearly grown-up women who *clearly* should have had more pride, if not sense, dressed as bolls of cotton, reclining chairs, or small aircraft. We'd call an emergency Tammy Club meeting so we could watch the pageant together and ridicule the contestants.

The red wigs ended up being too cumbersome (and attracted far too much negative attention in Gerald's case), so we wore them only when riding around in the convertible. We still donned our cat's-eyes whenever we felt a need to look mysterious—and trust me, five big ol' people wedged up in a car, wearing the same identical fancy sunglasses, did pose a mystery to any and all observers.

When Homecoming came along, I suggested we have our own float in the parade.

"Other clubs do it. Why shouldn't we?" I said at one of our meetings.

"That might be tricky," Tammy said. "The football team sponsors the parade, and they have to approve all the floats. We're not an official school club."

"Don't you worry your pretty little head 'bout *that*," Mary Bennett said, batting her eyelashes. "I have *ways* of persuading the football team."

True to her word, not only were we approved, but one of the players lent us a flatbed trailer, and a whole slew of them helped us build the float. They also brought the entire Tammy Club lunch from The Dog 'n' Suds.

"Man, those guys are helpful," I said to Mary Bennett as we were putting the final touches on the float an hour before the parade. "Did you pay them?"

"Nope," she said coyly. "They're motivated by the prospect of *other* rewards."

"Such as what, exactly?" I asked nervously.

"I just made them all a little promise that made them all

QUITE happy—and very willing to WORK, as you have seen. That's all you need to know right now—the float is perfect—you just leave that other stuff to me," Mary Bennett said with a sly grin and a wink.

I'd suggested we appear as the Tammy Queens in the parade—sort of a spoof of the Homecoming Court. All of us, except for Gerald, planned to wear old bridesmaid and prom dresses that Patsy embellished with sequins and feathers. Gerald was to wear a baby blue tuxedo and matching ruffledy shirt and SHOES, if you please, that he'd bought at a thrift shop.

A few minutes before the parade's start, Patsy was finishing up painting the "Tammy Queens" banner when Gerald accidentally jostled her elbow.

"Sorry, Patsy," he said, studying the banner. "Now the sign looks like it says 'Yammy Queens.'"

"Too late to fix it," I said, tucking a stray bra strap into my pink chiffon dress. A couple of football players affixed the banner to the float, and then helped us all get aboard. One of the players got behind the wheel of the truck towing the float.

"Those boys are leering at me," Patsy said, patting her wig as she took her place on the float. "Maybe my dress is too tight."

"I know what you mean," Tammy said. "Their eyes were boring a hole clean through me."

"It prolly had a little something to do with what I promised 'em," Mary Bennett said, pulling a long, white glove up her raised arm.

"The usual reward, I suppose?" Gerald said with a knowing smile.

"Well, I sweetened the pot juuuusssst a weeee little bit," Mary Bennett said, pinching her fingers together. The band had started, a signal for the parade line to begin. "I promised that all the Tammy Queens would give 'em blow jobs after the parade."

"What?" Gerald said, holding his belly as if he'd been punched. The rest of us exchanged horrified glances.

"Excepting Gerald, of course," Mary Bennett said. She grinned proudly. "Pretty effective, wouldn't you say?" with a palms-up swoop of her arms at the float and us.

"Are you out of your fuckin' mind!?" I exclaimed.

"Y'all put your eyeballs back in their sockets," Mary Bennett said evenly. "Them boys ain't ever gon' collect. Trust me. I have tons of experience with this kind of thing."

"Ummm, excuse me," Patsy said, a bewildered look on her face. "But what *is* a blow job?"

The truck suddenly jerked forward, and we were on our way.

"Don't you worry about that, Swiss Miss," Mary Bennett said. "Just smile pretty and wave your little Yankee heart out."

I can't remember ever having a better time than I did on that first float. We pranced, waved, and blew kisses. The way the crowd waved back and carried on over us, you'da thought we were gen-u-wine Miss Americas on that float. I hadn't been so full of myself since I was the first-grade Valentine Queen.

I looked across the float at my good friend Patsy and recalled our initial encounter over that first-grade crown—and her Peculiar Prowess way back then. She caught me looking at her and when I burst out laughing, she gave me a look that promised death if I told what I was thinking but joined my belly laugh—which we both declined to explain to the other Queens.

After the parade, Darla Hopkins, a bespectacled girl from the school paper, approached us saying she wanted a photo and an interview. We were only too happy to oblige and posed on the float.

"Y'all caused quite a stir," she said, after snapping a picture. "I think you gave the Homecoming Court a run for their money.

Tell me, how did you come up with your name, the Sweet Potato Queens?"

"What?" Mary Bennett said, a confused look crossing her face. "That's not what we're called."

"But I thought . . ." Darla glanced at the banner on our float. "You're right. I misunderstood. You're the *Yammy* Queens."

"That's *still* not right," Tammy said. "You see, Patsy messed up the banner—"

"Wait a minute. I *like* the sound of the Sweet Potato Queens. After all, we *are* as sweet as tea," I said.

Patsy nodded. "And we sure put away a lot of potatoes."

"I think it's time for a change," I said, "especially since we were such a big hit. As a matter of fact—"

"What in the hell do y'all think you were doing?" a red-faced Marcy Stevens said, flouncing over to our float in a long, formal white gown. She was the current Homecoming Queen, naturally. Her tiara was askew on her blond head.

"Excuse me," Darla said to Marcy. "I'm trying to conduct an interview here, and—"

"Look at the five of you," Marcy spat. "You've got a giant, a slut, a pansy, a maid, and a damn Yankee. What kind of Queens could you possibly be?"

Boy hidee. Marcy was ugly when she was mad. I couldn't believe how insignificant and puny she looked from my perch on the float. I looked that little hussy straight in the eye and with a regal sweep of my arm said, "We are the Sweet Potato Queens, and YOU are NOT!"

To my utter and everlasting surprise, Patsy stepped over to the float railing and smiled down at Marcy and said in a voice as sweet and Southern as you please, "You know, Marcy, hunny, little girls who look like YOU gen'lly have to be NICE—you ain't NEARLY good-lookin' enough to be such a fuckin' bitch." And then, as if to punctuate it, Patsy turned her back to Marcy and let one fly—the magnificent Poot had returned.

There was just the briefest moment of stunned silence as we all processed what had just happened, and then I'd have to say it was your basic pandemonium after that. We all blew Coke out our noses (which also seemed aimed at the hapless yet despicable Marcy), laughing until I thought we would surely pee our pants—and prolly THAT would end up on Marcy, too. She appeared to levitate for a split second, making unintelligible spluttering noises, and then she attempted to whirl around to leave in a big huff but of course she forgot she had on that big white dress. It didn't whirl quite as fast as she did, so she ended up practically hog-tied in her own homecoming gown and was flailing around in the grass trying without success to free herself, yowling in fury.

Gerald, whose mama raised him to be a gentleman always, even to mean-ass bitches like the one we saw writhing beneath us, jumped down from the float to help her. We thought we were gonna have to rescue HIM from HER. She reached out and grabbed one of his pant legs and hand-over-handed herself up off the ground, snarling like a crazed beast all the way. It looked like she might do him great bodily harm until she realized that Darla was focusing her camera on the Homecoming Queen in all her somewhat sweaty glory. With a venomous look and a parting snarl, she stomped away.

Then Darla looked up at us as if we really were Royalty. She even made a little curtsy as she asked if we would please, please, please—she would do ANYTHING—just let her be a Sweet Potato Queen. And just like that—a dynasty was born.

•

The Queens spent the next week or so on high alert, not sure which we were more afraid of: that Marcy Stevens would succeed in having us maimed or murdered, or that one of the football players was gonna try to "collect" on Mary Bennett's Promise. But Marcy gave us the wide and respectful berth we deserved (possibly because we made Darla ask Marcy, in a sweet, innocent voice, if she would like prints of the photos Darla had taken of her with the Sweet Potato Queens—just to let her know we Had Proof). And the football players followed us around in worshipful adoration—just in case there was even a Chance, I suppose.

•

The rest of our junior and senior years of high school passed faster than shit through a goose. Before I knew it, it was the last day of school, and I was sitting in the auditorium watching my friends pick up a slew of awards. Tammy got a certificate for being the lead soloist in the choir; Mary Bennett collected a trophy for best actress for her performance as Katherine in the school's production of *The Taming of the Shrew*. (She managed to pull off Shakespeare without a trace of a Southern accent, making us all wonder if her normal drawl wasn't exaggerated just a bit.)

Our darling Gerald received a huge loving cup for being the captain of the Quiz Bowl team, and Patsy was awarded several ribbons for her oil paintings—one a self-portrait in full Sweet Potato Queen regalia.

During lunch that day we all gathered under a big live oak (we'd long since abandoned the steps of the vocational building), and everyone was passing around their awards to a chorus of oohs and ahhs.

"Don't be modest, Jill," Mary Bennett said, holding her hand out. "Show us what you got."

"They don't hand out any kind of trophy or plaque for being

'Wittiest' and 'Class Favorite,'" I said softly. "They just call out your name—nothing to hang on your wall or put on your résumé. What good is it gonna do me that a bunch of kids liked me 'cause I could make 'em laugh? And that D I got in Algebra II—which was a GIFT, by the way, I shoulda flunked—means no college for me."

"You drop that crap right now, Jill," Mary Bennett said, shaking her head. "Who the hell cares about a bunch of dinky-ass dust-catchers from the trophy shop? You have so many other things going for you."

I tugged at the collar of my blouse. "Like what, for instance?"

All the Queens became unnaturally quiet. Nobody looked me in the eye. Why had I asked such an asinine question?

"You're a whiz at motivating people," Tammy said, her expression relieved because she'd finally come up with something. "You're the one who encouraged me to join the choir. You convinced Mary Bennett to try out for the school play, and persuaded Patsy to enter all those art shows."

"Remember how you staged a pep rally before my big Quiz Bowl meet?" Gerald said, patting his loving cup. "You even made me a breakaway poster to run through. I get misty-eyed just thinking about it."

"You're a born leader," Patsy said, nibbling on a blade of grass. "If the Queens had a president, you'd be it."

"And you're a helluva cook," Mary Bennett added. "Culinary history was made when you invented Pig Candy. Who else would have had the genius to combine bacon, brown sugar, and pecans?"

"Don't forget about Chocolate Stuff," Gerald said, smacking his lips. "We musta gone through a hundred pans of it in the last two years."

"I'm disappointed," I said, tossing about my hair, which was limper than usual from the June heat. "Not one of you assholes has said a word about my devastating beauty."

They all laughed. I'd *hoped* to lighten up the moment so they wouldn't guess how down I really was. All the Queens had plans to set the world on fire after graduation. Mary Bennett was moving to New York to conquer Broadway; Tammy was going to Nashville to be a country-and-western singer; Gerald had been accepted at Baylor to major in premed; and Patsy was moving to Atlanta, enrolled in art school. As for me, I was barely going to make a spark. I planned to stay in Jackson, and I'd found a pissy little temporary job as a receptionist at the Quick Weight-Loss Clinic. It was the only job I could get where I didn't have to wear a hair net.

I must have been absent when God handed out talents. And clearly that was the same day he gave out titties and big hair.

•

"Diamond bracelet, pearl necklace," Mary Bennett said, with a yawn, as she sorted through her graduation gifts at the kitchen table. "Those are the highlights—Daddy wanted to get me a new car, but I'm not ready to give up the Tammymobile."

"That's a hard act to follow," I said. "Makes my Timex and gen-u-wine leather wallet seem kind of puny."

Mary Bennett's father regularly brought her exquisite gifts, most of which she'd carelessly toss into a wooden chest and shove under the bed.

"What's your haul?" Mary Bennett said to Gerald, who was opening envelopes.

"Not too shabby," Gerald said with a grin. "I'm already at five hundred dollars, and I still haven't opened the cards from the Goldbergs or my Aunt Bernice and Uncle Irving."

"What's in here?" Mary Bennett said, picking up a package and shaking it next to her ear.

"I don't know. My pop handed it to me after the graduation ceremony," Gerald said. "You can open it if you want."

"Oh, goody!" Mary Bennett said. She stared at the object in her hands. "Well, this is interesting."

It was a book called *How to Flirt with Chicks*.

Gerald blushed. "My father's worried that I never have any girlfriends."

"Who does he think *we* are?" Mary Bennett asked.

"He means a *serious* girlfriend," Gerald said. "My father's old-fashioned, and wants me to date a 'nice Jewish girl.' He's been trying to push me toward one of my former Hebrew school classmates, Roseanne Cohen. She has a mustache."

"I wouldn't discount a mustache so quickly," Mary Bennett said. "Just means the girl has plenty of testosterone coursing through her veins. She's prolly a wildcat between the sheets."

"Roseanne's not my type," Gerald said dismissively. "What did you get for graduation, Patsy?"

Mary Bennett raised an eyebrow at Gerald's abrupt change of subject.

"I got a new easel, a book about portrait painting, and French-language tapes. Oh, I'd love to go to Paris one day," Patsy said. "Book" sounded like it rhymed with "spook."

"Don't know how you're going to *parlez-vous français* when ya still haven't gotten the hang of plain ol' Mississippi American," Mary Bennett said.

"Toast time! I 'borrowed' this from home," I said, unscrewing the top of a mason jar and pouring a small portion of liquid gold into each of our glasses. "Gen-u-wine moonshine, kids. Daddy knows a guy across the river who still cooks up a batch every now and then. It goes down smooth as silk, cured with a peeled apple, but it will kick your ass all over town if you're not careful."

"Where'd Tammy go?" Gerald asked, looking about Mary Bennett's spacious kitchen.

"Maybe she wandered off because we were talking about our graduation gifts," I said. "That was kinda insensitive. Her mama probably couldn't afford to get her anything."

"Oh, she got plenty of graduation presents," Gerald said. "Isn't that right, Mary Bennett?"

Mary Bennett shrugged. "I have no idea what you're talking about."

"Yes. I guess she probably did," I said with a smile. I'd forgotten about Tammy's "gift elf." When Tammy first joined our club she'd confessed that the main reason she hadn't come to school the day after the Key Club incident was because she'd run out of Marcy's house wearing a maid's uniform, and had left her only skirt behind. She owned some slacks and blue jeans, but the school's dress code prohibited girls from wearing pants. The next day "someone" left a basket on her doorstep brimming with brand-new skirts and dresses from The Tog Shoppe. The only person who could afford such an extravagance was Mary Bennett, but she never 'fessed up to it.

"We can't have a toast without Tammy," I said, plunking my glass down on the table. "I'll get her. I know where she is."

"Tell her to get her cute little ass in here so we can raise some hell," Mary Bennett said, sitting in a cane-backed chair, swinging her long, tanned legs. "I can't believe we're shed of that shitty high school, forever."

I went out back into the impeccably groomed yard. St. Augustine grass thick as a carpet was tickling my bare feet, and the air was perfumed with Confederate jasmine. A kidney-shaped pool shimmered like a cool blue oasis in the velvet darkness.

I saw Tammy in a tea-length white dress, standing between two boxwood hedges, gazing down the hill at a big, gray Dutch

Colonial blazing with light. Snatches of conversation and laughter drifted up from the house like bubbles from a champagne glass.

"Pretty view, isn't it?" I said. Mary Bennett's house was perched on one of the highest points in Jackson, and several of the stately homes could be seen from this vantage point.

"I guess," Tammy said, looking away quickly. "I just wanted a little air. It's so nice out tonight."

Pointing at Marcy's house, I said, "I heard some kids mention she was having a big graduation shindig tonight."

"Really? I hadn't heard," Tammy said, her eyes cast downward. She was one of the lousiest liars in the world.

Marcy's house did look enticing, glowing brightly like a lit-up birthday cake. But almost everything seems more attractive when you are outside looking in.

"I promise they aren't having as much fun as we are," I said. "Money won't buy a good time, ya know—and it sure as hell won't buy real friends."

"I know," Tammy said, smoothing the bell-shaped skirt of her graduation dress. It looked expensive and fit her beautifully, so I was sure it came from the "gift elf." She was dressed as if she belonged at Marcy's party.

"One day they'll be talking about you," I said. "They'll say, 'I used to know Tammy Myers in high school before she became a famous country-and-western singer.' At class reunions, they'll all be sucking up and clamoring for your autograph. They'll hope to God you won't remember how shitty they were to you."

"You think?" Tammy said, and I could tell by her tone that she very much liked this daydream.

"Someday, you'll have the power to fix 'em good. You could write a number one song called 'Marcy Stevens Deserves to Die,' but the truth is you won't care enough about her to humiliate her. After all, you'll be this huge star, rubbing elbows with George and Loretta, and she'll just be an aging perma-blond, small-town socialite with bad teeth and a cheating husband."

"Wow," Tammy said. "You have such a vivid imagination. It's almost as if this could be *your* dream."

I toed the grass with my sandal. "Well, it *was* my dream. When I was a kid I always wanted to be a Supreme, or at the very least a Pip, but unfortunately I was born white with the vocal talent of an under-laid cat in heat." I shook a finger at her. "That's why I'm counting on you to conquer Nashville so I can vicariously live my life. Swear to me you won't let me down?"

She gave me her first smile of the evening. "All right, Jill. I swear." She stood on tiptoe to kiss me on the cheek. "Thanks."

"Thank God, that's settled. Now, let's go inside—I brought a little something for a special toast."

The Queens drank like a band of gypsies that night, and after a raucous celebration that included dancing, skinny-dipping, and the rabid consumption of a vast array of decadent foods like Pig Candy, Chocolate Stuff, fried chicken, barbecued ribs, and big wads of cheese, we were all sprawled on the floor of Mary Bennett's rec room, surrounded by empty glasses, food wrappers, and a formidable pile of well-gnawed ribs and nekkid chicken bones.

Giddiness had given way to melancholy. I saw a pity party coming on as soon as Gerald started whistling "Leaving on a Jet Plane."

Mary Bennett was the first to lose it, possibly because she'd had the most to drink. "I don't know what I'm gonna do without my friends," she slurred. "After all, what's the point of being the most famous actress in the world if I don't have y'all to lord it over? Let's promise that we'll never lose touch with each other."

She dangled a bag of corn chips from her hand. "Swear on

this fag of Britos," she said, mixing her words, and of course we all swore, knowing how seriously Mary Bennett took her Fritos. She called them the Manna From Heaven.

There wasn't a dry eye in the house. Each of us solemnly touched the Frito bag and whispered, "I swear."

I was the last one to make the vow, and as I did, memories of the last two years zipped through my brain: dancing to "Land of 1000 Dances" until I wanted to collapse, eating until I thought I would burst, laughing until my sides ached, and riding in a convertible with the wind whipping through my wig, singing "Tiny Bubbles" (the Queens' theme song) at the top of my lungs. But most of all I remembered our long talks about our secret hopes and dreams—talks that were like stitches, knitting us together in a way that I thought would last forever.

I rose to my feet, glass in hand, and demanded they all join me in a toast. "Repeat after me," I said, "HERE'S to US . . ." They echoed it back to me, in tones more dutiful than enthusiastic, until they heard and roared the ending—of what was to become our battle cry—"and FUCK EVERYBODY ELSE!"

PART TWO

1974

Chapter 5

"You're up four pounds, Mrs. Mitchell," I said to the portly woman with a poodle cut who stood before me in an overtaxed satin slip. I'd guessed the news was going to be bad when she removed almost everything, including her bobby pins, before her weigh-in, hoping she'd somehow cheat the scale.

"I don't know why," she said, all red-faced and flustered. "I followed the diet to the letter."

Boy hidee, if I had a nickel for every time one of my clients said that, I could have bought my own weight-loss center.

One or two pounds up didn't necessarily indicate a cheater. Water retention could account for small fluctuations in weight, but *four pounds*? Mrs. Mitchell had definitely been face-first in the feedbag—frequently.

I consulted my clipboard. "So, you didn't have cookies, cakes, chocolates, or doughnuts?"

Her cheek twitched a little at the mention of "doughnut," and I knew I'd hit pay dirt.

"Now that I think about it, I recall I may have nibbled on a doughnut or two."

Make that one or two dozen *doughnuts,* I thought.

"But they weren't those heavy cake doughnuts. They were Krispy Kremes, and they were just light as air. I assumed they didn't count."

Ha! The things dieting women thought they could get away with! Snacks eaten on the run didn't count, and neither did "tasting" food while cooking it. Cokes and alcohol surely didn't count. "I just tinkle it right out," said one clueless client, who claimed ice cream didn't count either as long as it was nearly melted.

If women consistently deluded themselves about something as simple as the food they put in their mouths, what other gigantic lies were they telling themselves?

"Mrs. Mitchell, this diet is so scientific and delicately balanced that the slightest deviation can throw it clean off track."

"I'll try to be more careful," she said, slipping back into her blouse. "But it's hard to imagine that a couple of slices of cake would—"

"Cake?" I said with a raised eyebrow.

"It was *carrot* cake, which I assumed was perfectly acceptable since you people are always foisting vegetables upon me."

"After you get dressed, go in and see the nutritionist. She'll tweak your food list, and remind you of which ones aren't allowed."

People are always attracted to forbidden fruit, I thought as I closed the door to the weighing room.

"Speak of the devil," I said softly as I saw Tammy in the reception area, wearing her white nurse's aide uniform with her purse tucked under her arm.

"I was just coming to see if you were ready to have a little lunch," she said. "Wanta go to Miz Coleman's?"

Tammy never made it to Nashville after graduation. For the last several years, she'd worked in a gynecologist's office a couple of blocks away from the Quick Weight-Loss Center. She'd only intended to work there the summer after graduation, and take off for Music City in the fall. But then a teeny-tiny complication came up.

"It's going to happen," Tammy said breathlessly as the two of us left my office and trudged to Mrs. Coleman's Dream Kitchen, which was three blocks away. "He's going to leave his wife!"

The "he" Tammy was referring to was Dr. Deke Day, tanned, blond, and preppy—a poster boy for country-club living and therefore powerful juju to Tammy.

"Is the special today pork chops or country-fried steak?" I said. We'd only been outside for a minute, and I already felt a trickle of sweat at the back of my neck.

"I could see it in his eyes," Tammy said, taking fast steps with her size-five feet to keep up with me. "This time he really means it."

I stopped short and straightened my body to its full six feet one inch. Maybe she'd listen for a change.

"You mean as opposed to the fifty zillion times before?"

"He's at a medical conference for a few days, but he said as soon he gets back he wants to talk about the *future*."

"That doesn't mean a damn thing," I snapped. "Maybe he just wants to talk to you about giving him more blow jobs in 'the future.'"

She blushed, and tucked her hands into the pocket of her smock. "I don't care what you say. This isn't about sex."

"Bullshit, hunny! It is ALL ABOUT sex," I said in a low voice. We'd reached the entrance to the Dream Kitchen, which was a small gray building with loose roof shingles and peeling paint. The rule in the South generally is, the more pitiful the restaurant on the outside, the better the food was apt to be on the inside. That certainly was the case with Miz Coleman's.

We curtailed our conversation while we joined the cafeteria line. Two rather large women named Mamie and Caroline served up the food, and they didn't stand for the least bit of dilly-dallying. If you didn't say your order fast enough to please them, they'd likely scream, call you names, or short you on portion size. No one ever questioned their reign of terror—their food was just too damn good.

When I reached the head of the line, I hopped to attention and rattled off my order: "Country-fried-steak-fried-green-'maters-collards-corn-bread-sweet-tea-to-drink."

"You want lemon in your tea, sugar pie?" said Mamie in a saccharine voice as Caroline ladled up the food on my tray. If you followed orders and didn't bottleneck their line, Mamie and Caroline were gentle as lambs.

Tammy and I walked with our trays in hand, looking for an empty seat. We found a place beside the window and, as soon as I sat, Tammy proceeded to douse her food with pepper sauce without even tasting it first.

"By the time the others get to town, I'll probably be announcing my engagement," Tammy said.

The Queens were due in three days. I hadn't seen any of them (except Tammy) since the summer following graduation, although we talked on the phone and exchanged letters.

"Suppose hell freezes over, and Dr. Dick actually does leave his wife. What then?"

"We'll be together for always, instead of sneaking around,"

Tammy said, her eyes dancing like candle flames. "And I'll be the wife of a doctor! And please don't call him that."

I laid my fork down. "That's what it's all about, isn't it? It's not Deke you're interested in. It's that he's a *doctor.* Hang a stethoscope around a guy's neck and you're ready to drag his ass down the aisle. How can you give up your dream of being a country-western singer for a married man?"

Tammy shook ketchup on her home fries. "Honestly, Jill, I wish you'd stop nagging me about that whole Nashville thing. Do you know the odds of me succeeding? Talk about wanting the impossible."

"Yet you think it's more probable that your horny little doctor will leave his wife. Don't you read 'Dear Abby'? They NEVER leave their wives!"

"Keep your voice down," she said, looking about nervously. "And he *is* leaving her, I tell you. And, for your information, I'm very much in love with Deke. Yes, I like the fact that he's a doctor. And it's true I crave the security of a Professional man—with money. You would too if you grew up living hand to mouth the way I did."

"Even if he does leave her, it won't be the fairy-tale life you've been dreaming of," I said in a fierce whisper. "Everyone will treat you like a home-wrecker. Men will flirt with you in inappropriate ways, assuming you're a loose woman. Women will treat you like trash, because you've broken up a family. Meanwhile, the entire time you're married to your darling Dr. Day, you'll have to be on guard, because once a cheater, always a cheater, and pretty soon, you'll be the one finding lipstick on his collar."

Tammy violently shook her head. "The only reason Deke cheats on Linda is because she's completely frigid, and she doesn't understand him like I do."

"Gawd, Tammy. I can't believe you're swallowing the absolute oldest line in the whole book of 'Lyin', Cheatin' Sacks-of-Shit.'"

Thank heavens I'd met myself a steady-Eddie fellow. I took a quick glance down at my diamond engagement ring. It was dinky as all get-out, but my fiancé, Sonny, promised he'd get a bigger one down the road.

Tammy must have noticed me looking at my ring because she said, "Just think. We *both* might be brides this year."

"You wanna LOOK at food or you wanna EAT some, mister? Get outta my line 'til you decide what you want!" came a booming voice from the serving line. Mamie's metal spatula went sailing and made a noisy clatter when it hit the floor. The customers at the Dream Kitchen were so used to her outbursts, hardly anyone looked up except, of course, the guy she was aiming at.

I shoveled collards into my mouth and glowered at Tammy. "You'll be marrying Dr. Day when the last wild monkey flies outta his ass."

Chapter 6

The appliances in the kitchen are all from Sears and Roebuck's," the real estate agent said, sweeping her arm in front of a refrigerator as if it were a prize on *Let's Make a Deal*.

"Everything's so . . . green," I said with a frown. Ever since Marcy Stevens had dubbed me the Jolly Green Giant, I hadn't been overly fond of the color.

"Avocado," the real estate agent corrected me. "But if you don't like them, we have models with appliances that come in Harvest Gold."

The real estate agent was named Neecie Harrison, and she exuded feminine perfection—shoes matching bag, brows plucked into a perfect arch, hair curled into a neat bob.

Could I be a real estate agent? I definitely liked poking around in other people's houses. I pictured myself wearing a navy blue jacket and tossing around phrases like "Isn't this an adorable alcove?"

Sonny was in the den, sticking his head up the fireplace. He wanted me to go to college to be a health teacher, but I wasn't too hot on the idea. It'd take four years, and I wasn't particularly keen on school. Well, the truth was, I was dying to go but ever since I nearly failed Algebra II, I'd been too afraid to try it.

I was about to ask Neecie how long it took to be a real estate agent when Sonny emerged from the den.

"Is this the Phoenix?" he said.

"No, this is the Flagstaff. The Phoenix has an extra half bath and a foyer," Neecie said.

There were five models of houses in Oasis Flats, a brand-new subdivision in Jackson, and for some inexplicable reason, they were all named after cities in Arizona.

"That extra half bath might come in handy, but I like this floor plan better," Sonny said. "What do you think, hon'?"

Whenever I looked at Sonny I had to remind myself that though he was merely "nice-looking" as opposed to "handsome," there were several of his individual body parts that I adored. He had strong, square, decidedly masculine hands and perfectly honed forearms. His teeth were straight and white, he had well-shaped ears, and his calves were nicely sculpted even if he was bowlegged. He was also, truth be told, hung like Paw Paw's pony. Even so, while Sonny was well-intentioned enough, sexually speaking, it seemed as if he didn't even know about "the little man in the boat," if you catch my drift.

I smiled at Sonny—thinking of his more pronounced attributes—and said, "Whatever you think is best."

I was tired of looking at houses with small, claustrophobic rooms with low ceilings and not a lick of character. But, as Sonny had pointed out, they were reasonably priced, well built, and, most important, located in a good school district.

"Would y'all like to discuss it on your own for a bit?" Neecie said. "I have some paperwork I could do out in the car."

"Yes, thanks," Sonny said.

"Jill," he said after she left. "There's something I want to show you in the master bedroom." He took my arm and led me down the hall. We stood hand-in-hand on the powder-blue shag carpet, and he pointed to the blank wall. "Wouldn't that be the perfect place for an armoire?"

I frowned. Was it normal for a man to use the word "armoire"? Wouldn't it be more masculine to call it "one of those things that holds clothes"?

"Forget the armoire, Sonny. Why don't we try out the carpet," I said, toying with his belt buckle. "See if we like it?"

He batted my hand away. "Jill, I want you to concentrate. This house is an enormous decision. We're going to be living here for a few years, and I want you to be happy."

"Okay," I said with a pout. It was just as well. The shag carpet would have given me some god-awful rug burns.

"I think this house is cute as a button, hunny," I said, giving his arm a squeeze. If I could fake orgasm, I could certainly fake house-lust.

"Our home. Imagine the bed here," he said, pointing at a spot near the window. "The TV across the room. You and me watching Johnny Carson every night, and then afterward . . ." He waggled his eyebrows at me. "You know what."

"And the mirror goes here," I said, pointing up at the ceiling.

"Jill," he said, with the embarrassed smile of a guy who liked to dip his wick without having to discuss the urge with his future wife. She, apparently, should be more like Mary Poppins than Mae West.

"It all sounds perfect," I said.

"I also think the living room is the ideal size for entertaining."

"Who would we entertain?" I asked. We'd yet to make friends with other couples.

"People from the accounting firm. Clients."

Sounded like the opposite of "entertaining" to me, but being a good little fiancée I held my tongue.

"You've haven't said anything about the most important room in the house," he added.

"I just *said* it was perfect!" I said, gazing around the small, blue cube that was the master bedroom.

"I mean the kitchen!" he said, playfully poking me in the ribs.

It was more of a galley than a true kitchen, but as Sonny had pointed out many times, this was just our starter home. In the next few years, Sonny would be made partner at his firm, and we'd move to a bigger house. Sonny had our whole life plotted out on a legal pad: how many children we'd have (three), how we'd space them out (two years apart), and when he expected promotions. Before I met Sonny, my life had been like a pony on a carousel—measured ups and downs, all in the same little circle but amusing enough; now it was beginning to feel more like a mule, pulling a covered wagon doggedly across the prairie, with no trees in sight.

After a few minutes of discussion, we decided to make an offer. Sonny wrote Neecie a two-hundred-dollar check for earnest money.

We were going to celebrate by doing "you know what" at Sonny's apartment. As Sonny shed his jockey shorts and folded them into a neat square, I was reminded of the first time I'd ever had sex with him. We'd been dating for about four months and after one particularly sweaty and scintillating make-out session, he grabbed my hand—which was slipping down the waistband of his khakis—and said, "Jill. Let's stop for a minute. We need to talk."

He sounded so serious I spat a piece of hair out of my mouth, tucked an errant titty back into my bra, and trained my eyes on him.

"I'd like to make love with you, but I want it to mean something. I want it to be a step toward strengthening our commitment."

I'd never heard a guy actually say "we need to talk" before. That and "commitment" coming out of a guy's mouth within sixty seconds of each other sent my mind reeling.

"Do you understand what I'm trying to say?"

There was a smooth click in my mind, like a key turning the tumblers of a lock. *This is a relationship.* This is what braces, hair curlers, Mark Eden breast exercises, and reading Harlequin romances had been leading up to.

Of course, once I knew what I was dealing with, I stepped right on up to that plate.

"Yes, Sonny," I said. "I think I do."

"Good," he said, tenderly touching my cheek. "I would like you to spend the night with me tomorrow, and we'll consummate our devotion to each other."

I flinched at the word "consummate" (it sounded like a kind of soup to me) but figured I just wasn't accustomed to a man using real words. This one had a whole six letters more than I was used to hearing from any guy.

I showed up at the appointed hour, and Sonny greeted me at the door, smelling like he'd performed a full-immersion baptism in cologne.

"Jill," he said, awkwardly pecking my cheek. "You look wonderful!"

He led me into the apartment. Henry Mancini was playing on the stereo, and champagne cooled in an ice bucket on the coffee table. From the living room, I could see into the bedroom, and I saw that the covers were pulled back. The only thing missing was a glowing neon sign blinking TONIGHT'S FEATURE: SEX!

"Are you hungry?" he asked, his forehead shiny with perspiration. "I originally thought we should eat first, and then it occurred to me that we might to be too bloated afterward and—"

Don't say bloated! I wanted to shriek. Bloated was not a sexy precoital word.

"We'll eat later," I said quickly.

"Would you like a glass of champagne?" he said, shifting into debonair gear.

"Champagne would be just lovely."

"Champagne it is," he said.

He returned with two glasses and handed one to me. Peering over the top, he said, "I've been thinking about you all day long."

We finished our champagne and he wordlessly led me into the bedroom.

It would be the first time I'd ever made love on a bed. My previous sexual encounters had taken place in the backs of cars, in a storeroom, and once hanging off the swim platform of a ski boat in the middle of a lake (which I discovered is a lot better in theory than in practice. Who woulda thunk there was such a thing as too much moisture?).

Foreplay ensued, sweet-little-nothings were exchanged, and disrobing went without a hitch. I'd purposely worn a dress with a zipper, so I'd slip out of it like a greased pig. (Stop it! Don't think about pigs, greased or otherwise.)

I remember feeling extremely relieved when it was over. Sonny held me in an awkward way, as if his embrace was motivated by something he'd heard—"women love to cuddle after sex"—rather than something he really wanted to do. And apparently the cuddling thing was about the only woman-pleasing kinda thing he'd heard about.

"I have to go to the bathroom," I said, extracting myself from his arms. I started to take the sheet with me—like I'd seen women do in the movies—not being at all interested in him having an unobstructed view of my ass this early in the deal. He didn't seem too keen on lying there splayed out nekkid either, so I just sort of backed out of the room while he pretended to be otherwise distracted while I performed this ridiculous maneuver.

"Did you climax?"

I was so young and self-conscious about my body that his question seemed overly intrusive, as if he had asked me, "Do you fart much?"

"Yes," I lied.

"I'm glad," he said, and the delight on his face was so apparent that fibbing seemed like the right thing to do.

•

Now I had no idea how to break the truth to him and here we were, buying an avocado tract house and about to get married.

"Just think. This is the first time we're doing it as property owners," Sonny had said, just before he entered me. And a little mortgaged piece of earth moved that night—at least for Sonny.

Sometimes when we were making love I'd try to think sexy thoughts, hoping something climactic actually would happen for ME, but unfortunately nothing ever did. I tried so hard, one night I nearly called him "Elvis," which clearly would have stirred things up but prolly not in a good way.

Still, I mostly enjoyed making love with Sonny—it was just sorta comfy. His body was firm, and he smelled like Lifebuoy soap. I liked being close to him and having our limbs tangled together. My favorite part was when Sonny reached orgasm. For a split second, I'd look at his face and think, that's the real Sonny, but then he'd melt away as quickly as he'd appeared.

Later, as Sonny was reading *Time* magazine in bed and I was filing my nails, I said, "I wonder how long it takes to be a real estate agent."

"I don't know. Why?"

"I'm just weighing different options. I'm not sure if teaching is for me."

"Real estate agents work nights and on Saturdays," Sonny said, lowering his magazine an inch to glance at me. "That would be a problem with children. We really should stick with our original plan." The magazine went back up, as if that was the end of the discussion.

Chapter 7

"There's something I want to show you," Tammy said, giddy with excitement.

She startled me. I'd just gotten back to our apartment from the Piggly Wiggly and was stashing a box of Little Debbie Swiss rolls behind a row of tomato soups in the pantry. I hid my treats because Tammy had a terrible sweet tooth and would gobble them up in a single day.

Tammy didn't even notice the Little Debbies, she was so worked up. She seized my hand and said, "Come on. I just got it today, and it's just so beautiful."

I followed her into her room, which looked like a shrine to Dr. Dick. Photos of the two of them covered her dresser and were thumbtacked to a bulletin board. In all of them, Tammy had her hand pressed to Dr. Day's chest, as if claiming him as spoils.

There was a small table near her bed where she kept all her Dr. Day mementoes—movie ticket stubs, matchbooks from restaurants, dried flowers, and a stack of greeting cards he'd given her over the years. I also knew that her two top drawers were stuffed with teddies, panties, and nighties that she donned exclusively for his benefit. Around the house she wore an oversized "Archie Bunker for President" T-shirt, holey granny-panties, and a ratty butt-sprung bathrobe.

Despite sleeping with a gynecologist, she wasn't having any orgasms either. I'd asked her about it a few months after I first started having sex with Sonny and she'd said, "I'm not sure. Sometimes I get a pleasant tingling during sex. That's probably an orgasm, don't you think?"

"No," I'd said. "I think it's like sneezing—you'll *know* it when you're having it."

"Look!" Tammy said, holding a long white dress encased in a see-through plastic garment bag. "I have to take it out for you to *really* appreciate it."

I blinked in confusion. "Is that a fuckin' wedding gown?"

"Not just any wedding gown," she said, unzipping the bag and pulling free the dress. "It's *my* wedding gown, and it's the most beautiful one they had at Marla's House of Brides. Look at the detailing. There must be a million seed pearls."

"Oh, my God," I said, sinking onto her twin bed and knocking to the floor a three-foot pink teddy bear, a Valentine's gift from Deke. "He did it. Dr. Dick actually left his wife. I've been wrong all along."

"I told you not to call him that!" Tammy said, spreading out the train. "Of course, it's not exactly official, but I *know*—"

"Wait a fuckin' minute. Whaddya mean it's not official? Has he left her or not?"

"Jill! Deke's still in Boston at that medical conference," she said, with a thin laugh. Dimples dented her cheeks. "I told you that when he comes back, I'm *positive* he's going to give me an engagement ring."

"So why in the world do you have a wedding dress?"

"Well, it's inevitable that Deke and I are going to get married, so I'm just thinking ahead. Marla's was having a sale, so I bought it."

"Tammy—"

"I've decided that when he comes home, I'm going to wear it." She shook the gown at me. "It looks so pretty on. I'm convinced that when he sees me in this dress, he'll understand how badly I want to be his wife."

"Oh, God, Tammy," I said softly. "I think he already knows that."

"He *wants* to marry me," she said, stroking the dress with her hand. "I know he does. I can hear it in his voice."

"Let's put the dress up," I said gently. "You don't want to spoil it."

"I know you have doubts, but you just don't *know* him like I do." Her eyes were bright and hard, like quartz crystals.

"I bought some Little Debbies, and *Laugh-In*'s on tonight," I said. Tammy had clearly crossed some line that made it impossible for me to argue with her. "You wanna watch it with me?"

"No, I think I'll tidy up in here," she said, tugging on the sleeve of her blouse. "Besides, I don't want to get involved in a show because Deke is gonna call tonight."

I left her alone and ended up reading the latest issue of *Good Housekeeping* (Sonny had given me a gift subscription) instead of watching television. I couldn't believe Tammy was doing this. Through her door I could hear occasional snatches of "Lara's Theme" coming from the music box that Deke had given her. The evening passed quietly with not a single phone call. When I glanced at the clock and saw it was eleven, I decided I'd check on her.

"Tammy," I said, lightly knocking on the door, "I'm going to bed."

I thought she'd fallen asleep because she didn't answer, but then she said, "Good night. Sleep well."

"Tammy, are you all right?"

"I'm great," she said, but her voice sounded thick, as if she'd been crying. "I forgot that Deke had a dinner function tonight. I'm sure he'll call me tomorrow at work."

"'Night, Tammy."

Chapter 8

"I have one final question before I can perform your wedding ceremony," Reverend Mixon said, his kind watery eyes searching mine.

Shit! Here it was—the question I'd been dreading ever since we'd started the premarital pastoral counseling. He was about to point a finger at me and say, "Have you remained pure before marriage or become the devil's harlot?"

Should I lie, confess, or plead the Fifth?

"No need to look so alarmed, Jill," Reverend Mixon said. "I just want to know how you feel about the word 'obey.'"

I let out a long sigh of relief.

"Obey? You mean as part of the wedding vows?" Sonny asked. He and I had been holding hands for so long that both of our palms were slick with sweat.

"Some women have asked me to omit the word from the ceremony," Reverend Mixon said. He chuckled. "They think it's old-fashioned."

Sonny let go of my hand and squeezed my shoulder. "Jill's very traditional. She's not one of those wacko women's libbers."

His comment irritated the shit out of me. While it was true I considered bra-burning a fool's errand, I absolutely agreed with the whole premise of the movement—how could Sonny be so oblivious to that? But, since this was our last counseling session, I didn't want to make waves.

"I suppose it's just a word," I said, the very picture of a dutiful fiancée.

A twinkle of approval came to Reverend Mixon's eyes. "I guess I'll see you on Sunday, then."

Sonny got up, but I lingered.

"Was there something else, Jill?" Reverend Mixon said.

What do you think our chances are? I wanted to ask, hoping for his seal of approval. Had he ever refused to do a wedding because he thought a couple was too mismatched?

"Nothing," I said, picking up my pocketbook.

As we strolled to Sonny's Buick in the church parking lot, he asked, "When did you say those friends of yours, the Sweet Peas, were arriving?"

"They're the Sweet Potato Queens," I said, sliding in after Sonny opened the door. He had painstakingly covered the seats with clear plastic. It was stiff and yellowing from months of Mississippi heat.

He turned the key in the ignition and stretched his arm across the back of the seat as he backed out of the parking lot. My daddy used to do the same thing when he drove me to school, and the heaviness of his arm behind me always made me feel safe.

"I still don't understand about this Gerald person," he said. "Are you sure he's not an old flame?"

It made me smile to think of Gerald as being an old boyfriend of anyone's, and I suppressed a chuckle at the word "flame," thinking of another meaning entirely.

"No. Gerald and I never dated. We're just very good friends."

"What sort of guy spends his high school years around a bunch of girls?" Sonny said, puffing up his chest. "That's what I want to know."

"You'll like him," I said. Truthfully, Gerald would probably give Sonny the creeps and Gerald wouldn't have two words to say to Sonny. Gerald had always hung out with us—there weren't any guy-type buddies in the picture, no hunting trips, bar fights, or hot cars to talk about.

"So there's Tammy . . . ," Sonny said, frowning. He sorely disapproved of Tammy's affair with Dr. Day. "And there's Patsy, an artist in Atlanta, and Gerald, who dropped out of medical school to move to San Francisco—what's that about? And who's the other one?"

"Mary Bennett. She's an actress in New York," I said, twisting my engagement ring. "She can be kinda—ahh—flamboyant."

I could easily imagine Mary Bennett sidling up to Sonny and saying, "So, you gettin' much, Sonny-boy?"—just to see the look on his face.

And it wasn't like I could ask her to tone herself down. Hell, no! You did *not* try to muzzle Mary Bennett—not unless you wanted her to be ten times more brazen than usual.

"An actress," Sonny said in a disapproving tone. "All your friends sound a bit *odd*. I hope they're not too weird at the wedding. Clients will be there. And my folks."

"They'll be fine," I assured him. After all, the Queens weren't in high school anymore. Surely everyone had matured over the last few years. Life couldn't be moonshine and Fritos forever.

•

"There she is!" Mary Bennett said, grabbing at least two inches of cheek flesh from my face and squeezing hard. When she let go, I stepped back to take her in.

She wore a geometric-patterned dress and tights. Her hair was cut boyishly short, like Twiggy's, which brought all kinds of interesting angles to her face.

"You look fabulous!"

"And you look"—she paused as if she were trying to conjure up a compliment—"like someone's wife." Her nose wrinkled ever so slightly when she said the word "wife."

I looked down at my clothing. I was wearing a pink cotton blouse with a Peter Pan collar, a khaki dirndl skirt (Sonny didn't like women in pants— "only 'hippie scum'" wore blue jeans), and canvas shoes. Instead of wearing my hair in its customary messy bun, I had it pulled back from my face with a black hair band.

"Of course she looks like a wife," Tammy said, who was standing on the steps behind me. "She's gettin' married in two days."

"Tammy!" Mary Bennett said. "I didn't even see you there. And get a load of you, hunny." She took in Tammy's familiar teased hair, heavy makeup, and tight dress. "You're exactly the same."

"Why, thank you," Tammy said, patting her hair, basking in Mary Bennett's attentions and obviously taking it as a compliment. "You look like a fashion model," Tammy gushed.

"Wait until y'all see Geraldine," Mary Bennett said, motioning us inside. "You're goin' to flip out! Come on in."

She led us into the kitchen, where an unfamiliar bearded man sat at the table. He had long, bushy dark hair tied back with a piece of leather and wore purple-tinted John Lennon–style glasses. He wore a tight, faded Iron Butterfly T-shirt that showed off his toned pecs and biceps.

"That cannot be—" I began.

"It is!" Mary Bennett said, whipping off the stranger's shades. There was Gerald, blinking back at me, his eyelashes as long as ever.

Tammy gasped, and I slapped my cheeks. "Oh, my God!"

"Pretty wild, huh?" His voice was huskier than I remembered.

"What's with the hair?" I asked. "It used to grow straight out, like an Afro."

"When it grows long enough, it falls down into big, fat, hippie hair," Gerald said, fingering his ponytail.

What if he had so much hair he wouldn't be able to tuck it into his Queen wig? But we were too old for all that. Come to think of it, I wasn't even sure where my wig was.

I gave him a hug and got a snoot full of patchouli oil.

"Are you holding, Geraldine?" Mary Bennett demanded, hand on hip.

"Maybe," he said from behind his beard.

"Give it up," Mary Bennett said, thrusting out her palm and tapping her foot impatiently.

Tammy and I exchanged a glance. We had no idea what they were talking about.

Gerald rifled through a fringed pouch hanging from his shoulder.

"Is that a pocketbook?" Tammy asked with a laugh.

"It's a *bag*," Gerald said, as if it was completely obvious. "Everyone in the Haight has one. We all need a bag"—he withdrew a rolled-up plastic baggie and held it up triumphantly—"to hold our bags."

"Colombian Gold?" Mary Bennett said, watching Gerald hungrily.

"Better," Gerald said, unrolling the baggie on the table and looking up at her with a smug smile. "Maui Wowie."

"Is that marijuana?" Tammy asked with alarm.

"The very best. Roll us a fatty, Gerald." Mary Bennett slapped a package of strawberry rolling papers on the table, and Gerald took out a thin, pink square and licked it along the top.

"Y'all do get high, don't ya?" she said.

"Every once in a blue moon," I lied, deliberately avoiding eye contact with Tammy, who knew I'd never even seen the stuff. "Aren't you worried about your father catching us?"

"He's in Paris stuffing his face with croissants and wooing his latest conquest," Mary Bennett said, idly flicking a Bic lighter with her thumb. She was sitting forward in her chair, her elbows planted on the table.

"I see," I said with a nod, watching Gerald spread a large portion of marijuana on the rolling paper, and then with one hand, dexterously rolling it up into a fat-bellied joint.

"Show-off," Mary Bennett said, plucking it from Gerald's hands and waving it under her nostrils. "Mmmmmm, baby, come to mama."

"Where's Patsy?" I said. I couldn't keep my eyes off the joint. This was a first for me.

"She called. Her plane's late. She won't be here for another half hour or so," Mary Bennett said quickly. She lit the joint and inhaled deeply. "Primo weed," she said with a cough as she passed it to Gerald, who made a loud sucking sound as he inhaled. Then Gerald wagged it at Tammy and me. "You two want a toke?" he asked.

"Sonny and I are planning on having children," I said, quickly. "So I better not."

"I'm with Jill," Tammy said with her arms folded across her chest. "I'm involved with a doctor, and he wouldn't approve."

Great clouds of smoke billowed out of their mouths as they both burst into laughter.

"God, when did y'all get so uptight?" Mary Bennett said.

When did you and Gerald turn into hippie scum? I thought, but a small voice inside my head wanted to know when *I* turned into *Sonny,* so I said nothing.

"All right, chickadees," Mary Bennett said with a sigh. "I can see this is making y'all uncomfortable so we'll hold off."

Gerald stubbed out the joint and tucked the pot back into his pouch. The room fell into an awkward silence. I couldn't recall a time when four Queens were in the same place and the noise and laughter wasn't deafening.

"So why don't you tell us about your commercial, Mary Bennett," I asked. "Sounds so exciting."

"The only reason I'm doing it is to pay the bills," Mary Bennett said in a weary voice. "It's for Dainty and Dry deodorant. What a crap product!"

"I use Dainty and Dry," Tammy said brightly. "It's effective, and has a very nice fragrance."

"Maybe *you* should do the stupid commercial," Mary Bennett said. Her eyes were lazy red slits.

"I think Mary Bennett is trying to say that deodorant is a completely unnecessary product," Gerald said. "What's wrong with a person's natural scent? Why do we have to cover it up?"

"'Cause it's stinky?" Tammy said, holding her nose.

"I don't wear deodorant," Gerald said. "Haven't for years."

"Remind me not to sit next to you at the rehearsal dinner," I said, hoping to lighten things up.

"Ha, ha," Gerald said, but there was no levity in his tone.

Mary Bennett leaned back, clasped her fingers on her flat

stomach, and said, "Why don't you tell us about your old man, Jill?"

I was grateful for the change in subject, so I forged ahead. "His name is Norman, but everybody calls him Sonny, and he's an accountant. We just bought a house in Oasis Flats. He wants me to go back to school to be a health teacher, because—"

"Another Pleasant Valley Sunday, down in status-symbol land," Gerald sang softly.

"I have that album. It's the Monkees," Tammy said. She looked at Mary Bennett and Gerald with triumph in her eyes. "See, I'm not completely ignorant about this counterculture stuff."

"The Monkees are far from counterculture," Gerald said. "They're a creation of Madison Avenue—a vehicle for selling sugary breakfast cereals to the masses."

"Then why are you singing their song?" I said.

He gave me a pointed glance. "I thought it was apt."

"Instead of singing, why don't you *say* what you mean, Gerald?" I said, narrowing my eyes.

"Give it a break, Gerald." Mary Bennett stifled a yawn. "Jill can't help it. Jackson's twenty years behind the times. I was trying to find a decent radio station 'round here and all I could pick up was gospel, country-western, and Burt fuckin' Bacharach."

"What's wrong with Burt Bacharach?" Tammy demanded. "His songs are piped into the doctor's office."

"Egg-zactly," Mary Bennett said with a nod of her head.

"I don't see what Burt Bacharach has to do with anything," I said.

Gerald looked me square in the eye. "Your life is Burt Bacharach, Jill."

"What he means is that your life sounds sorta bland. Establishment," Mary Bennett said.

"I *know* what he's saying," I said, roughly. "And I'm with Tammy. I don't think there's a damn thing wrong with Burt Bacharach. Do you think everybody's life is supposed to be like Jefferson Airport?"

"That's 'Airplane,'" Mary Bennett said, sniggering.

"Who cares?" I said, pushing my chair away from the table. "I don't think there's anything wrong with getting married, buying a house, and planning a future. That's what people do. You can't sit around smoking pot the rest of your lives. Who are *you* to judge me?"

"Damn. Y'all are killin' my buzz," Mary Bennett said with a groan.

"But the question is, *whose* future are you buying into, man?" Gerald asked, leaning back in his chair. "Yours, or the one society is dictating for you? Women don't have to be baby factories anymore. They can have their own identities and lives."

"I personally don't understand what's up with Gloria Steinem." Tammy dabbed on lip gloss. "She's way too pretty to be one of them libbers. They don't even shave their pits."

"Look," I said. "I *have* my own identity, and I don't know what you're trying to prove—"

"I'm just trying to save you from a lifetime of oppression," Gerald said.

"Oh, Queens!" came a voice from the hall. We all turned to see Patsy sauntering into the kitchen, wearing a red wig and cat's-eye sunglasses and carrying a big greasy sack. "Oh, my goodness! It's so great to see all of you! And look what I brought!" She plunked the bag in front of Mary Bennett.

"More pot, I hope," Mary Bennett said. She eagerly peered inside and then dropped it on the table as if it were hot. "Oh, Gawd! Get this away from me or I'll puke."

"What's wrong?" Patsy said, a puzzled look on her face. "It's your favorite, Pig Candy. I know it's cold, but—"

"Mary Bennett's a vegetarian, and so am I," Gerald explained. "We refuse to eat the flesh of innocent animals. It turns our stomachs."

The room fell silent. We surveyed each other with uneasy glances as if we were strangers.

"Well," I said, after a moment. "I can tell my rehearsal dinner is going to be a real hoot, seeing how it's being held at the Sizzlin' Steakhouse."

Chapter 9

How in the world did you get tied up with such a bunch of wackaloons?" Sonny demanded. I was curled up in a corner of my couch, watching him wear a groove into the carpet.

"They're not *all* like that. What about Patsy? She's perfectly—"

"*One* out of four," he said. "That's nothing to brag about, and I can hardly understand her. Obviously, she has some sort of speech impediment."

"She doesn't have a speech impediment. Her mama's from Minnesota, and the Southern accent just never really took hold for her."

He stopped his pacing, and glared down at me. "You're missing the point. That Mary Bennett was bad enough. Her skirt barely covered her be-hind, and she's crude."

"Crude?" I said with a puzzled tone. I'd actually been surprised at Mary Bennett's uncharacteristically subdued behavior during the rehearsal dinner.

"She said 'blow job' within earshot of my mama. Mama graciously pretended not to hear, but it was obvious from the appalled look on her face that she had."

Sonny's daddy cussed like a sailor, so it was hard to imagine that one little "blow job" from Mary Bennett would make his mama's precious ears wither, but I held my tongue.

"But *nothing* could prepare me for Gerald," Norman said, holding his middle as if the thought of Gerald made him physically ill. "As if his freakish appearance wasn't bad enough."

Gerald, bless his heart, had made an effort to dress appropriately. He'd worn a navy blue blazer, a white button-down shirt, and khakis, but nothing could be done to make his long, unruly hair look conservative.

"But that wasn't the worst of it. Not nearly," Norman said with a shudder.

This is where Sonny calls Gerald a pansy, a mama's boy, or a sissy, I thought with a sigh. Homophobes are so predictable.

"He quits Baylor Med School to study philosophy at Berkeley," Sonny said, his face awash in color. "And you know what *that* means."

"Enlighten me," I said wearily.

Norman's voice lowered a pitch. "Drugs. Everyone knows that all those swamis and yogis are heavy LSD users. That's how the Beatles got hooked on the stuff. I read about it in a magazine. And *Berkeley,* well . . ."

I sorely doubted Sonny had his facts straight, but I wasn't in the mood for an argument. Suddenly I was extremely tired.

"Sonny, listen I—"

"Bottom line is this," he said, pointing a finger at me. "I don't want that commie-pinko fag at my wedding. My boss and colleagues will be there. His presence will reflect poorly on me, on both of us. Let that gutter-mouthed Mary Bennett attend if you must, but I'm putting my foot down when it comes to that freak Gerald."

His cheek muscle and right shoulder were jumping. Whenever he was wound up, Sonny jerked like a string puppet.

"You want to bar one of my oldest friends from our wedding?" The thought of feet being put down was disquieting to me.

Sonny sat down beside me and gently clasped my hand. "Be honest with yourself. Gerald may have been a buddy of yours a long time ago, but he's not anymore. You've even said how different he is now."

"Yes, but—"

"Sometimes we grow apart," he said. "You and Gerald have completely different values. Y'all have nothing in common anymore."

The last few things Sonny had said made sense, but as disconnected as I felt from Gerald, I still couldn't imagine uninviting him to the wedding. He'd flown in from San Francisco just for me.

"I'll call him for you if you'd like, sweetie," Sonny said, obviously sensing I was close to caving in. "Just give me his number."

If Gerald didn't come, Mary Bennett probably wouldn't either. I'd seen them whispering and rolling their eyes at the rehearsal dinner and I was almost certain they'd been talking about me. Did I really want to exchange sacred vows in front of them, knowing they thought my life was all a big, boring joke? It would be much simpler to let Sonny take care of this problem, the way he already handled most other things in my life.

But out of the blue came a mental image of Gerald as he was in high school—with frizzy hair and that blue outfit he wore in our first parade. Maybe the Gerald I'd known and loved didn't exist anymore, but if I didn't want him at my wedding, I should have the guts to tell him myself.

"I'll speak to him."

"You promise?"

"I said I *would,*" I said quickly. "You should go home. I need my rest. You don't want a bride with big dark circles under her eyes."

"I know you'll do the right thing. You're a sensible girl." Sonny kissed me on the cheek. "Just think. By this time tomorrow, we'll be Mr. and Mrs. Norman Butts."

I winced at the sound of my soon-to-be last name and shooed him out the door.

•

After Sonny was gone, I stared at the phone a full fifteen minutes before I got up the courage to even pick up the receiver. The dial tone buzzed in my ear for so long that a recorded voice came on.

"If you'd like to make a call, please hang up and dial again. If you need assistance—"

Bang! Bang! Someone was knocking on the front door. Tammy must have forgotten her key. She was supposed to meet Dr. Day right after the rehearsal dinner to talk about their "future," but things must have really blown up for her to be home this early. I dragged myself to the door. I really wasn't up to listening to her caterwauling the night before my wedding.

"Keep your panties on," I said as I swung open the door. Mary Bennett, Gerald, and Patsy stood under the pale yellow glare of the bug light.

"We need to talk," Gerald said, his hands stuffed into the

pockets of his bell-bottoms. He'd changed into a scruffy Led Zeppelin T-shirt and water buffalo sandals. Mary Bennett still wore the bright orange minidress she had on at the rehearsal dinner. Patsy stood slightly apart from them. Her nose was red, and she was honking into a handkerchief.

"I agree," I said, ushering them inside.

The three of them sat in a stiff row on my sofa. Gerald was the first to speak.

"I've decided—rather *we* decided—that we won't be attending your wedding." His eyes were unreadable behind his glasses.

"By *we,* he means Mary Bennett and himself," Patsy said, breathlessly. "A herd of stampeding elephants couldn't keep me away."

"It's not personal, hunny," Mary Bennett said. "We were just getting a nasty vibe at the House of the Dead Cows. Your old man kept staring at us like we were three-headed snakes in a freak show. Gave us the heebie-jeebies."

"Yeah, man," Gerald said with a nod. "It was a paranoia party, and we weren't even stoned."

"I keep telling them they're being ridiculous," Patsy said, her voice high and thin as if near the breaking point. "We're the Sweet Potato Queens and that means we're family. You'd be devastated if Gerald and Mary Bennett didn't come to your wedding. Right?"

I slid down the wall, utterly exhausted. "Maybe we should just—"

The ringing of the phone caused me to jump. I reached over to the end table to pick it up.

"Hello?" I said. The line sounded dead. "Hello," I repeated, this time louder. "Who is this?"

Seconds of silence ticked by. Ordinarily I would have hung up, but something made me hang on for a little longer. Finally, I heard a sound, faint as a baby's sigh.

"Jill?" the voice said.

"Tammy? Is that you?"

There was more silence, and then a gasp, as if the caller was summoning the last vestiges of her strength.

"Jill, I took some . . . pills. Sleepy," she slurred.

"Tammy? Where are you?" I demanded.

Patsy, Gerald, and Mary Bennett gathered around me in a tight knot, their bodies tensed as they listened to my end of the conversation.

"I shouldn't have done . . . mistake."

"Tammy!" I was screaming now. "Where are you?"

More silence—a deadly quiet that seemed to stretch into forever. Then there was a click and the sound of a dial tone.

"No!" I said, throwing the receiver to the ground. "Why did you hang up?" Then I lunged for it and quickly replaced it in its cradle. "Ohmigod! She might call back again. *Please* call back!"

"What happened?" a white-faced Patsy asked.

"Tammy took some pills," I said, bolting to Tammy's room. The others followed on my heels. "She was supposed to see her boyfriend tonight. He's married, and it must have gone to shit." I pawed through the memorabilia on her table, sending matchbooks and play programs flying to the floor.

"Where did they usually meet?" Mary Bennett asked.

"Different places. Motels. She was never very specific," I said, as I pulled open a dresser drawer hoping to find some clue to her whereabouts.

Gerald put his hands on my shoulders. "Slow down a minute. This isn't doing any good. Think! Is there anyone who would know where she went tonight?"

"Well, Dr. Day," I said, tears coursing down my cheeks. "But he won't tell us anything, he's—"

"The fuck he won't!" Mary Bennett shouted. "Come on. We've got to get to his house, pronto! He'll by God tell us where she is. Do you know where he lives?"

"North of Yazoo Road. A couple of streets from your old house," I said.

•

A few minutes later, the tires of Mary Bennett's convertible screeched as we slid to a stop in front of Dr. Day's darkened Victorian mansion.

"It's ten o'clock. He's probably in bed. What if he won't answer the door?" I asked.

"Didn't you say he's an ob/gyn?" Mary Bennett said.

"Yeah," I said.

She grabbed a sweater that was lying in the backseat and wadded it up into a ball. "So how could he possibly turn away a pregnant woman who's in the last stages of labor?" She handed it to Patsy. "Swiss Miss, you've got the most innocent face. Stuff this under your shirt and make like you're preggers. Knock at the door while we hide in the bushes."

Patsy obediently tucked the sweater under her shirt and headed toward the front porch. We followed.

She mashed the doorbell several times, and after a few moments a light illuminated the entryway.

"Who is it?" said a gruff voice from behind the door.

"Please help me," Patsy shouted helplessly. "My baby's coming right now! I can feel the head! I can feel the head!"

"What?" Dr. Day said, swinging open the door and surveying Patsy. He was wearing a plush burgundy bathrobe and matching slippers. "You're not one of my patients."

"The baby's coming, Dr. Day. Ooooh! The pain." Patsy was so into her role she dramatically clutched at her stomach, causing the sweater to fall onto the porch. "Oh my God! It's here," she said, reaching down to pick it up. "Congratulations to me. It's a cardigan!"

Dr. Day narrowed his eyes. "What the hell is going on!?"

At that, the rest of us scrambled out of the hedges.

"We need to talk with you, *Deke,*" Mary Bennett said with an edge, arms planted on her almost nonexistent hips.

"What do you want?" Dr. Day said, fear flitting across his face as he eyed us. His glance rested on Gerald. "I'm calling the police."

"Not so fast, Buckwheat." Mary Bennett took a step forward. "We'll be on our way just as soon as you tell us where Tammy is."

"Tammy who?" Dr. Day said. He took a quick peek over his shoulder. "How dare you come here this late at night—?"

"Tammy Myers," I said, edging closer to the door. "Your nurse's aide. The one you fucked tonight. I don't know what you said or did, but it must have been horrible, because she just called saying she'd taken a lot of pills. She was so disoriented she couldn't tell me where she was."

A brief look of alarm flashed in Dr. Day's eyes, but it was replaced with hard-jawed denial. "This is ridiculous! Of course I know Tammy Myers, but our relationship is strictly professional, and—"

"Honey? Is everything all right?" A female voice floated down from a long, curving staircase behind Dr. Day.

"Everything's fine, Linda," he shouted up. "It's just someone who's lost. I'm giving them directions." He lowered his voice to a harsh whisper. "If you don't leave this very second, I'm going to—"

"You're not going to do a goddamn thing except tell us

where Tammy is right this second," I said through gritted teeth. I held up a photograph of him and Tammy kissing. "I'm sure *Linda* would be very interested to see this photo of you acting *professional* with one of your employees. If you don't tell me where the hell Tammy is *NOW,* I swear to God, I'll run this straight up those stairs to *your wife* and then I will personally see that it's published in the society page of the *Northside Sun*."

Dr. Day's complexion, which had previously been a motley purplish-red, was now the hue of curdled milk.

"She's in room 107 at the Sleepy Time Motel on Fifth Street," he said. "Are you satisfied?"

"Not entirely," Gerald snapped. "Call an ambulance to meet us at the motel. If you don't, I'm sure your wife will just love looking at that picture while she counts her alimony."

"There's plenty more," I said. "Do you understand?"

"Suck my dick, you bitch," Dr. Day said through gritted teeth.

"DICK? Hunny, PLEEZE, you ain't got a dick—all you got's a little dust flap to keep the dirt outta your pussy! Now you back up from us and call that ambulance before I start screeching LINDA!" Gerald hissed with uncharacteristic venom.

"I'll phone right away," Dr. Day said, in a defeated voice.

Moments later the four of us pulled into the parking lot at the Sleepy Time Motel.

"What a dive," Mary Bennett said as we took in the string of decrepit cinder-block buildings with peeling paint, the drained and mildewed pool, and the yellowed grass littered with beer bottles and cigarette butts. "If there's anything worse than a lying jerk, it's a cheap lying jerk."

"I'm going to find Tammy's room," I said, bounding out of the car as soon as it came to a stop. I heard the whine of a siren getting closer. "Y'all go to the office, and see if you can get a key."

I didn't wait for a response, but instead ran around until I saw a faded "107" painted on a rusty metal door. It was slightly ajar.

"Tammy?" I said, pushing it open. The only light in the room came from an orange-shaded floor lamp in the corner. Tammy was stretched out on the bed, wearing her wedding dress. There was a foul odor and a bib-shaped vomit stain down the front of the dress.

"Tammy," I said again, shaking her shoulders. Her nostrils flared as she took quick, shallow breaths. Panic fluttered in my belly when I saw that her lips and fingernails were a deep shade of blue. "Come on, Tammy! Wake up."

I heard footfalls behind me. Two male paramedics rushed into the small, dank room.

"Do you know what she took?" asked one. He had to shout to be heard over the wheeze and rattle of the air conditioner.

"Some kind of pills." I spotted a small brown vial on the nightstand table, and pointed. "I bet this."

I stepped outside to let the paramedics do their work. The rest of the Queens approached me, accompanied by a scowling man with a basketball midsection.

"Damn-it-to-hell," he said, breathless from the short walk. "This ain't good for business. Why'd your friend choose *my* motel to off herself?"

"Maybe she got depressed staying in such a rat hole," Mary Bennett said.

"He's not worth the energy," I said to her just as the paramedics were rushing out of the room with Tammy strapped to a gurney.

"How is she?" I asked as they passed.

"Her vital signs are weak, but she's alive," the paramedic said briskly, as he and his partner loaded Tammy into the ambulance.

A couple of other sleepy-eyed motel guests had come out of their rooms to see what the fuss was about.

"The lady fainted," the owner said to them. His pockmarked skin was the color of Swiss cheese under the neon glow of the Vacancy sign. "Go back to your rooms. There's nothing to see."

"Can I ride along?" I asked, shielding my eyes from the spinning red lights on top of the ambulance.

"Not enough room," said the same mustached paramedic who'd answered all my other questions. "But you can follow us to University Med Center."

•

The Queens and I perched on the plastic chairs under the overly bright fluorescent lights of the emergency room waiting area. The pungent smell of rubbing alcohol and anesthetics made my nose run. I kept glancing at the entrance to the examining rooms, waiting for Tammy's doctor to appear.

"I've been reading the first paragraph of this article, 'I Am Joe's Prostate,' for the last hour," Mary Bennett said, tossing aside a year-old copy of *Reader's Digest*.

I nodded. None of us had been able to do much but stare into space.

Two seats down, a baby with an arm wrapped in gauze shrieked while his mother tried to soothe him. He'd been crying on and off since they'd arrived.

"I need to get out of here for a minute," Gerald said, abruptly standing up. "I saw a vending machine in the hall. Can I get anybody anything?"

"Not unless they have Scotch and water," Mary Bennett said with a yawn. An unshaven, gin-doused old man who'd been dozing startled to attention at Mary Bennett's comment.

"Go back to sleep, old-timer," Mary Bennett said. "They

ain't selling anything stronger than stale Cheetos 'round here."

Just as Gerald was about to leave, a thin-faced doctor with five o'clock shadow trudged into the waiting room clutching a battered clipboard.

"Who is here for Tamara Myers?" he asked.

"We are," the Queens said in unison.

"She'll be okay, except for a little soreness in the throat," he said, approaching us. "We pumped her stomach, and now she's sleeping it off."

My muscles, which had been knotted up like old, sun-dried fishing lines, now slowly untangled with the doctor's good news.

"Can we see her?" I asked.

The doctor shook his head. "She's on the psych floor. No visitors until noon tomorrow."

Psych floor. The two words hung in the air. Of course, I *knew* that Tammy had tried to kill herself, but it was awful to think of her being locked up.

"Thanks, Doctor," I said. Various manifestations of the same followed from the rest.

"Let's get the hell out of here," Mary Bennett said, brushing off the back of her skirt as if she'd picked up something nasty from the chair.

"I'm too wired to sleep," Gerald said. "Is there anywhere we can go this time of night?"

"I know the perfect place." I said. "But it ain't exactly vegetarian-friendly."

"Screw that," Mary Bennett said, with a flick of her hand. "Every cell in my body is crying out for grease and plenty of it."

•

"Little squares of pure heaven," Gerald said, a bulge of Krystal burger in his cheek. We were hunkered down in a booth eating from a tray stacked high with fragrant undersized hamburgers. "Nothing better on this continent."

"Even better than hooch?" I asked, trying to be hip.

Mary Bennett and Gerald swapped a guilty look and grinned.

"We're sorry, Jill," Mary Bennett said, her smile a squiggly line of embarrassment. "While you were in the ladies' room, Gerald and I were discussing it, and . . . we may have acted a bit shitty when we first got here."

I folded my arms across my chest. "Are you referring to the way you treated me and Tammy like a pair of backwater hicks who don't know their asses from their elbows?"

"Yeah," she said sheepishly as Gerald nodded. "That's pretty much what we were referring to."

I let out a deep sigh, and contemplated the crisp French fry in my hand.

"Well," I said, swabbing it in gobs of ketchup. "If you can forgive me for thinking the two of you were a couple of drugged-out hippie freaks with questionable fashion taste, then I guess I can forgive you. And of course, we ARE backwater hicks who don't know their asses from their elbows, so there's that . . ."

Gerald laughed so hard he had a near-nasal Coke experience but swallowed just in time. "That's the Jill I know and love. Get over here! We haven't had us a real hug since I arrived."

I stood and held out my arms to Gerald, and we locked our bodies into the most breath-squeezing bear hug in the entire world. I caught a strong whiff of patchouli, but also smelled another more familiar scent that transported me straight back to high school.

"Brylcreem!" I shouted, stepping back from him. "I can't believe you're still using that stuff!"

Gerald dropped his chin and smiled in the bashful way I'd remembered. "I buy it by the case. Even free-flowing hippie hair needs that 'little dab'll do ya.'"

I laughed and flung my arms around him, burying my face in his neck.

"Hey, y'all," Mary Bennett said, tapping me on the shoulder. "Think I might be able to sneak into this love fest?"

"And what about me?" Patsy demanded. "Don't leave me out."

Gerald and I dropped our arms to let them in, and all of the Queens huddled together into one big, weepy, lopsided, groping embrace.

"Geeze," Mary Bennett said, breaking free from the group. "I love y'all to pieces but the smell of onions is getting mighty thick in here—or was that you, Poot?"

"You better hush about that right now, missy—she just had ten Krystals—you know she's working up a paint-peeler!" Gerald laughed.

Patsy glanced at her watch. "Shit! Jill, it's one o'clock! We gotta get your ass home. You need your beauty sleep for the wedding."

"The what?" I said. I'd been so involved with Tammy and the Queens, it was as if the last few years of my life had been erased from memory. "Oh, yeah. I'm supposed to get married tomorrow—uh, today."

Suddenly Norman "Sonny" Butts seemed like a remote acquaintance from somebody else's life. Who was this man who folded his tighty-whities before sex? Who'd planned an extremely detailed itinerary of our upcoming honeymoon in Biloxi, going as far as to pencil in the times for sex? Who'd barred dear, sweet Gerald from the wedding because he didn't fit in with the other guests? More important—who the fuck was the woman who had so readily agreed to marry that man?

"The wedding," Mary Bennett said, glancing uncomfortably at Gerald. "We'll come if really you want us to."

"Sure," Gerald said. "Sonny seems like a decent sort, a little on the stuffy side but—"

"I think we just expected someone a little different for you, Jill," Patsy said. "Not that Sonny isn't a decent catch and all, but—"

I stiffened. Even ever-agreeable Patsy didn't like Sonny?

"Out of curiosity," I said softly, "what sort of guy do you see me with?"

"Somebody fun, and spontaneous, and funny—or at least somebody who knows YOU'RE funny," Gerald said.

"Egg-zactly," Mary Bennett said. "Somebody who makes things happen and has a zest for life!"

"And somebody with a heart as big as yours," Patsy said, spreading her arms wide. "Somebody as wonderful as you, only with bigger biceps."

I felt as if they were talking about a stranger. When I packed my Tammy wig in the attic shortly after I met Sonny, what other parts of myself had I boxed up and hidden away?

•

"Jill?" Tammy said, her eyelashes fluttering as I stood over her. She blinked rapidly as if adjusting to the light. Her gaze made a jerky sweep of the room.

"Oh," she said with a soft exhale. "All the Queens are here."

"Damn straight we are, gorgeous," Gerald said, squeezing her hand.

Tammy touched her red curls, most of which were matted to the pillow. "I bet I look like dog doo." Tammy's infamous potty-mouth had been severely curtailed by the disapproval of the inexplicably prim Dr. Day. His own adultery somehow passed muster on his moral scale, but to hear a woman swearing was simply intolerable to the man. Go figger.

"No you don't," I said, gently stroking her clammy forehead. "You look fragile, and beautiful. Like Camille."

"I don't feel beautiful," Tammy said in a raspy voice.

"Can I get you anything?" I asked. "Water, a cold towel, hard candy?"

"A straitjacket," Tammy said flatly. Her eyes flickered to the wire-meshed windows.

"Don't fret, hunny," Mary Bennett said. "There's no shame in being sent to the loony bin. Everybody goes a little crazy now and then."

"That's right," Patsy added. "All the world's greatest artists have gone mad at one time or another."

Tammy managed a weak smile. "Well, I musta been crazy as an acre of snakes." She cast her eyes downward and sighed. "You were right, Jill. Deke never had *any* intention of marrying me. He came back from the conference to tell me that his so-called frigid wife is pregnant with twins. He told me we should lay low for a while." Tammy snorted. "And he fired me. That's the 'future' he had in mind for me, unloved and unemployed."

"That bastard!" Gerald exclaimed.

"I'm so, so sorry, hunny," I said.

"I am, too," Tammy said, tensing her fists. "I'm sorry I wasted five years of my life on that worthless jerk. And I'm mad!"

"You *should* be mad," Gerald said, pumping his fist. "Anger's a good thing!"

"As soon as I took those pills I knew I'd messed up," Tammy continued. "I tried to vomit, and guess I managed to get some of them up. Then I called you. I was so groggy by that time. Thank God you were home. I was afraid you might have been out and . . ." Her eyes grew large. "Wait a minute," she said, glancing at the clock on the wall. "You're supposed to be getting married right now! Don't tell me you put off your wedding on account of me?"

"No, no, no," I said softly. "It wasn't because of you."

Several hours earlier I'd stopped by Sonny's to tell him the wedding was off. I cried the entire time. Part of me desperately wanted Sonny's hand to guide my decisions, the way my daddy had as a child, but I knew I was the only one who could decide the true direction of my life. Otherwise, I might just disappear altogether. The Queens comforted me after I had broken it off and spent the rest of the morning informing all the guests, the minister, the photographer, and the caterer.

"What happened?" Tammy asked.

"Nothing," I said. "Marrying Sonny just didn't seem like the right thing to do anymore. It never was."

"I'm glad, Jill," Tammy said with a definitive nod of her chin. "I *never* thought he was the right guy for you."

"You, too?" I asked in amazement. "Why didn't you say something?"

"Well, I've been so preoccupied with Deke I couldn't think of anything else," Tammy said. "And . . . I'm just not used to *you* making stupid mistakes. You've always given everybody sensible advice. I just figured you knew what you were doing."

The others nodded in agreement.

I shook my head in disbelief. The Queens certainly saw me differently than I saw myself.

"Believe you me, I'm as good at screwing up my life as anyone else here," I said. "If you think I'm making a stupid mistake, y'all need to tell me. I might initially tell you to mind your own fuckin' business and drop dead while you're at it, but I swear, I still want to hear it. Do y'all promise?"

"We promise," the Queens said in unison.

"Same goes for me," Gerald said. "If I'm fixin' to screw up, I'd like to know, and you're the only people I can trust to tell me."

"Me, too," Patsy said.

"I'm in," Tammy said with a sigh. "Not that I always listen. I tuned Jill out this time around."

"Sounds like a fine plan to me," Mary Bennett said with a grin. "We Queens gotta look out for each other."

"Here's to US," I said, putting my hand out. The Queens stacked hands on top of mine and we laughed as we completed it, "and fuck EVERYBODY ELSE."

•

"I don't know about y'all, but it seems to me that the good Dr. Day got off a wee bit too easy," Mary Bennett said as she backed her convertible out of the hospital parking lot. "Don't we think he should suffer just a little bit more?"

"Yes," Patsy said, bobbing her blond head up and down. "He deserves a good stab in the ass with a sharp stick."

"I agree," Gerald said. "But what could we do to get back at him without getting ourselves in trouble?"

Suddenly a fiendishly diabolical plan began to swirl in my brain.

"I might have a little something in mind for our dear Dr. Dick," I said. "There's a hardware store a few blocks from here. Why don't we swing by?"

•

Three days later Tammy was released from the hospital. It seemed only fitting to pick her up wearing our cat's-eyes and red wigs. (Mine had a small bald patch on one side from where the moths had gotten to it.)

It was a pretty June day. Blue and pink hydrangeas bobbed

like big balloons in dozens of yards, and the air smelled like line-dried sheets.

Tammy rode shotgun. A hospital bracelet still encircled her slender wrist and her complexion was a tad on the wan side, but after cruising with the Queens for a few minutes, singing our anthem, "Tiny Bubbles," color blossomed in her cheeks.

"We have a surprise for you," I said, squeezing her arm. "A gift from all the Queens."

"As if all those flowers and trashy cards weren't enough?" Tammy said with a grin.

"This is an *extra* special surprise," Mary Bennett said, a strand of red hair flying into her face. "It's a present you'll be sharing with the entire city of Jackson."

"It's a group effort!" Patsy shouted from the backseat. "We all contributed."

"You've certainly roused my curiosity," Tammy said.

Mary Bennett slowed to a stop as she neared the main road leading to Dr. Day's office.

"There," she said, pointing to the block letters spray-painted fluorescent pink on the overpass. "Isn't it a thing of beauty?"

Tammy's eyes followed Mary Bennett's finger. "Omigod!" she said, cupping her mouth. Muffled squealing sounds came from behind her hand, and her torso heaved. The Queens traded worried looks. Had we gone too far?

Tammy dropped her hand. With eyes shiny with tears, she said, "This is, by far and away, the sweetest thing anyone has ever done for me. I just love it! *Loooove* it!"

"Hopefully it will be around for a very, very long time," I said, admiring our handiwork. "Our dear Dr. Dick will get to see it every morning when he goes to work."

"What lyrical alliteration," Gerald mused, as he read the message on the overpass: "'Dr. Deke Day has a dinky dick.'"

"It's a work of art," Tammy said, gazing dreamily at our graffiti. "And TRUE—but there's prolly not room on that sign to describe his other problem."

"What?" we asked in unison.

A wicked giggle escaped her lips. "Well, didja ever try to put a marshmallow in a parking meter?"

PART THREE

1979

Chapter 10

Isn't she lovely? Isn't she won-der-ful?" sang the incredibly handsome, broad-shouldered man sitting next to me at the Diabetes Association Annual Fashion Fling. Sadly, I was the not the inspiration for his serenade. His dark blue eyes were fastened on Tammy, who was strutting down the makeshift runway in the middle of the community center.

"Tammy is wearing a silk bomber jacket, Jordache jeans, and hot pink shoes from Candies," said the emcee, reading from an index card. "All are available from J.B. White's. Doesn't she look divine?"

"Yes!" yelled out my table companion. He stuck his pinkies in his mouth and let out a long, shrill whistle. "She's breathtaking."

"Gee, Bob," I said, leaning toward him. "Maybe you should ask her out for a date."

He flashed me his bright, white movie-star smile. Bob was wasting his time teaching high school English; he would have made a great underwear model.

"Oh, Jill," he said. "I'll bet you think I'm some kind of idiot, huh?"

"No more so than the average guy," I said.

"I just can't believe she's my wife!" he said. "Every morning I thank God for her."

Bob's affection for Tammy reminded me of a little boy with his very first BB gun. I smiled at him, wondering if I'd ever have a man so completely moon-pied over me.

Tammy approached the table, fresh from her runway stint. "How was I?" she asked, her eyes darting with excitement.

"Cheryl Tiegs is a dogball compared to you," Bob said, rising from the table and enveloping her in his arms. "You were the hit of the show, baby."

"You really think so?" Tammy asked.

They started nuzzling and whispering to each other, creating a bubble around themselves as lovers often do. Tammy's happiness was blindingly evident. She had a positively worshipful, not to mention handsome, husband and a killer job. If I hadn't loved her so much, I would no doubt have been annoyed that her life was as frothy and colorful as an episode of *Happy Days*.

"Can I get y'all a drink?" Bob asked, even though the line now snaked halfway across the room. He'd walk barefoot through fields of broken glass just to wait on his wife and me, as a mere extension of her wonderfulness.

"Oh, yes. A wine spritzer would be yummy!" Tammy said gratefully.

"I think I'd like a Jack and Seven with lots of lemon." I paused. "On second thought, hold the Seven. And the lemon."

"Coming up," Bob said cheerfully. The two of them kissed quickly but passionately before he departed.

"Okay, give me the unvarnished truth," Tammy said. "How did I *really* look?"

"Like a wave over a slop jar," I said in a teasing voice.

Tammy's mouth fell open in horror.

"Oh, come on, Tammy. You *know* you looked stunning—you just like hearing it over and over."

"I guess . . . I'm just being . . . I don't know. It just that I'm kind of long in the tooth for *modeling*."

"Twenty-eight is hardly old," I said, although I'd been feeling the pangs of my own advancing age lately. After all, twenty-eight was only a few heartbeats away from thirty, the age at which we then believed death began.

"Tammy Myers? Is that you?" said a woman with a long face, large Chiclet-like teeth, and heavy blond hair pulled into a ponytail. She reminded me of a sweet little palomino I'd ridden as a child.

"My *married* name is Tammy Hollingsworth," Tammy said, slightly raising her left hand from her lap. She wore the patient and mildly flattered expression of a person who is accustomed to being recognized in public. "But yes, that's me."

"My husband and I watch you every morning. He won't go out the door until he hears what Tammy has to say about the weather."

"Well, thank you very much," Tammy said, beaming.

Tammy worked at WJBW as the weather girl. She was so pretty and personable that she'd become something of a local celebrity. The station even sold logo umbrellas that said "Tammy predicts showers."

"I didn't know you did charity work. That's so wonderful! We sure could use a little help with this year's Hair Ball."

"Really?" Tammy said, her eyes glinting with glee. Despite the relatively disgusting name, the Hair Ball was *the* charity event in Jackson. It was a benefit for the local chapter of the Humane Society.

"Yes," continued the woman, who wore a skirt covered with pink and green whales. "We're having a planning meeting Thursday at seven p.m. at my house. I'd *love* for you to come. I'm not the chairwoman per se, but I'm sure that won't be a problem. Let me jot down my contact information for you." She found a pen in her purse and wrote a phone number on a cocktail napkin.

"I'll check my schedule and make sure I'm free," Tammy said.

"Oh, forgive me. My name's Stacy Albright," she said. "I hope you can come. We really need people to help with fund-raising. Our slogan this year is 'Cough it up for the Hair Ball.'" She let loose a loud, braying laugh. "What did you say your husband did?"

"I didn't," Tammy said, toying with her oversized hoop earring. "Bob is, uh . . . an academician."

"Really? My Doug taught at the medical school for a few years, but he couldn't resist the lure of a lucrative private practice. It's a good thing, because I just adore shopping. Tammy, it was a pleasure." She tossed off a bye-bye wave. "Hope to see you Thursday."

"I jest ado-o-ore shop-pin'," I said, mimicking Stacy's voice after she left. "Please tell me you aren't planning on going."

"It's the Hair Ball, Jill! I've wanted to attend forever. If I'm on the planning committee, I'll surely get an invitation."

"It should be called the H-e-i-r Ball," I said, spelling out the name. "Practically everyone there is covered up in Daddy's Money."

There was no *way* I'd be able to talk Tammy out of being on that committee. With her high-profile job and cute-as-a-button husband, maybe Tammy had finally "arrived" in the way she'd always hoped.

"We'll see," Tammy said. "So, how's work going?"

"Not great," I said with a sigh. "I thought my promotion to manager would make a difference, but I'm still under Penny's thumb. I keep telling her we need to discuss exercise with our clients, but she's resistant. Thinks it would be a turnoff to 'em."

"I've gotta admit, I don't find all that sweating and huffing and puffing very appealing."

"Appealing or not, exercise is the only way to keep weight off."

"You're so good about all that. Walking every day. Lifting those heavy barbells over your head." Tammy shuddered.

I knew from previous discussions that she considered weight lifting to be unladylike and believed that one day I was going to wake up looking like Charles Atlas.

"I have plenty of time to exercise," I said, "since my social life is about as lively as a Quaker funeral."

"You've only been divorced six months. It takes a little while to get back in the swing of things."

I nodded. Shortly after jilting Sonny, I met and married a guy named Warren, despite some trepidation from the Queens. He was the opposite of Sonny, wild and irresponsible. I finally ran him off after he quit his sixth job and maxed out all my credit cards.

"I could ask Bob if he knows anyone to set you up with."

"I hate blind dates," I said, peering at the line to the bar to see what kind of progress Bob was making with our drinks. "I also hate being the only one without a boyfriend or a husband. But, a boyfriend who sucks is NOT better than no boyfriend at all. Anyway, when the Queens get here tomorrow, Mary Bennett will be yammering about that actor she's been howlin' at the moon over, and Patsy will be gabbing nonstop about Jack."

"You won't be the only Queen without a man," Tammy said. "There's Gerald."

I laughed. "You're right. I'll have Gerald to commiserate with."

Chapter 11

"We are family!" Mary Bennett sang as she boogied over to the table. She was wearing a shimmering pink disco dress. "I got all my sistahs with me."

She squealed and hugged Patsy, Tammy, and me in quick succession. We were seated in a part of the Stardust Discothèque called the Mellow-Out Lounge. It was much quieter than the main room with the dance floor, but we could still feel the thumpata-thumpata of the music surging through our bodies.

"Actually, one of our 'sistahs' is missing," I remarked. "Where's Gerald?"

"Geraldine's coming later. And guess what? He's bringing his hunny bunny," Mary Bennett said with a sly wink.

"What?" I gasped.

"It's high time," Patsy said. "I thought he'd never come out of the cupboard."

"I think you mean *closet*, Swiss Miss," Mary Bennett said with a chuckle. "But you're right, it did take him a while to figure out what we've known all along. My gawd, he's been living in San Francisco now for years."

We all nodded. Gerald never talked about his sexuality, and we'd never pressed him about it, not even the brazen Mary Bennett.

"He called to tell me he was bringing someone tonight," Mary Bennett said, settling herself on a padded stool. "He was all giggly about it, too. Sounded like a schoolgirl."

"It's 1979," I said, raising my Jack Daniel's. "Queer is in!"

"You don't think he and his friend will be kissing, do you?" Tammy said with a scowl. "I'm no Anita Bryant, but I don't want to see two guys with their tongues down each other's throats, either."

"Would it hurt your feelings if I pointed out that you're completely full of shit?" I asked. "How many times have I had to watch you and Bob swap spit?"

"That's different," Tammy said with a sniff. "Kisses between the opposite sex are completely natural."

"Tammy Hollingsworth," I said sternly. "It's taken our dear little Gerald twenty-eight years to finally express his *own* completely natural sexuality, and you want to begrudge him a few smooches with his sweetie?"

"Here! Here!" Mary Bennett said, raising an empty glass. "You tell her, Jill."

"You're right, you're right," Tammy said in a contrite voice. "I'm sorry. Please don't tell Gerald—it was just a momentary lapse into ig'nant dumbass—I don't even know where that came from!"

"For a minute there you sounded like SONNY BUTTS," I said with a shudder.

The last time the Queens had been together was two years ago, for Patsy and Jack's wedding in Atlanta. Jack, a defense attorney, is a huge, strapping blond from Wisconsin, and when he and Patsy got together they talked so fast we could hardly understand a word. But there was always plenty of cheese on hand.

Mary Bennett handed the waitress her credit card, ordering a gin and tonic and every appetizer on the menu for us to share. "Gerald is just going to have to listen to the reruns. I cain't wait to hear what's going on with y'all."

"I have some big news," Patsy said, her cheeks even pinker than usual. "Jack and I are expecting a little bundle."

"Boon dull?" Mary Bennett said with a raised eyebrow.

"Bundle!" I translated. "Patsy's in the family way."

"You've done got yourself knocked up, Swiss Miss?" Mary Bennett grinned. "Well, ain't you sump'n. Congratulations! We need to celebrate. A whole round for the table and your very softest drink for our little friend here," she said to waitress, who'd just returned. "On me."

"Miss," said the waitress, who wore a low-cut, short leopard-print dress. "I'm afraid your credit card was declined."

"Really?" Mary Bennett said. "That doesn't sound right. I could have sworn—"

"I'll get it," I said, handing over my American Express. "You're always picking up the tabs."

"Just this one time," Mary Bennett said, shaking her finger at me. "So when is this little Yankee due?"

"Six months, in December," Patsy said, rubbing her small swell of a belly. "And Mary Bennett, this baby won't be a Yankee. He or she will be born in Atlanta as a true-blue Southerner."

"Sorry, hunny," Mary Bennett said. "But jest 'cause a cat has kittens in the oven doesn't make 'em biscuits. But don't you worry—I'll still love the little beester anyway 'cause he'll be *your* Yankee."

We gabbed about the baby for a while. Talked about possible names. Patsy favored Katrina for a girl and Olaf for a boy. Mary Bennett said that either of those names would be a serious handicap for a child growing up anywhere in the South, particularly Georgia, and suggested Bubba for a boy and MaryBubba for a girl.

Once we'd exhausted the topic of Patsy's baby, Tammy fixed her gaze on Mary Bennett and said, "So let's hear about this new boyfriend of yours. The actor."

"Brian is sublime," Mary Bennett said, swirling her straw in her drink. "We met in an off-off-off-Broadway production called *Bald*. It's a spoof on the musical *Hair*, and the entire cast wears bald caps. It's kind of sexy, 'specially in the third act when everybody gets nekkid."

Tammy gasped. "You take your clothes off onstage?"

"Get your tonsils off the table, hunny," Mary Bennett said. "It's all in the name of art. Besides, showing your bare hiney in public is the latest thing. Think of all those people going around streaking. The human body is a bee-you-ti-ful thing."

"You wouldn't say that if you worked in a weight-loss clinic all day long," I said drily. "But let's get back to Brian. Tell us about him."

"He's tall, dark, and handsome," Mary Bennett said with a winsome sigh. "He thinks the sun shines out my ass and he is an absolute MINK in bed—Jill, hunny, he knows ALL ABOUT 'the little man in the boat'!"

I squealed—with a mixture of delight for the good fortune of my friend and a twinge of embarrassment over my former sexual naïveté.

After a round of laughs at my expense, the ensuing silence at the table was so thick you could have carved it up like a Thanksgiving turkey.

"Well," I said, wagging my eyebrows at Mary Bennett. "I guess you know what we're all thinking."

"We're sorry," said a shame-faced Patsy. "We shouldn't have."

"Yes, we should, and we're dying to know—what's WRONG with him?" I said, laughing.

Mary Bennett's mouth puckered into a frown. "I am deeply disappointed in all of you." She took a quick swig of her cocktail. "I'll have you know there is absolutely NOTHING WRONG with Brian—he doesn't have a record, he's never even been arrested; he's not married, never done that, either; he doesn't live with his mama or his big butch sister; he doesn't have any children, tiny dogs, OR parrots; he doesn't collect stuffed animals—and, he's not a vegan! There's NOTHING WRONG with this one, I swear—and y'all, for the first time in my life I think I might be in love."

After Mary Bennett's rhapsodizing over the seemingly flawless Brian, Tammy sang Bob's praises (Patsy and Mary Bennett had never met him because they'd eloped) and talked about her job and how much fun she was having wearing cute little costumes on the air, i.e., a down jacket and earmuffs when it was cold and a bright red raincoat with matching boots when the rain was raining. And on the weekends, she had a regular singing gig at the piano bar in the University Club. Bob would sit at the bar, watching, listening, and worshipping.

"Jill," Patsy said when Tammy took a breath. "What've you been up to?"

They were all staring at me, and I was reminded of the last day of high school when the rest of the Queens were showing off their trophies and I was empty-handed.

"Well, I do have some news," I said, grinning.

The Queens leaned forward in their seats with interest.

"I renewed my driver's license a couple of weeks ago and, believe it not, this picture is even more hideous than the last—I look just like that big fish on the front of the sports page today, MUD CAT."

"Oh, Jill," Mary Bennett said, punching my arm. "Listen to you—will you EVER stop putting yourself down? Nobody gets a good driver's license photo—I think it's against the law, and it's universal. There must be some special photography school they send those folks to—and if they accidentally take a flattering picture, they fail. Mine makes me look like I have no teeth!"

"She's also being modest," Tammy said. "Jill got promoted at the Quick Weight-Loss Center. You're looking at their new manager."

Tammy's announcement was met with hearty approval—way more than my piddling little accomplishment deserved.

"Enough already," I said finally. "It's not like I discovered the cure for cancer or anything. They *had* to promote me. I've been working there since high school."

And with Penny, the raging bosshole, *I sure as hell don't have a whole lot more authority,* I thought.

"There's Gerald!" Mary Bennett said suddenly. She waved her hand. "Over here."

Gerald swished over to our table. Gone were his long locks and hippie clothes. His hair curled around his ears, and he wore a tweed jacket and a turtleneck, looking every inch the professor that he was. Mary Bennett gave him a noisy smooch on the cheek. "Gerald just got his Ph.D., so we're going to have to call him doctor now. Maybe you can give me a private examination later, Dr. Gerald?"

"Maybe," he said, not playing along as usual. He was blinking rapidly and his hug felt stiff and perfunctory.

"Where's your hunny?" Mary Bennett asked.

"The restroom," he said, looking nervously over his shoulder. "We can't stay long. I promised my parents we'd stop by their house in an hour or so."

So that's why he was so uptight. I knew his father had worried about Gerald's lack of girlfriends. He must have "come out" to his parents earlier, and now they'd be meeting his love interest for the very first time.

"Let's get you a drink," Mary Bennett said, patting the stool next to her. "I know this is a big, big step, bringing your sweetie home to meet everyone."

"I'm a wreck," Gerald said, sagging onto the stool. "Could you . . . ? Would you . . . ? Just be a little . . ."

"I know egg-zactly what you're trying to say, sweetheart. Fret no more," Mary Bennett said. "We Queens are going to be on our best behavior for your hunka hunka burnin' love. You hear that, Swiss Miss? Keep those off-color remarks to yourself."

"I'll wash my mouth out with soap and not even rinse," Patsy said with a laugh.

"We'll be as wholesome as a troop of Girl Scouts," I said, putting my right hand over my heart and raising my left.

"That's good because . . . oh, there she is," Gerald said, jumping up from his stool.

"He calls his boyfriend 'she,'" Mary Bennett whispered. "Isn't that precious?"

"Ladies," he said, gesturing over an imposingly tall black woman with an impressive shelf of a bosom and enormous feet. "I'd like you to meet my girlfriend, Sheila."

"Girlfriend?" I repeated, trying to understand. I could see the questions in the other Queens' eyes.

"Actually," Sheila said, her voice booming throughout the lounge, "Gerald proposed to me a month ago, so technically I'm his fiancée."

"That's right," Gerald said, blushing. "I haven't gotten in the habit of saying 'fiancée' instead of 'girlfriend.'"

"No biggie," Sheila said, brushing imaginary lint off Gerald's jacket. "In a couple of days you'll have to switch to 'wife,' anyway."

Our faces must have given voice to our confusion. Gerald clarified it: "We've decided to elope—run over to Livingston, Alabama, and just DO it. They've been marryin' fifteen-year-olds from the tristate area ever since I can remember—let's see how they handle US!"

After some awkward congratulations from the Queens, Gerald proceeded to introduce us to Sheila individually, and I could tell that everyone was trying very hard not to seem too shocked.

"How long have you two been seeing each other?" Tammy asked.

"About a year," Gerald said with a tight smile.

"Men!" Sheila said with a harsh laugh like a seal's bark. "It's been eleven months, thirteen days, three hours, and"—she glanced at her watch—"seven minutes."

Sheila had deep grooves around her mouth, like a lifelong smoker, and pronounced crow's feet. It was my guess that she was at least ten years older than Gerald.

"How did y'all meet?" I asked.

"We both teach at San Francisco State," Sheila said. "I teach in the new Women's Studies department."

"You don't *sound* like you're from California," Mary Bennett said.

"I'm from Jersey," she said, her "Jersey" sounding like "Joisy."

"I miss the East, but I think California is a better place to raise kids. Bunny agrees." She elbowed Gerald. "Right, bunny?"

Bunny/Gerald nodded sheepishly.

Under normal circumstances at a Queenly gathering, one of us (probably Mary Bennett) wouldn't have been able to resist ribbing Gerald about his "bunny" nickname. As it was, nobody said a word.

"Excuse me, dear," Gerald said in an overly formal tone as he rose from his chair. "I need to visit the facilities."

"Go ahead, bunny," Sheila said. "Us girls will just chitchat."

Gerald left, and Sheila gave us all a broad smile, revealing teeth dotted with bright red lipstick. "I'm so thrilled to meet all of you. Gerald talks about you constantly. I told him, 'Gerald, what's up with all these women friends? Should I be jealous?' He says to me, 'Dumpling'—that's what he calls me in private—'don't get yourself into a swivet. I haven't shtupped any of them. They're my best friends in the whole world.' I'm so lucky to have a man like Gerald who isn't afraid to be in touch with his feminine side, and is capable of having platonic relationships with members of the opposite sex."

"It's a rare thing in a man," I said with a weak smile.

"Gerald's special all right," Tammy said, and Patsy nodded along.

"He is a PRIZE!" Sheila said. Her hair was so lacquered with spray, not a strand stirred when she moved her head—it was preternaturally perfect, and there was something vaguely disturbing about it.

Mary Bennett, who'd kept curiously quiet, lit a Virginia Slim and stared contemplatively at the smoke rings.

"I have a personal question for you, Sheila, dahlin'," she said.

Tammy, Patsy, and I traded glances of alarm. We'd heard *that* tone before.

"Fire away," Sheila said with a wave of her manicured hand. "I'm used to sensitive topics."

"Good." Mary Bennett smiled. "I was just wondering if it ever occurred to you that Gerald might be a wee bit *too* much in touch with his feminine side? That he might, in fact, be as gay as a goose? Because the truth is, when Gerald told me he was bringing his sweetie here, I quite frankly expected a Sherman, not a Sheila."

I gulped back a gasp, and Patsy gripped the arms of her chair. Tammy's face was two shades paler than normal.

"I hear you, Mary Bennett, and I don't mind your frankness," Sheila said, with a seemingly unfazed expression. "I agree Gerald might have some latent desires, but his wish to be a Jewish family man, respected by his parents, is far stronger."

"What about you?" I surprised myself by asking. "Why would *you* want to marry a man who's probably gay?"

Sheila put a hand to her belly and said, "Tick-tock. Tick-tock. I'm almost forty, Jill. You girls might not understand this now, but one day you will. There's more important things in a relationship than mind-blowing sex."

"Well, this group would prolly dispute THAT, hunny," Mary Bennett said, "but have you thought about how his family is gonna react—I mean, you not being Jewish and all?"

We all got quiet. The only sound was the whirring of the blender behind the bar, and the muffled boom-boom of the bass from a Donna Summer song next door.

"Lift those chins, girls," Sheila said, brightly. "Your dear Gerald is ecstatic, I promise you. This is a good thing for everyone!"

"Here he comes," Patsy said, taking a sip of her ginger ale.

"Did y'all have a nice visit?" Gerald said as he sat.

"We did, bunny!" Sheila said, pecking his cheek. "Your girlfriends are such sweeties. We were gabbing away like old pals."

"Good. It's very important to me that everyone I love gets along."

•

"Could I stay at your place tonight?" Mary Bennett said, touching my elbow just as everyone was leaving the disco. "We're painting the inside of the house, and the fumes will make me sick."

"Of course," I said, picking up my purse from our table. "But you're going to have to sleep in a double bed with me. My apartment is ti-ny and there's no guest room."

"It'll be like a slumber party! Besides, I'm used to close quarters living in New York."

Mary Bennett followed me home in her convertible from high school. She always drove the Tammymobile when she was back home. I was thrilled it was still running. The red leather seats and gleaming chrome brought back so many fond memories.

"Get comfy," I said to Mary Bennett as I switched on the living room light. "I gotta pee."

Mary Bennett made herself at home. She stretched out on my spindly saggy sofa, legs dangling off one end. When I returned, her nose was deep into my journal.

"Whatda hell do you think you're doing?!" I asked.

"Well, you didn't have any magazines, and your TV's all snowy," she said, licking a finger as she turned a page.

"Hand it over."

"This is funny stuff," Mary Bennett said with a snicker. "Have you ever thought about being a writer?"

I snatched the journal from her hand. "Have you ever thought 'bout mindin' your own fuckin' business?"

"Hell no," Mary Bennett said, swinging her long legs around

so she faced me. "That's why I'm racking my brain trying to decide what we're going to do about Gerald."

I sat in the only other seat—a rattan chair that hung from the ceiling. It had looked cute in the store, but its swaying sometimes gave me motion sickness.

"I've heard of gay guys getting married and having children. Maybe Gerald—"

"Horse shit!" Mary Bennett said. "Marriage to that woman would be like locking him up in a cage. He needs to run free—get all wild and woolly. I know!" She snapped her fingers. "We should take him to a gay bar the night before his wedding."

"Too obvious," I said, rocking back and forth. "Besides, don't you think he sampled that scene in San Francisco?"

"He used to be into *drugs*, not the gay scene. He probably got high, hoping to lessen his attraction to men. I'll bet he's never even been in a gay bar before."

"We actually have a few right here in Jackson now—I've been, had a blast," I said. A thought suddenly came to me. "There *is* this fabulous gay guy who works out at my gym. He's the most gorgeous creature you've ever seen, not to mention the nicest. He's the minister of a nondenominational church that meets in an empty store downtown. Maybe he could talk to Gerald."

"We could have a bachelor party for Gerald and have this guy jump out of the cake!" Mary Bennett said.

"I think subtlety is the key here. Let me give it some thought and . . . Lord have mercy!" The combination of the spinning chair and three Jack Daniel's (Seven and lemon held) were making me queasy.

"Excuse me," I said, hotfooting it toward the bathroom. "Oh, Lord, I think I'm gonna lose my lunch."

"Can I do somethin', hunny?" Mary Bennett said, following on my heels.

"No," I said, shooing her off. "I've always considered pukin' to be a very private affair."

I was in the bathroom a good while, squashing my cheek against the coolness of the tile floor. Mary Bennett had called out to me a couple of times to make sure I was still breathing, and I'd moan a reply. After a half hour or so the room quit lurching, and I thought I could pick my face up off the floor.

I rose on rubbery legs, brushed my teeth, and turned off the bathroom fan that I'd turned on earlier to drown out my gagging. I was about to open the door when I heard a high-pitched cry.

"But, Daddy. I'm down to my last few dollars. You can't cut me off."

Mary Bennett's voice sounded so desperate and childlike I scarcely recognized it. In all the years I'd known her, I'd never heard her cry.

"I can't do that, Daddy. Please don't ask me. I love him. Don't hang up!"

The room was suddenly silent. I slowly opened the door and saw Mary Bennett sitting cross-legged on the sofa, desperately trying to choke back tears.

"Mary Bennett, is there anything I can do?" I asked gently.

"I've always considered a pity party to be a very private affair," she said in a ragged voice.

I sat next to her, and hugged her neck. She melted into my chest, crying softly. After a few moments she lifted her head and said, "Pleeeze don't tell the others, okay?"

I nodded. "Do you need some money? Warren pretty much cleaned me out, but I do have a little bit of savings—"

"Hush, Jill," she said, putting a finger to her lips. "I wouldn't take a cent from you. The convertible is in my name, so I can sell it if I absolutely have to. There's this fellow in the neighborhood who's always had his eye on it."

"The Tammymobile," I said sadly.

"Well, I won't sell if I can help it, but don't think one more thing about it. One day I'll have enough money to buy us the biggest, flashiest convertible in the entire world. Screw Daddy's money! I'll make my own."

"I guess there wasn't really any painting going on at your house."

She shook her head. "When I told Daddy about Brian, he had 'his people' check him out—found out he's a mostly unemployed actor, just like me, and swore he would NOT support TWO of us—that the Man should be the Provider and all that crap. Said that until Brian got a real job or I ditched him, I'd not get another penny. Told me I could get a job and support his sorry ass if I wanted to but he'd be damned if HE was gonna pay for another MAN to sit on his butt claiming to be an 'actor'—oh, fuck it. Forgive me for fibbin'. I didn't want to burden you with my problems. And there really ISN'T anything wrong with Brian—he's a good, honest, hardworking man—only it's harder to GET the work than do it, and Daddy just doesn't understand . . . I'm sorry—you don't need to hear all my troubles."

"But Mary Bennett, that's why you *have* friends."

That started her blubbering all over again. "I can't lose Brian, Jill. He's my first."

"I know," I said, lightly scratching her back. "The first love is the strongest."

"Not just that," Mary Bennett said, pulling away and staring up at me, her eyes fringed with damp lashes. "He's my first *everything.*"

"You don't mean . . ."

"Yes, I do," she said with a solemn nod.

"But Mary Bennett, in high school—"

"All an act," she said, biting her bottom lip until it turned white from her teeth marks. "My daddy was sleeping with anyone in a skirt, so I figured I would fight back by sleeping with anyone in pants. Trouble was, I was too scared to actually go through with it. But that was the beauty of high school, you didn't have to actually *do* the dirty deed to get credit for it, you just had to act like ya did."

"Oh my God," I said, gently grasping her wrist.

"Brian understands me," Mary Bennett said. "It's like he's got those X-ray glasses from the back of the comic book, and can see straight into my heart. No man's ever been able to do that—none's ever cared enough to even try. He is the only man I ever believed *really* loves *me*." A brittle laugh escaped her lips. "It's ironic, ya know. The one time Daddy pays me any attention is the only time I wish he wouldn't."

"I'm so, so sorry, hunny."

"That's all right," she said, scrubbing away her tears with her fists. "Ever since I was a little girl, my dream was to please my daddy—make him proud of me—but this time, I'm gonna have to please myself."

Chapter 12

"The thrill is gone," I sang in a melancholy voice as I slipped files into their proper places in the cabinet.

"Jill!" My boss stuck her head inside my office, reading glasses dangling from a chain around her neck. "Could you come here for a minute?"

"Sure, Penny," I said, banging shut a drawer. I strode to her office and saw Mrs. Dickerman sitting in one of the rounded-back chairs across from Penny's desk. Mrs. Dickerman had on a pair of bright blue shorts that accentuated the network of fine veins running through her pale, fleshy legs. On her feet she wore rubber flip-flops, and one of her toes was wrapped with a bandage. I scooted into the chair next to her and nodded a greeting, but she didn't meet my eye. The mood in the office was decidedly frosty and grim, and I was pretty certain I was fixin' to get an ass chewin'.

Penny's eyes were blue and chillingly cold, and her hooked nose looked sharp as a hawk's.

"Jill, did you happen to notice the injury to Mrs. Dickerman's big toe?"

"Yes, ma'am," I said.

"Do you have any idea how she got that injury?"

"No." *But I'm sure you're going to tell me.*

"She dropped a can of cream of celery soup on it," Penny said. "Does that ring a bell?"

"I don't think this is *entirely* Jill's fault," Mrs. Dickerman said with a whimper. "After all, my hands were slippery. I'd been moisturizing with Jergen's."

I knew exactly what this was all leading to. At a recent weigh-in, Mrs. Dickerman complained that even though she'd lost twenty pounds, her upper arms were still mushy. I'd shown her a triceps exercise that would help battle those batwings, and suggested that she hold a soup can for added resistance.

"What's our slogan here at Quick Weight-Loss Center?" Penny demanded.

"'Lose weight without exercise.' But Mrs. Dickerman wanted to—"

"Jill," Penny cut me off in warning. "Mrs. Dickerman, I'm very sorry about your toe, and I'm sure Jill is, too. She had no business recommending such a dangerous exercise." She held out a piece of paper. "Here's a coupon for five dollars off your next visit. We'll see you in a week."

Mrs. Dickerman shuffled up to the desk to get her coupon. Her eyes slid guiltily in my direction. I knew she hadn't intended to get me into trouble.

"We have a problem, Jill," Penny said after Mrs. Dickerman left. "I should fire you. You've been warned not to discuss exercise with clients. Showing Mrs. Dickerman an arm exercise right after our last talk was insubordination, pure and simple."

"I'm sorry," I said, knowing better than to argue.

Penny twisted a paper clip in her hand. "However, since you've been here ten years and this is the first *real* problem I've had with you, I'm going to give you one more chance. But, as punishment, I'm demoting you. Christy will now be our new manager."

I nodded, not trusting what I might say. Christy was three years younger than me and had worked at Quick Weight-Loss Center for only six months. She kept a Magic 8 Ball on her desk and was always consulting it for important decisions, being too uncoordinated to flip a coin and also having trouble deciding whether to choose "heads" or "tails." The Magic 8 ball was a real time-saver for ol' Chris.

•

"You're in a foul mood," I said to Tammy, pumping my arms as we circled the walking track around the YMCA. I slowed my pace to a near crawl so she wouldn't have to walk alone. Patsy and Mary Bennett were so far ahead you couldn't tell who they were.

"I am *perspiring*," Tammy said, flapping her arms like a chicken. "And the other girls are a mile away—we're missing all the latest rumors. Why don't we just go somewhere and EAT. Hunny, now, tell the truth—wouldn't you *really* rather sit around in some nice air-conditioning—with a tableful of sweet, salty, fried, and au gratins with a big side of delicious gossip?" she pleaded. "Lord, I know I would. I despise all this sweat—it's disgusting!"

"That's the idea," I said. "You're supposed to work up a sweat—there's simply no other way to get in shape."

"Huh! I don't know that I *want* to change my shape. I think men prefer curvy women. My daddy always said the only use he had for a *skinny* woman was to take a message to a *fat* one."

She'd been squawking the entire fifteen minutes we'd been walking, and I was getting more resentful by the minute. It was *my* turn to be in a dark mood. I was the one with the miserable job. I was the one who spent night after lonely night in a narrow-ass bed while Tammy cuddled up to her cutie-pie Ken doll. What the hell did she have to be crabby about?

"Guess who called last night?" Tammy said, her lower lip jutted out so far a pigeon could have perched on it. "Stacy. That's who."

"Stacy?"

"The Hair Ball girl. Remember? Turns out she called the chairman of the ball to tell her about me, and the chairman told her they didn't have any openings on their stupid committees so my services wouldn't be needed."

I paused for a moment to shake a rock loose from my Adidas. The sun was just coming up, and the grass was glittering with dew. "Count your lucky stars. They probably would have had you stuffing envelopes or some other mind-numbing chore."

"Guess who the chairman of the Hair Ball is? Marcy Stevens!" Tammy said, spitting out the name. "Only it's not Stevens anymore, it's Highsmith. She married the president of Highsmith Insurance. No openings, my ass—Marcy just didn't want *me* on the committee. It's the fuckin' Key Club all over again."

"I hate her—hope she dies," I said offhandedly and started to walk again. It didn't even register that Tammy had slipped back into her true trash-talking ways. I'd been the one to suggest an early-morning trek, but I was no longer in the mood; my legs and mind felt heavy.

"It doesn't matter," she said bitterly from her own world. "You can have a great job and a red-hot husband, but you can't ever get away from assholes like Marcy. She probably laughed herself sick at the idea of the loser from high school trying to be a part of her precious Hair Ball. She's just been WAITING all these years to get back at me for her Homecoming Humiliation."

"So what?" I said, without my usual patience. "Even if she's trying to snub you, who is *Marcy* to you anymore? Frankly, I'd love to have seen her face when Stacy told her that she wanted YOU on her committee! I bet she nearly shit, and now she's prolly in a complete meltdown that Stacy will find out about Homecoming and *she'll* be humiliated all over again—we can only hope."

A startled look appeared in Tammy's green eyes, as if she were trying to process my question. In the meantime, Patsy and Mary Bennett had backtracked to join us.

"I'm pooped," Mary Bennett said, grabbing her bony knees and stretching. "Why don't we take a little breather and go over our plans for tonight?"

We arranged ourselves around a picnic table a few feet away from the dirt track.

"Why don't we quit altogether and just talk about what all we're gonna *eat* tonight? That's about the only planning I'm interested in," Tammy said, mopping her damp forehead with the tail of her T-shirt. "Even dogs have sense enough to go lie down in the fucking shade when it's so damned hot—I ain't walkin' another step on this stupid track today. Now, who's bringing what tonight?"

•

As soon as there was a satisfactory list of enough fat-filled foods to give Tammy hope for the future, our conversation turned to the raft of questions raised by the return of Gerald with the mystifying Sheila. Was there anything to be done about the situation? An hour later, and sick of sitting on those hard bench seats, we were no closer to an answer.

Chapter 13

Mary Bennett's boyfriend, Brian, was like hot fudge for the eyes. My glance slowly traveled all over him, from his black velvet eyes to his taut tan biceps.

"Earth to Jill!" Mary Bennett said, snapping me out of my Brian-induced trance.

"Was I staring?" I asked.

"Let's put it this way," Mary Bennett said. "If lookin' was eatin', there wouldn' be nuthin' left of MY boyfriend but a greasy spot and some crumbs. Get a grip on yourself, girl—you act like you've never seen a gorgeous man before!"

"Mary Bennett, you're embarrassing me," Brian said in a low, smooth, oboelike voice. "I'm pleased to meet you, Jill, and, for the record, I didn't feel like you were staring at me."

"I was gawking all right," I admitted. "Usually I'm a little bit sneakier."

"Brian's so used to being gawked at he barely notices," Mary Bennett said. "Ain't that right, hunny?"

"I don't notice because I'm too busy lookin' at you," Brian said, grinning.

Mary Bennett rapidly waved a hand in front of her face as if she were hot. "You hear that? That's the kind of thing this man says to me all day long! Bless his heart, he's under some kind of delusion that he's in love with me."

"It's a delusion I hope I never recover from," he said, slipping an arm around her waist.

"There he goes again!" she said, shaking her head in wonderment. "What am I gonna do with this poor hapless soul?"

"A kiss would be nice," Brian said.

"That's fine, hunny," Mary Bennett said. "But no tongue—I promised Jill I'd go easy on the mushy stuff tonight."

I laughed. It was obvious that Mary Bennett was ass-over-teacups in love with Brian. Despite the occasional pang of something very like jealousy, I was happy she'd finally found the right guy.

As the party wore on, the Queens went out of their way to make me feel a part of things, mainly by foisting their sweeties on me. I'd danced with Jack three times, Brian five, and Bob six. Any more dancing and my feet were going to fall off.

I'd decided to take a breather at an umbrella table near the pool when Sheila approached me.

"Oh no," I said, taking off my shoes and rubbing my feet. "You're not going to ask me to dance too, are you?"

"Not unless you want me to," she said with a laugh. She pointed at my shoes. "You have the right idea! My feet are killing me, too."

"Those are cu-u-u-te shoes," I said, admiring her glittery purple platforms. "But they don't look very comfy."

"They're torture devices. It's amazing what we girls will do in the name of fashion." Sheila dropped one shoe. It landed next to mine, and I blinked in shock. My size tens looked like itty-bitty elf shoes next to Sheila's.

"My feet are as big as barges," Sheila said, obviously noting my surprise. "I have to custom order them. All my life I've wanted tiny feet. When I was twelve, I actually bound my feet like Japanese women used to do, but it didn't help."

"I know exactly how you feel. I once bought size seven shoes and forced myself to wear them even though they pinched like hell. I kept thinking my feet would shrink to fit the shoes."

"Big-girl woes," Sheila said, smiling at me companionably. She tugged on her hair, which shifted unnaturally. Mary Bennett was right. Sheila was definitely wearing a wig. I wondered if, in addition to the big-foot blues, she also suffered from the heartbreak of skinny hair. If so, she was in damn good company.

Tammy approached us, gathering her hair up into a ponytail. "You think we'll swim later on? It's as hot as the hammered-down hinges out here."

"Back to the Baptist Youth Group version of cussin', Tammy? I swear, I miss the girl who woulda said 'It's as hot as P-FUCK out here and I am fixin' to git my cute little ass in that nice cool water!' I thought she was back today out there on that track—y'all shoulda heard her, I swear," I said, laughing.

"I didn't bring a suit," Sheila said.

"Hunny, you won't need one," I said. "SOME of us may try to fool you with Pollyanna-talk, but we *all* still love to skinny-dip."

"Oh dear," Sheila said, covering her large chest with her hands. "I guess I'm the modest type."

That was a bit hard to swallow since she was once again

wearing a dress the size of a hanky, but I guess it's a big leap from dressing seductively to not dressing at all.

"You could always swim in your bra and panties," I said.

"Not me." Sheila dropped her voice to a whisper. "I never wear panties to a party. Panty lines, you know."

"Never?" Tammy said, wide-eyed.

Sheila nodded.

"No panties to a party," I mused to myself. "What an intriguing notion."

"You Can't Hurry Love" blared from the speakers and all three of us said in unison, "THE SUPREMES!"

Tammy and Sheila dragged Bob and Gerald to the makeshift dance floor underneath the shade of an enormous live oak. Mary Bennett and Brian were already jiggling up a storm, as were Patsy and Jack. I was the only one without a partner. Clearly, the hour of appeasing the decrepit old maid was over.

A chorus of "Poor Pitiful Me" rose up in my head. I decided it was time for a little self-medication in the form of a margarita. As I headed to the kitchen, a well-muscled man wearing a leopard-print loincloth burst out from behind a clump of azalea bushes.

I let out a surprised yelp, followed closely by a "What the fuck" as I tried to figure out what an ersatz Tarzan was doing in Mary Bennett's backyard. His hand was pressed above his brow as if searching for someone. When his eyes rested on me, he gave an ear-splitting jungle yell and started shimmying toward me in time with the music.

"Jill?" he said when he reached me.

"Ahhh, yeah?"

"You bring out the beast in me!" he shouted, and off came the loincloth. He wore skimpy animal-print underwear underneath, and started undulating in front of me. I looked over his shoulder. All the Queens had stopped dancing and were now grinning at me.

"Might as well give them their money's worth," I said, joining jungle boy in his hot-and-heavy mating dance while the Queens shrieked and hooted.

"Jill Conner," shouted another male voice from behind the bathhouse. He tooted on a whistle. "You're under arrest!"

I sensed immediately he was not a real Jackson police officer when I saw his tight little ass and six-pack belly, unenhanced by Krispy Kreme doughnuts.

"What's the charge, Officer?" I asked in a falsetto voice.

"You're so sexy, you're illegal, baby!" he said, launching into his striptease dance.

During the next half hour, a mailman dropped by (whose special delivery package was contained in his G-string), as did an astronaut who promised to send me to the moon. It turned out each Queen had hired a stripper so I wouldn't feel left out at the party. I had to admit that four gyrating near-nekkid men definitely did lend a festive touch to the occasion.

After the strippers left, and the stereo was in between songs, Brian tapped a spoon against the rim of his beer mug to get everyone's attention.

"I'd like to thank the Queens for this lovely evening," he said, in a feigned prim but nonetheless sexy baritone. "Now I know why Mary Bennett always wants to come home to Jackson."

The Queens whistled and hooted in response.

"Secondly, I have a question I wanted to ask Mary Bennett, but I have to clear it with the Queens," he continued. "I want to ask for her hand in marriage, but I'd like your blessing."

He needed no such thing—it was plain that Mary Bennett was going to marry him no matter whether we approved or not, which we did, with all our hearts. I, on the other hand, did think of another related and very important matter that needed to be settled first.

"Not so fast, Buckwheat," I said, holding up a hand. "We'll be needing to see the ring first."

Brian nodded, and withdrew a box from his pants pocket and handed it to me. I motioned for the Queens to gather 'round. I opened the box and there on a bed of deep burgundy velvet glittered a gorgeous antique diamond of sufficient size and clarity befitting any Queen. We all oooohed and ahhed our approval.

"This is one fine-ass piece of joo-ry," I said, handing it back to Brian. "The girl is all yours."

Mary Bennett let out a whoop, and ran to her man's open arms. They proceeded to break every PDA rule in the book until we all shouted, "Get a room!"

By two a.m., Bob had bailed out and gone home. Brian was snoring in a lounge chair, Jack was passed out facedown in a clump of clover near the pool, and I had no idea where Sheila was. The Queens and I were still dancing and laughing, feeding off each other's energy.

"Pee break," I said, stumbling my way toward the back entrance of the house. I pushed open the door that opened to the guest bathroom and saw Sheila inside. She was standing in front of the toilet holding up her dress, and she had spoken the truth. She definitely didn't wear panties to a party. Within the next two seconds, it dawned on me *why* she was *standing* in front of the toilet with her skirt hiked up.

"Excuse me," I said quickly, backing out the door. Sheila turned around and that's when I saw it. It was king-size, just like everything else about Sheila. I was so shocked by the sight I screamed.

"Oops!" Sheila said, pulling her dress down over her formidable member and flushing the toilet. "I guess my little secret is out."

My scream brought the Queens running, with Gerald in the lead.

"What's wrong, Jill?" he asked.

"Gerald, honey," Sheila said, "Jill just met Mr. Shaft."

"Mr. Shaft?" Gerald said with a blush. "How did that happen?"

"It wasn't a formal introduction," I said. "I walked in on him in the bathroom."

"Who is Mr. Shaft?" Mary Bennett asked.

"There's no point in hiding it anymore," Gerald said with a sigh. "Sheila isn't a she. She's a he. Mr. Shaft is . . ."

"The reason I screamed," I said.

"Wait a minute," Tammy said, trying to process all of this with her tequila-addled brain. "You're a man!" She pointed to Sheila. Then she looked at Gerald. "And you're a man so that means . . . you're gay!" Tammy said, a bit unsteady on her feet. "Glad that's finally settled."

"Why would you try to keep this from us?" I asked.

"It's not like we haven't suspected it," Mary Bennett said, and Patsy nodded.

"Really? How long?" Gerald asked.

"Since we first met you. When did YOU finally figure it out?" Tammy said with a snort.

"I guess I knew I was different than other boys since I was a little kid," Gerald said. "In college, I managed to numb those feelings with drugs, but then one summer, I went to Fire Island with some friends who 'knew' about me—even though I didn't—and we went to something called The Invasion where all the men dress like women and go on boats to this beach bar that once tried to kick out a gay couple and—"

"He met me," Sheila said, in a voice several octaves lower. She took off her wig and put a protective arm around Gerald.

"I'm William—and I'm not really into drag, but for The Invasion and a few other special occasions, I become Sheila."

"What was the point of trying to fool *us*?" Mary Bennett asked gently. "Did you think we'd disapprove? And really, William—lovely to meet you, by the way—you can't really think you look like an actual *woman* in that getup. I don't want to hurt your feelings or anything, but you just ain't exactly what we'd call 'girly.'"

"I *was* going to tell you," Gerald said. "But then I heard Brian and Jack were going to be here, and I didn't feel comfortable coming out around all those guys."

"Then I suggested I come to Jackson as my stage persona," Sheila said. "Gerald liked the idea!"

"I didn't know if he could pull it off," Gerald said with a smile. "But when Sheila fooled everyone at the disco, I thought maybe she'd be able to fool my parents, too. Then they'd finally get off my back about not having a girlfriend. I was going to tell y'all about Sheila. Eventually."

"But then Mr. Shaft outed us," Sheila said with a guilty smile.

"I should have figured it out when I saw Sheila's shoes," I said, shaking my head. "Never in my life have I seen a woman with feet bigger than mine."

"Hunny"—Patsy leaned in to William and said in a girlfriend-to-girlfriend tone—"next time wear a turtleneck to hide your Adam's apple—and check your teeth for lipstick before you leave the ladies'."

"I'm just so relieved it's out in the open with y'all," Gerald said, squeezing his lover's large well-manicured hand. Standing up, he said, "Would y'all excuse me for just a few minutes? There is something I have got to do right this second before I lose my nerve—even if it is two in the morning." And he went into the house.

We were having a good laugh with William about the events of the weekend when Mary Bennett suddenly gasped and said, "Oh my God—WHAT was it like with Gerald's parents? Do you think they suspected?"

Gerald reappeared at that moment, shaking with laughter, and said, "No worries on that score. I just got off the phone with them—felt terrible for wakin' 'em up in the middle of the night, but I just could *not* wait another second to BE who I AM—and God bless 'em, they said in their hearts they'd always known about me and they knew about William the second we walked in. They were just waiting for the right time to bring it up. Mother said whatever we wanted to do was fine, but if 'Sheila' was scheduled for any more appearances, she's insisting on giving her some fashion and makeup tips! William, they don't even care that you're not Jewish—they just want us to be happy."

William stood up and declared that he would convert if it would make Gerald's mama happy. "If Sammy Davis Junior can do it, so can I."

With eyes brimming, Gerald said, "Y'all, I intend for William to be a big part of my life. What I said about us eloping . . . well, nobody will marry us legally, not even in Livingston, but we're together—forever—no matter what."

"We couldn't be happier for you guys," Patsy said.

"That's the truth," Tammy said.

"Ditto!" Mary Bennett said.

"And it's not like we're losing a Queen," I said with a smile. "We're gaining a drag queen! Welcome to the family, Tammy Willie-Sheila!"

PART FOUR

1982

Chapter 14

"Three more pounds down," said Sean Kelly, patting his diminished midsection as he stood on the scale. "I'll be able to fit into my Speedo this year."

"If you own a Speedo," I said, recording the weight in his chart, "I advise you to throw that sucker into the incinerator and bury the ashes. I'll let you in on a little secret. No man alive, not even Sean *Connery*, looks sexy in a *Speedo*."

"You just haven't seen *me* yet," he said with a wink as he hopped off the scale. Sean had devilish green eyes and a weathered face splashed with hundreds of freckles. Two years before, when he'd first visited the weight-loss center, he'd weighed two hundred and fifty pounds and had been recovering from a triple bypass. Now he was a lean one hundred seventy-eight pounds and healthy as a mule.

"Miss Susan might not approve of me ogling you in your swimsuit," I said, referring to his wife of forty-five years.

"In Sue's book you can do no wrong. 'Jill saved your life,' she always says to me. I think she's even written to the pope nominating you for sainthood." He pumped his arms up and down as if he were jogging. "I'm up to fifteen miles a week now."

I put a finger to my lips and shook my head.

"Don't sweat it," Sean said. "The wicked witch of weight loss was leaving just as I was coming in."

I'd tried to follow Penny's rules after she threatened to fire me, but two days later a client burst into tears because her weight was coming off so slowly. She wanted to whittle down to a size eight before her wedding, but she didn't have a chance in hell without exercise.

That's when I started scheduling coffee dates with clients who were frustrated by the program. I now had more personal training clients than I could handle.

"When are you going to quit this place and become your own boss?" Sean asked, handing me his credit card.

"Any day now." I hadn't quite screwed up the courage to give up the steady paycheck.

"I've heard that before," Sean said. "By the way, will you do me a favor? My buddy Malcolm is putting together Jackson's very first St. Paddy's Day parade. You think you could hang a flyer in the window?"

"Parade?" I said, snapping to attention. "With floats and candy-throwing and beauty queens gliding by to wave and blow kisses?"

"That's the idea."

"Where do I sign up?"

Sean chuckled. "You want to be in the thing?"

"You better believe it, Buckwheat. Me and the world-famous Sweet Potato Queens will be the highlight of that parade."

"Can't say I've ever heard of any 'world-famous' Sweet Potato Queens."

"Mark my words, once you meet us you'll never forget us."

"I'm looking forward to it," Sean said, stuffing his wallet into his rear pants pocket. "St. Paddy's is my favorite day of the year. Susan will make some kind of inedible low-cal, low-fat, but somehow Irish-type food and I'll console myself by guzzling mugs of green beer."

"Make that light beer," I said, pointing at the scale.

Sean made a grumbling sound. "You're just plain ol' mean. Just mean."

•

The next step was coaxing the Queens to come to Jackson for the parade. I hadn't seen them together since we'd gathered in Atlanta a few years ago for the birth of Patsy's son, Mack. The parade would be an ideal opportunity for a raucous reunion.

I spoke with Patsy, who said she'd be thrilled to come. Then I dialed Tammy's number, and as usual the phone rang and rang. I'd been trying to catch her for the last several days. Just as I hung up, Penny came into my office and slapped a copy of *Soap Opera Digest* on my desk.

"Isn't this your friend, the actress?" Penny asked, proving herself to be a chronic eavesdropper.

I opened the magazine and saw a color photo of Mary Bennett sitting in a wing chair, wearing a lacy black dress with enormous shoulder pads. She was filing her blood-red, talonlike fingernails and staring haughtily into the camera. The title of the story read, "Mary Bennett Manning Cast as the Queen of Mean on New Evening Soap Opera *Eagle's Cove*."

"Good gawd almighty," I said. "I knew she was up for a big

part, but I didn't know she'd gotten it. I can't believe she didn't tell me!"

"Look," Penny said, pointing to the second paragraph. "'Mary Bennett Manning, who will star in NBC's *Eagle's Cove,* claims that, in real life, she's nothing like her backstabbing character Electra Frostman. "I'm just a sweet little ol' magnolia blossom from Mississippi."' The article also says she's been stepping out with her co-star Grant Frazier. Have you seen him? The man is sizzlin' hot, is all I'm sayin'."

"You can't trust one word written in that rag," I said. "Mary Bennett happens to be engaged."

Penny gawked at me, awe in her eyes. "I just can't believe you're best friends with someone who's on TV. If she ever comes here for a visit, do you think I could meet her?"

"She doesn't come home that often," I said. There was no way I was going to introduce Mary Bennett to a ditch-witch like Penny.

"I'd probably be so starstruck I'd babble like a baboon."

Kinda like you do now, I thought.

"I've never known anyone who's been on TV before. Will you call Mary Bennett and ask her for an autographed picture? I love my soaps."

I sighed. Unfortunately Penny was still my boss, and I had a vested interest in keeping her happy.

"All right. I'll have her send one out."

"Why don't you call now?" she said. "Never mind the long-distance charge. Talk as long as you like. Have a little gabfest on my dime."

I didn't feel like talking to Mary Bennett with Penny breathing down my neck.

"It's still pretty early on the West Coast. I'd better wait."

"It's ten a.m. in California," Penny said, in a snippy tone. "I don't know why you're being so difficult about this—maybe you're not such big buddies with her after all."

"Hold your water," I said, reluctantly picking up the phone. "I'll give her a holler." Maybe I'd sneak in a mention about the St. Paddy's parade while I had her on the horn.

I dialed, listening to several rings droning in my ear. Finally I heard a click.

"Hello," said a weary voice on the other end.

"Brian? This is Jill. I was trying to reach Mary Bennett."

"Hi, Jill," Brian said in curt voice. "Mary Bennett isn't here." He paused for such a long time I thought he'd hung up. "You heard she got the part, didn't you?"

"Yes! I just found out."

"That changed everything. She's moved out. We split up."

"You're kidding."

"I'm afraid not. It was for the best. Let me give you her number at the studio. I don't have her new home number."

Had fame gone to Mary Bennett's head? Maybe that's why Brian sounded so abrupt. She'd broken his heart.

Chapter 15

I chewed my fingernails down to the quick as I watched Bob read my essay. He chuckled a few times, and I had to restrain myself from leaping up out of my chair and saying, "Which part made you laugh?"

After a few minutes, he looked up from my pages and started to rub his temple.

"It gave you a headache, didn't it?" I said. "I don't know why I asked you to read my pitiful little chicken scratchings. I'm not cut out to be a writer. You could dangle a participle right under my nose, and I'd never know it. I wouldn't recognize a gerund if it bit me on the butt."

"Jill!" Bob said with a smile. "Calm down. I really liked it."

"You did?" I said, resisting the urge to dance the cancan right in the middle of his classroom.

"I think it's ready to be sent out."

"Sent out? What do you mean?"

"You do want it published, don't you?"

"Published?" I said, dramatically clutching at my chest. "You mean in print, out there . . . for complete strangers to ridicule?"

Bob chuckled. "You won't be ridiculed. Writers usually write to be published."

"I told you! I'm *not* a writer. Writers wear pince-nez and ascots and trade bon mots at Elaine's. They're tortured souls who drink whiskey straight from the bottle. . . . Although come to think of it, I could probably cozy up to the whiskey part, and what the fuck is a pince-nez, anyway?"

"This is funny stuff. Humor's one of the hardest forms of prose to pull off," Bob said, handing me my pages. "You're a writer—like it or not."

I tried to imagine myself saying, "I'm Jill Conner, a writer." It sounded as credible to me as saying, "I'm Jill Conner, pop singer and part-time proctologist."

An Amazonian blonde, wearing an add-a-bead necklace and painted-on Bonjour jeans, sashayed into the classroom.

"Mr. Hollingsworth, do you have a minute?" There was so much sickly sweet hanging off her words, it made 'em all have several extra syllables. "I have a question about my term paper."

"Sure, Tiffany," Bob said. "Fire away."

"I'd best git," I said, unfolding my six-foot frame from the student-size desk.

"Don't leave," he said. "I'll only be a minute."

Adolescent girls today seemed far more sultry than when I was coming up. Bob's high school crawled with so many pouty-lipped, hip-swinging sex kittens it looked like the site of a Lolita convention. It was a miracle teenage boys could concentrate on anything beyond their pocket rockets.

Tiffany was especially comely. As she chatted with Bob, she kept tossing her long, blond hair over her shoulder and rotating the end of a pencil between her shiny pink lips. Tammy told me female students were constantly slipping perfumed notes into his briefcase.

Bob, on the other hand, was blind to their charms. He acted as if every woman on the planet was a snaggletoothed troll compared to Tammy. His desk had several framed pictures of the two of them, and after several years of marriage he still sent flowers and wrote her steamy love poems.

"Thank you SO MUCH, Mr. Hollingsworth," purred the junior seductress just before she wiggled out the door.

"Sorry about that. Where were we?"

"You said something about publication. Maybe I'll try the *Fish Wrapper Gazette*."

Bob shook his head. "Come on, Jill. Have a little faith in yourself."

"I can't help it! The idea of anyone but close friends reading my stuff makes the hairs on the back of my neck stand up." I stood to leave. "I appreciate your time, but I should let you get back to work. Say hello to Tammy for me."

"If I ever see her," he said with a sad sigh. "She's always working. She's given up her singing gig and is angling to be a full-fledged news anchor."

"She didn't mention it to me." Tammy hadn't said a word about work. She'd been too busy bubbling over about a new pair of diamond earrings.

"I hope she and I can spend some time alone before I leave." Bob was in the army reserves, and was shipping out in a couple of days to Fort Dix, New Jersey, for his field training.

"I guess the diamond earrings were a good-bye gift."

"Earrings?" Bob said, perplexed. "What earrings?"

A feeling of dread stirred in my gut—telling me that something rotten this way comes.

"What am I saying?" I said, banging my forehead with the palm of my hand. "That wasn't Tammy. I'm getting her mixed up with one of my clients."

"Oh," Bob said, accepting my line of bullshit with nary a raised eyebrow. He was so trusting, so innocent. "Jill, will you look after my girl while I'm gone? I worry about her so much."

"You got it. No problem," I said, mustering up a reassuring smile. Obviously Bob had not given Tammy those diamond earrings, so the question banging around in my little brain was, where the hell had she gotten them?

•

I sat around a table in the meeting room of the Jackson Public Library listening to a squeaky-voiced twenty-three-year-old graduate student named Fred read a section from his novel-in-progress. The work was entitled *One Man's Journey.* It was about an intrepid photographer named Fernando who had women constantly throwing themselves at him. The novel read like a series of *Penthouse Forum* fantasies strung together. Fred, however, considered his manuscript to be a groundbreaking work.

"Comments?" said our workshop leader, Louis, after Fred finished reading. Louis was in his forties and had a long gray ponytail.

"You misspelled 'turgid,' dear. It's 't-u' not 't-e,'" said Bonnie. She was a retired schoolteacher who wrote poems about nature, her latest being "Ode to an Orchid." "I also thought the setting for the scene was original."

"You understood the symbolism, didn't you?" Fred asked, blinking behind smudged eyeglasses. "The bank vault represents how Fernando seals off his innermost feelings." He went to explain all the other nuances and metaphors that might have escaped our inferior little minds.

"Where's the plot?" said Norah, who always sounded angry. She wrote aggressively feminist haikus about areolas and labias. "Am I the only one who is wondering when something's going to happen besides sex?"

"It doesn't need a plot, Norah," Fred said very slowly, as if he were talking to a dim-witted child. "It's a literary novel."

"I agree with Norah," Louis said. "You should consider adding some conflict. The scene reads a little static."

Louis wrote wonderful short stories, one of which had been published by a literary magazine called *Ploughshares*. He was also finishing up a novel.

I was too shy to comment. After all, what the hell did I know about writing novels? I just scribbled "good effort" on the bottom of Fred's pages and handed them back to him.

"Do you have anything today, Jill?" Louis asked.

I'd brought an essay about all the crazy diets my clients went on (cabbage, stewardess, grapefruit, and the ever-popular pink weenies and ice cream) and had planned to read it, but couldn't bring myself to share it with the others.

"Not this week," I said. "But I *do* have a question. If, on the off chance, I ever wrote an essay good enough to be published, where would I send it?"

"*The New Yorker,* or *The Atlantic Monthly,*" Fred said, impatiently.

"*Guideposts* takes essays," Bonnie said. "So does *Reader's Digest.*"

"Actually," I said, taking a deep breath, "I was thinking of something a little bit less intimidating."

"Good for you, Jill," Louis said with an approving nod of his head. "Learn to walk before you run. Why don't you try that free circular in town? It's called *The Diddy Wah Diddy,* and they publish essays."

"Thank you, Louis," I said. "I'll look into it."

I don't know why I lied. I had no intention of submitting my work anywhere. I wasn't near ready yet.

•

"Gerald?" I said, squinting through the peephole. He stood on my stoop with a very fat dachshund on a leash. I immediately flung open the door. "What a fabulous surprise! This must be the infamous Kitchie Koo."

Every year Gerald and William sent Christmas cards with Kitchie posing in the center like a beloved child. Gerald claimed he warmed the dog's Alpo and fed him with a sterling silver spoon.

I hugged him, and he stiffened in my arms.

"Are you okay?" I said, after I dropped my embrace.

"Can we come in?" His expression was somber.

"Absolutely!" I said, beckoning him inside. "It's great to see you. Where's William?"

Gerald sat ramrod straight on the couch but allowed Kitchie to jump up on his lap. It was the first time I noticed he had dark crescents under his eyes, and he was unshaven.

"Did the two of you have a falling-out?"

Gerald didn't answer right away. His features were so still they could have been cast in plaster of Paris.

"You could say that," he said in a barely audible voice.

"Do you want to talk about it?"

"No," he answered immediately and vehemently. Judging by the sound of his voice, it must have been a bitter breakup.

"Is there anything I can do?"

"I've quit my job at the university in San Francisco. There's a position at Jackson State. It's an adjunct professorship but it could turn into full-time. I've also rented an apartment here."

I knew Gerald was close to becoming tenured in San Francisco. It used to be all he could talk about, so I was shocked to hear he'd left his job.

"I wanted you to know I was back in town. Naturally, I'd like to get together with you and Tammy."

"Of course," I said, sitting beside him. "Sometimes it helps to get these things off your chest. See this," I said, grabbing one of my ears. "This is one big, ol' floppy listening device. It is right here, waiting for you to talk into it."

Gerald placed Kitchie on the floor and stood. "I'll be glad to gab all you want. But there's one thing I won't discuss, and that's William. Understand?"

"But—"

"I mean it, Jill. I never want to hear his name mentioned again."

Chapter 16

"I was going to call and tell you about getting the part of Electra, but I guess you already know!" Mary Bennett's voice said on my answering machine. I had left a message about the parade at the studio. "I would love to be in the parade. As a matter of fact, I think I'll come in a few days early so I can have some time with you and Tammy. We've got a lotta catching up to do!"

I was so pleased Mary Bennett had decided to come home for the St. Paddy's parade, I forgave her for calling me at home during work hours, knowing full well I wouldn't be there. I had a sneaking feeling she didn't want to talk about what had happened between her and Brian just yet. Obviously, she didn't know anything about William and Gerald, which kind of surprised me. If Gerald were going to confide in anyone, it would be Mary Bennett.

I made my daily phone call to Tammy, listening to the familiar trill of the phone ringing, when I finally heard her say a harried hello.

"It's about damn time."

"Jill?" Tammy said, not sounding at all pleased to hear from me. "I thought you were someone else. I can't talk long. I'm expecting a call."

"Well, that's a fine greeting to someone you haven't spoken to in a coon's age. Can we get together later on?" I'd planned to interrogate her about the diamond earrings. "I know Bob's out of town, and I thought—"

"I'll call you," Tammy said in a hurried voice. "I need to hang up now."

"Just two quick things." I proceeded to tell her about the St. Paddy's Day parade.

"Sounds like a blast," Tammy said. "Count me in."

"Also, guess who has moved back to Jackson?"

"Jill! I gotta go." *Why was she so desperate to get me off the phone?*

"This is important. It's Gerald. Something happened between him and William. He's in a terrible state—"

I heard the dial tone. I was talking to empty air. Tammy had hung up on me.

•

The month before the parade flew by. I had a couple of strained dinners with Gerald, who still seemed absolutely miserable. Despite much gentle coaxing on my part, he remained stubbornly closemouthed about William. I was pleased to see him perk up a bit when I mentioned the St. Paddy's Day parade, and he'd promised to participate. He mentioned he was going to a support group, but refused to tell me any details. I was just grateful he was talking to someone.

Tammy joined us only once and begged off early, saying she had an early-morning meeting, but when I passed by her house on the way home from the restaurant her car wasn't in the driveway. What was she up to—and more important, how bad was it gonna fuck up her life?

I didn't have much time to worry about Tammy's shenanigans. I was working harder than a one-legged man in a butt-kicking contest keeping up with all my personal trainer clients along with my regular job, and doing a little bit of writing on the side.

After downing a couple of glasses of excellent red wine, I'd stuck several of my essays into an envelope and addressed it to Buster Henry, the editor at *The Diddy Wah Diddy*, but hadn't gathered the courage to toss it in the mailbox yet.

•

"Before we start reading, there's something special I want to share with you," said Louis. There was a foiled bottle of sparkling grape juice on the table and several Dixie cups.

I felt a pang of disappointment. I'd been hoping to dive right in. I had promised myself an entire bowl full of my world-famous raw chocolate chip cookie dough if I managed to muster the nerve to read out loud my latest essay. I'd gone over it by myself several times before the meeting, and the last time, my cheeks hadn't gotten hot with mortification. I was even a tiny bit proud of it.

"This is a huge moment in my life, and I wanted to share it with my fellow writers," Louis continued. "Today, I received a letter from New York's most powerful literary agent, Bunky Lazar."

"Bunky," Fred repeated in a hushed, respectful tone. Both Bonnie and Norah nodded in recognition.

"I haven't opened it yet." His voice was shaky with emotion. "I wanted to wait until you, my esteemed colleagues, were gathered around me."

It was flattering to be identified as Louis's colleague even though he hadn't yet read a single word I'd written. The others must have felt likewise, because they were beaming up at him from their chairs.

"Here goes nothing." Louis slit open the envelope with the blade of a pocketknife. Bonnie and Norah grasped hands. Fred made a gulping sound.

"I don't think I can read this," Louis said with a nervous chuckle. "Would you do the honors, Jill?"

The others shot me irritated looks. I could practically read their thoughts. Why should the newbie get such a great honor? She doesn't even contribute to the group.

"Certainly," I said, uncomfortable at having all their eyes upon me.

"Dear Author," I began.

"Louder!" Fred said, cupping his ear.

"Dear Author!" I repeated.

"Hear that?" Bonnie said, clapping her hands. "Louis is a real-live author now."

I continued. "Thank you for sending us your manuscript. I've had a chance to review your work, and have decided . . ." My voice slowed as I continued to read. "I'm not the right agent for this project, and therefore . . . I cannot offer you representation."

"What?" Louis said, in an almost inaudible voice. The others were too dumbstruck to comment.

"Do you want me to continue?" I asked.

Louis nodded very slowly, as if in shock.

"Please understand publishing is a subjective business and taste and judgment may vary among agents. Also forgive this form letter. Due to the volume of submissions received, it's impossible for me to write personal rejection letters. Best of luck with your writing. Signed Elizabeth Primrose, assistant to Bunky Lazar."

No one spoke. I carefully folded the letter and tucked it back into the envelope.

"Well," Louis said in a ragged voice. "Clearly I thought the outcome was going to be slightly different."

"You were robbed!" shouted a wild-eyed Fred.

"What a brutal business this is!" Norah said in a small, scared-sounding voice.

Bonnie's mouth was a crinkly line of distress. "The letter says publishing is subjective, dear. Maybe you should send it to another agent."

"I wanted Bunky," Louis said. "He's the best in the business."

"I'm so sorry," I said.

"This isn't the end of the world," Louis said, his voice cracking slightly. "I've heard of writers who paper their walls with rejection letters. It's a rite of passage. It's . . . uh—" His brave front started to fray. I thought he was going to either cry or get sick. "Would you excuse me for a moment?" Then he fled the room.

"Good going, Jill," Fred hissed.

"Hush, Fred," Bonnie said. "It's not her fault."

I picked up my papers and my purse. "Good night, everyone," I said, knowing I was never coming back.

As soon as I got home, I tore up the letter to *The Diddy Wah Diddy* and threw it in the trash. If someone as talented as Louis had problems getting published, I didn't stand a chance. Writing was far too risky.

•

"Y'all are a sight for these sore eyes!" Mary Bennett said, looking every inch a rising star in a raw silk pantsuit, wearing expensive-looking shoes and carrying a Chanel handbag.

I hoped Mary Bennett's visit would help snap Gerald out of his funk. After all, they were both going through breakups.

"How was your flight?" I asked.

"De-vine," Mary Bennett said. "I kept the first-class stewardesses on their toes, fetching Bloody Marys. Gerald, don't just stand there with your dick in your hand. Come here and hug my neck!"

Gerald shuffled over to her and gave her a perfunctory embrace.

"You help Mary Bennett with her luggage," Gerald said to me. "I'll bring the car around to the passenger loading area." Then he plodded out to the parking lot.

"His face was so sour it could turn buttermilk," Mary Bennett said. "What's wrong with him?"

"He and William have apparently split," I said, as we headed for Baggage Claim. "And don't even try to bring it up. He's totally clammed up about it."

"Poor baby," Mary Bennett said. "If that guy broke Gerald's heart, he'll have me to answer to."

"I don't know *what* happened, but it wasn't like it was just 'some guy.' It was the love of his life—it was his precious WILLIAM. This is HUGE, I'm telling you—Gerald refuses to talk about it. He's been going to some kind of support group."

"Oh, for Pete's sake. He's already GOT a support group: the Queens! All he needs is our loving devotion, a pan or three of Chocolate Stuff, some Pig Candy, and a couple of shots of te-kill-ya. He'll be as right as rain."

"I think it's more complicated than that."

"No it isn't. When someone knocks you down, you gotta get

right back up. No point in wallowing in it." She stopped short. "Where's Tammy? Why isn't she here to meet me?"

"Good question. I called to tell her you were coming home, but I can never catch her."

"But she's coming to the parade?"

"She promised. All of the Queens will be there."

We reached the luggage carousel and Mary Bennett chattered about the show and her co-stars. Never once did she say a word about Brian.

"By the way, I've moved," she said ever so casually. "I'll have to give you my new number."

"I know. How do you think I got the number to your studio? I spoke with Brian."

"You did?" She flinched slightly. "What'd he say?"

"That y'all had broken up. You *were* going to tell me, weren't you?"

"Of course! It just didn't seem really important. I'm already dating someone else. I'm going out with Grant, my co-star."

"Not important? You were *engaged* to Brian. You've been together for three years."

"That's right. And it took me only three days to get over him. There's my bag!" She grabbed a pink suitcase from the carousel. "Are we ready? Let's find Gerald."

"Is that all you're going to say?" I asked in an incredulous voice. "The two of you were so much in love!"

"Sometimes things can change overnight," Mary Bennett said firmly, as if the matter was closed.

•

"Where's Gerald?" Mary Bennett said, looking impatiently at her watch. "He was supposed to be here fifteen minutes ago."

It was two days before the St. Paddy's parade and we'd

agreed to meet at a neighborhood bar to discuss final parade preparations. Tammy, as usual, had begged off, saying she had to work late. *Liar, liar, pants on fire.*

"Maybe he forgot. He's so unreliable these days."

Mary Bennett had been in Jackson for three days, and nothing she could say or do had any effect on Gerald's mood.

"I hope he comes soon." She smiled. "I have lit-tle sur-prise for him. The night before last I was brainstorming, and I think I came up with a foolproof way to cheer him up."

"There he is!" I said, pointing to the door. Gerald stood for a moment in the entrance, blinking in the dim light of the bar. When we waved him over, he ambled toward us.

"He walks like a ninety-year-old man," Mary Bennett said with a sigh. "But I have something that will put a little starch in his shorts."

"What is it?" I whispered.

"You'll see." She smiled mysteriously.

"Hello," Gerald said, greeting us with a limp wave of his hand.

"Hi, handsome," Mary Bennett said. "How we doing tonight?"

"Okay," Gerald said as he sat. "I'm a little tired."

"Me, too, hunny," Mary Bennett said, smothering a yawn. "Me and Martin were up all night havin' phone sex. Let me tell you, that man can heat up the lines."

"Martin?" I asked. "I thought you were dating Grant."

"I am," Mary Bennett said. "I'm also dating Martin, who is my nutritionist; Rodney, who is my publicist; and André, who is my acupuncturist. I believe in sharing the love."

"It sure didn't take you very long to get over Brian," Gerald said. There was recrimination in his voice.

"Easy come, easy go," Mary Bennett said with a shrug. "Words to the wise. There's just too many men in this world to get all worked up about just one. And speaking of men, here comes one of the finer examples." Mary Bennett signaled to the man who'd just entered the bar. "Over here, Gaylord." She smiled at Gerald. "Don't you jest love that name—it CAN'T be real, of course, but isn't it just so deliciously descriptive?"

Gaylord was tall, with platinum blond hair and chiseled cheeks—facial and otherwise. He wore a muscle shirt and very tight—*very* tight—leather pants.

"Hi, Mary Bennett," Gaylord said in a whispery baby voice. "I hope I'm not late."

"You're right on time, hon," Mary Bennett said. "This is my friend Jill, and this"—she waved her arm with a flourish—"is Gerald."

Gaylord covered his cheeks with his hands. "Oh, she's adorable!" he squealed to Mary Bennett, obviously referring to Gerald. He smiled at Gerald. "You're adorable."

"Thank you," Gerald said, his eyes darting nervously.

"I understand you're having a hard time, sweetie," Gaylord said. "A little birdie tells me your heart's been broken."

Gerald looked panicked. "Mary Bennett."

Gaylord clamped a hand on Gerald's knee. "Calm down, sweetie. I can help to ease your pain," he said in a low, seductive voice.

"That's our cue to go," Mary Bennett said with a wink. "Come on, Jill."

"Mary Bennett," Gerald said through clenched teeth, his face awash with fright and fury.

"Hush now," Gaylord said to Gerald. "You're getting yourself all worked up—and THAT is MY job."

"Have fun, boys," Mary Bennett crooned as she departed the table. I followed behind her.

"I don't know about this, Mary Bennett," I said. "Gerald was *really* upset."

Mary Bennett turned around. "Don't you fret. Gaylord is a professional. My manicurist highly recommended him. I flew him in from Hollywood especially for Gerald. I'm putting him up in the penthouse at the Jackson Hilton. That's where he's supposed to take Gerald tonight."

"You mean Gaylord's a prostitute?"

"They like to be called escorts these days, but yes, that's what he is. Don't look so shocked. He's very high-class."

"I don't think Gerald's ready for something like that," I said as we left the bar.

"It's exactly what he needs," Mary Bennett said firmly. "Moping around hasn't done him a bit of good. He needs to cleanse his palate. Believe me—if there's one thing I know about, it's palate-cleansing."

We'd reached my car in the parking lot when someone called out Mary Bennett's name. It was Gerald, stomping toward us.

"Hey, Gerald," Mary Bennett said, squinting in the dusk. "What are you doing out here? Get back inside with Gaylord."

"Don't you *ever* pull something like that again!" Gerald said, seething. "I've never been so pissed off at you in my entire life." He jabbed a finger in my direction. "Were you in on this too?"

"Don't give Jill a hard time," Mary Bennett said. "She didn't know diddly about this. I can't, for the life of me, understand why you're having such a hissy. Didn't you find Gaylord attractive? I thought he was cute. I even thought he kinda looked like a white William."

"What is wrong with you?" Gerald said, the cords of his neck standing out. "Do you think you can just HIRE a replacement for William? That I can just switch my affections to some hooker, some streetwalker, some WHORE?"

"No need to shout," Mary Bennett snapped. "I was just trying—"

"I should have expected this!" Gerald shouted. He was so upset I feared he was going to stroke out on us. "Look at you! You've only been broken up with Brian for a few weeks and you're already fucking every guy you know."

"First off, Gaylord's not a streetwalker," Mary Bennett said with a defensive jerk of her chin. "He's a high-priced call boy. As for me, I have never denied being a woman of loose morals."

"No you haven't," Gerald said, his tone getting more scathing with every word. "I used to find your behavior amusing, even when I knew it was just an act, but now it just seems pathetic. Maybe I could overlook your whorish behavior if you possessed other qualities I valued. But it's clear to me from your recent actions that you lack any sensitivity or empathy. You're as empty inside as that character you're going to play on TV."

For the first time ever, Mary Bennett seemed too stunned to speak. The parking lot was so dark I couldn't read her face.

"Gerald really didn't mean that," I said quickly. "He's just upset."

"Don't put words in my mouth, Jill," Gerald said. "You don't know Mary Bennett like I do. You have no idea what's she's capable of."

•

It had been two days since Mary Bennett and Gerald's big blowup and I couldn't reach either one. I intended to go forward with the parade, even if it was just going to be Patsy, Tammy, and me.

I was pulling the seams out of an old prom dress when Patsy called to say she couldn't make it to the parade. Her son Mack had a fever, and although his condition wasn't dangerous, she didn't feel comfortable leaving him behind.

"I'm so sorry, Jill," Patsy said, tearfully. "I can't tell you how much I was looking *forward* to this trip."

My heart sank. That left just me and Tammy, and I hadn't heard from her in days. The float was going to look mighty sparse.

"Give the little guy a kiss from his Auntie Jill," I said, trying to sound chipper.

•

The day before the parade, I came home from work to find my answering machine blinking. I sensed impending doom when I pressed the PLAY button and heard Tammy's voice.

"Hi, Jill. It's Tammy. I'll try to make it to the parade, but I'm not sure I'll be able to get off work. I'll try my best."

"No! No! No!" I shouted, deleting the message. I didn't want to hear another word.

After Tammy's phone call, my mood grew darker than a stack of black cats. I was so down, it was the first time in my life that the thought of a big, sticky pan of Chocolate Stuff didn't cheer me up; but I made one and ate it anyway—preventive medicinal measures. I spent the next couple of hours boo-hooing into my pillow and listening to Babs belt out "Don't Rain on My Parade."

Finally, after I'd drained out every last bit of moisture from my tear ducts, I felt the urge to spill my guts. I grabbed a pen and wrote until my arm ached and my fingers were numb. I scrawled about my disappointment over the parade and Mary Bennett and Gerald's fight, but then I moved on to questions that had been niggling at me for a long while: Why couldn't I find a decent man? Why did I settle for bums? Why had I stayed in the same crappy job for over twelve years? Why didn't I have any confidence in my writing ability? The only area of my life worth a flip was my friendships with the Queens, and now our friendships seemed to be falling apart.

Seeing all my disappointments in black and white was like being hit in the face with a wet squirrel. If I was so mizzable, why didn't I do something about it?

Pick something in your life, I told myself. *Anything, just one teensy thing, and work to change it.*

Ever since high school, when surrounded by friends, I had felt and acted like a Queen. The question was, could I be a Queen—for myself—all by myself?

Chapter 17

When I parked my car on State Street, my mouth went dry and my heart felt like it was playing the drum solo in "Wipeout." I struggled with my carryall, which contained my wig, sunglasses, and some other necessary supplies.

My skintight prom dress hampered my walking as I approached the area where the parade participants were lining up. I waved at my client, Hamp Avery, who owned the flatbed trailer that was the base of the float.

"Hey, Jill," he said with an easy grin. Hamp was in his mid-fifties, broad-shouldered, with a bit of beer belly we were trying to get rid of. "How does she look?"

A couple of nights before, Hamp had attached six-foot banners to each side of the trailer with duct tape. The space seemed so vast and lonely. It begged to be filled with a passel of prancing, waving Queens—a "bevy of buxom beauties," as we liked to call ourselves. I would be a bux-less bevy of one up there.

"Looks sharp," I said to Hamp. "I really appreciate your help."

I glanced around at the other participants. The Shriners were lining up their miniature cars. There was a high school band dressed in green-and-gold uniforms, and the Rude Boys had a large float festooned with enormous papier-mâché shamrocks. The Krewe of Kazoo was out in full force, dressed as flamingos and randomly humming into their kazoos. I was the sole free agent in the mix except for a couple of kids on bicycles.

"When are the other girls getting here?" Hamp asked.

"They ain't comin'," I said, tugging my Tammy wig onto my head. "It's just gonna be me."

The banners snapped in the wind. It was a typical March day, blustery as all get-out.

I adjusted my cat's-eye shades on my nose and stepped on the tongue of the trailer and clambered on board. Hamp handed me my carryall, saying, "Good God Almighty, gal. Whatcha got in here? Rocks?"

"A twenty-pound bag of sweet potatoes."

"What for?" he asked.

"I thought I'd lob them at the spectators."

"I think you're supposed to throw candy or beads. Who's gon' want a sweet potato?"

"These aren't *ordinary* sweet potatoes. They're autographed by me, the boss queen of the Sweet Potato Queens."

Last night, after I made the executive decision to appear in the parade all by my lonesome, I also decided to appoint myself boss of the Queens for my extreme bravery. Obviously there were no dissenters.

The boom box was in place, and I slipped in a cassette tape of the song "Tiny Bubbles." I'd hit the PLAY button as soon as we started moving. My plan was to toss taters with one hand and blow bubbles with the other. I'd also try to sneak in a little preening, hand-waving, and cavorting. I planned to be busier than a one-armed monkey with six dicks, leaving me no time to ponder to what extent I was making a world-class fool of myself.

"You look pretty regal up there, your majesty," Hamp said.

"Thank you kindly, sir," I said, trembling ever so slightly as I practiced my wave.

A few minutes later we were ready to roll, and my stomach lurched as we pulled out of the prep area.

It's not too late, I thought. *You can still take a flying leap off this trailer if you want.*

But I didn't. I stood my ground, bubble wand in one hand, sweet potato in the other. In moments, we were on the parade route proper, and passing by the skimpy crowds. Dozens of pairs of eyes stared at me, and just as I was about to pitch a potato, I froze up—locked up, pulled up lame—as all Queenly thoughts vacated my brain.

I could almost read the onlookers' thoughts. Who was the weird lady in the red wig and prom dress, standing stock-still with a sweet potato in her hand?

I'd freaked out because something was missing. After a moment, it occurred to me what it was. I'd forgotten the music! I bent down to press PLAY and heard Don Ho singing, "Tiny bubbles in the wine. Make me happy. Make me feel fine."

The familiar words and music served as an on switch, launching me into action. I tossed my potato, blew my bubbles, pranced across the flatbed, wiggled my hips, waved, and cavorted.

I could see people watching me. Some smiled. Others laughed. A few pointed. After a few run-throughs, I performed like a well-oiled machine. Toss, blow, prance, wiggle, wave, cavort. People started chasing after my sweet potatoes instead of staring at them with bewilderment as they landed near their feet—or dodging them as they zinged past their heads. They were scooping them up—they were catching them on the fly and laughing—they all wanted a little piece of me. I was a hit!

"Oh my God! You must want to skin me alive."

I turned my head to see Tammy climbing up on the trailer, wearing a lime-green bridesmaid dress.

"I'm sorry I'm late," she said, righting her crooked cat's-eyes.

On the one hand, I was delighted to see her. On the other, I wanted to say, "Take a hike, sister, I was handling this gig fine on my own."

"Never mind that," I whispered. "Just do your thing." After a short while, Tammy fell into rhythm with me and the two of us caused an even bigger stir in the crowd. Folks whistled and waved. Just before we reached the governor's mansion, site of the judging stand and the most important spot on the parade route, I heard a familiar drawl: "Give me a leg up, would ya?"

"Mary Bennett?" I said, leaning down to pull her aboard. Behind her stood Gerald and Patsy. All three were dressed in full Queen regalia.

"What the . . .?" I asked, but of course there was no time for them to answer. Our public was waiting.

With the five of us aboard the float we ran out of sweet potatoes almost immediately, so we started blowing kisses instead. It didn't escape my notice that Gerald and Mary Bennett kept to opposite ends of the float.

The parade ended all too quickly. We could have performed for hours. In my book, adoration is as good as Blue Bell ice cream. There ain't no such thing as too much of that, either. When the truck came to a halt, I dropped my regal facade and hugged the Queens' necks.

"Butter my butt and call me a biscuit! Y'all made it after all."

"Well, I called everybody to tell them I was going to miss the parade," Patsy said. "Gerald said he'd decided not to go and Mary Bennett said she'd changed her mind. I couldn't get in touch with Tammy. That did it. I told Jack he was going to watch Mack. Luckily his fever was nearly gone."

"After I talked to Patsy, I decided it wasn't fair to break my promise to be in the parade," Gerald said.

"I couldn't bear to think of you doing this by yourself," Mary Bennett said. "So I flew all the way back from L.A."

"But she *was* alone!" Tammy said, eyes flashing with pride. "I was late too and there was Jill up on the float all by herself, shaking her booty. It didn't seem to bother her one bit."

"That took some balls," Gerald said.

"Looky here," Mary Bennett said, bending over to pick something up. "Here's a sweet potato we missed." She squinted at the message written across it in Magic Marker. "Hey, I didn't notice when I was tossing 'em, but this one is signed 'Jill Conner, Boss Sweet Potato Queen.'"

"I held an election last night," I said with an impish grin. "Guess who won in a landslide victory?"

Mary Bennett slung an arm around my neck. "Frankly, I can't think of a better person for the job. What's your first royal edict, Boss Queen?"

"Hmmm," I said scratching my chin. "I proclaim the Queens go hence immediately and forthwith and engage in group consumption of copious amounts of fried food and adult alcoholic beverages."

Mary Bennett cut her eyes nervously in Gerald's direction. "I don't know, I should probably—"

"I can't, Jill. I—" Gerald said.

"The Boss Queen has spoken!" I said, and then in a pleading

tone. "Just for a little while. You owe me for being late for the parade."

The guilt card worked like a charm, and both Gerald and Mary Bennett finally agreed to come along.

The five of us alighted from our float, only to be surrounded by a small knot of fans.

"That looked like so much fun," said one young woman, holding a sleeping toddler. "Are you doing this next year? I'd love to be on the float with you!"

"Me, too," said a silver-haired matron.

"Wannabes," Tammy whispered to me in a snippy tone.

"The more the merrier, is what I say," I whispered back. "Besides, what good is it being a queen, if you don't have a few subjects sucking up to ya?"

Chapter 18

"Who would have thought to deep-fry a pickle?" I said, dangling the delectable appetizer above my lips. "It's sheer genius."

"I'm a gumbo gal myself," Mary Bennett said, dipping her spoon to get the last bite of the fragrant roux. "What's this place called again?"

"Hal and Mal's. Mal is the one who organized the parade, and his brother Hal is the king of all soups," I said in between bites. "Used to be a merchant's warehouse in the fifties." I swept my arm around the restaurant with its exposed ceilings and brick walls. "Later on, they'll have live music for some dancing."

"I can barely walk, much less dance," Tammy said, looking over the remains of her supper, which included a catfish po'-boy, red beans and rice, and a fat wedge of Mississippi Mud cheesecake.

"You would *not* believe what I saw in the men's bathroom," Gerald said as he slid into the red vinyl booth we all shared.

"There ain't much I haven't seen in that department," Mary Bennett said out of habit.

"I was talking about the *décor,*" Gerald said coldly. "It's an Elvis-themed bathroom, and the urinals have motorcycle handles."

Our waitress approached the booth. "Are you the world-famous Sweet Potato Queens?"

"Yep," I said. "Word sure gets around fast."

"The gentleman at the bar would like to buy your table a round of beers," said the waitress.

Sean, who was seated on a stool, lifted a mug.

"That had better be light beer, fella," I hollered to him. "Why don't you come over here and join us?"

He shook his head. "Gotta get on home—my queen is holding supper for me. Just as predicted, y'all were the hit of the parade."

"Thanks for the good word and the beer," I said, blowing him a kiss.

"Cold beer, fried pickles, and Elvis memorabilia," Patsy said. "You couldn't ask for more in a restaurant. Maybe Hal and Mal's should be the o-fficial Sweet Potato Queens hangout. How does that sound to you, Boss Queen?"

"Marvelous," I said, sopping the last fried pickle with Come-Back sauce. "We've been so busy stuffing our faces, we haven't had a chance to catch up. What's new?"

"Jack and I have a new addition," Patsy said. She'd lived in Atlanta for so long she was starting to sound like a native.

"Again?" Mary Bennett's eyebrows jumped. "Y'all are going at it like a couple of rabbits."

"Not that kind of addition. You guys would have known

about that," Patsy said with a giggle. "We added a bedroom and a bath to the house—so we'll have more room for those *other* additions."

We made the proper noises over Patsy's new addition and the prospect of those Other ones, but after that, everyone got quiet.

"Anything else? Anyone?" I said.

"Well, not to toot my own kazoo," Mary Bennett said, "but there's been talk of me starring in a made-for-TV movie. I've been looking at scripts."

"Fantastic," I said, and the others chimed in, except for Gerald. There was much chatter about plot and possible co-stars, but after the topic had been exhausted, the table was silent again.

"Does that cover everything?" I said. The room seemed thick with conversational elephants that no one was mentioning.

"Kitchie Koo has finally learned to make umps outside," Gerald said, staring into his napkin. "I'm relieved. My apartment's been a minefield."

The Queens all clapped enthusiastically over Kitchie's new-and-improved bowel control, except for Mary Bennett, who was pushing crumbs around her plate.

"Anything else?" I looked at Mary Bennett, hoping she might be in an air-clearing mood.

"I gave you a made-for-TV movie," Mary Bennett said, defensively. "What more do you want?"

"All right, then," I said, crumpling my napkin. "I have a few things to say."

I launched into a long monologue about my frustrations with my job, and all the doubts and fears I had about my writing. Finally, I shared with them my new vow to take some risks—to put myself out there and see what happened.

"My very first one was appearing in the parade by myself," I said. "I was scared shitless, but the parade is only gonna be once a year and I was determined I was NOT going to miss it just because y'all weaseled out on me. I would have spent the whole year pissed off at y'all for costing me my parade, so I just by God HAD my parade, and it felt good. I'm very proud of myself. Of course, it just made it perfect when y'all DID show up—but I learned I can make my own cake and eat the sumbitch, too!"

When I finished, no one said much of anything.

"I didn't mean to bend your ears like that," I said, self-consciously. "I just—"

"No," Mary Bennett said, shaking her head. "We needed to hear it. Who knew you had so much angst churning inside of you? Bravo for speaking up!"

"Yeah, Jill," Patsy chimed in. "I think we've sorta monopolized the whining over the years. I'm glad you shared your troubles." She twisted her hands in her lap. "By the way, you were right on the money. I *was* holding back. I'm actually a little worried about Jack. It was my birthday last week, and he gave me a blender—and a few nights recently he's come in real late and slept in that new bedroom."

Every mouth at the table plopped open.

"It's a bad sign, isn't it?" Patsy said. "I worry that he's falling out of love with me."

"It's a sign that he's a complete igmo," Mary Bennett said. "Men who give appliances to women as gifts should be shot, or at the very least maimed."

The other Queens rang in, agreeing that giving a blender for a birthday was a grave husbandly infraction, on a scale equal to but not greater than answering in the affirmative when asked, "Do I look fat in these blue jeans?" We all just kinda let that sleeping-in-the-guest-room thing sorta lie there on its own.

"Thanks for spilling, Patsy," I said, rubbing her shoulder. "That was courageous of you."

"Well, I guess everybody here knows that me and what's-his-name broke up," Mary Bennett said.

"Brian," Gerald said.

"Right," Mary Bennett said. "Unfortunately, *some* people think I'm callous because I have made a healthy choice to move on with my life instead of clinging desperately to my past."

Gerald threw down his napkin. "What's so healthy about treating people as if they were disposable?"

Tammy and Patsy swapped puzzled looks. They had no clue about what was going on.

"Not disposable, but certainly *replaceable*," Mary Bennett said in clipped tones. "Or do you think it's healthier to sulk around acting miserable, dragging everyone down with you?"

"I am sorry if I haven't felt like being your happy little side-kick lately," Gerald said sarcastically.

"I am just saying that this sad-sack act is a waste of fuckin' time. If you're so moon-pied over William, do something! Quit acting lower than a snake in a tire track. Swallow your pride and patch things up, for godsake. Give the boy a call."

"I can't call him," Gerald said tersely.

"I'd like to know why the hell not? False pride won't get you anywhere," Mary Bennett said.

Gerald sat motionless. His eyes were staring straight ahead, but they didn't seem to be registering anything around him.

Gerald faced Mary Bennett. "I can't call William because . . ."

"Go on," Mary Bennett said. "Spit it out! You'll feel better."

"Because William is dead!" he shouted. "There! Are you satisfied?"

Mary Bennett was the first to break our stunned silence. "DEAD?! Oh my God, hunny—I'm so sorry, Gerald. I didn't know. Please forgive me." She reached across the table to stroke his arm.

Gerald jerked away from her. "Don't touch me!" Then he gulped and swallowed a sob, and looked up at us with tortured eyes.

"No one should touch me," he said in a barely audible voice. "William had AIDS, and it's entirely possible I have it too." Gerald tore out of the restaurant, leaving a table full of very confused and very, very sad Queens.

PART FIVE

1987

Chapter 19

"I'll just come out and ask it," I said to the gorgeous specimen of manhood sitting across from me, who was at that moment slicing into a pink slab of prime rib. "Do you have a criminal record?"

The specimen (whose name was Ross) chuckled, showing off a set of pristine white choppers that would make an orthodontist swoon.

"I must confess," he said. "Yesterday, I got a ticket for double-parking."

"Check!" I said, pretending to summon the waiter.

He rested his well-chiseled chin in the palm of his hand and gazed at me through the flickering candlelight. "Are you the suspicious type?" he asked.

"It's just become a standard courtship question ever since I went out with a guy who got arrested for fraud—right in the middle of his shrimp scampi. Stuck me with the bill."

"How did you meet him?"

"One of the Queens saw his personal ad that said his hobby was 'creative writing,' so she thought we were made for each other and answered the guy ON MY BEHALF, but without benefit of anything like my PERMISSION. Set up a date with him and sent me to meet him—with me thinking he was some long-lost good buddy of hers. Turned out his passion for 'creative writing' didn't extend much past 'hot checks.'"

"So I guess you don't put much stock in the personals, huh?"

I laughed, barely concealing an underlying snort.

"I guess the answer is no," he said, leaning forward to pour more wine in my glass.

"I've heard so many horror stories about the personals I learned to decode the ads. For instance, men who say they're seeking 'confidential relationships' are always married with six kids. 'Open-minded' is a code word for 'into trick-fucking.' 'Affectionate' means they'll try to feel you up in the movie line, and guys who say they're 'teddy bears' need two seats on an airplane. I told Tammy she could read 'em if she wanted to but if she ever tried to fix ME up with one of 'em again, she might not live to tell the tale."

"Good," he said. "It sounds kind of dangerous. No telling what kind of shady characters you might encounter. I don't know why a stunning woman like you would have to meet men that way. I'd think you'd be fighting the guys off with an ax handle."

"Aren't you a flatterer?" I rose from the table. "Would you excuse me? I need to powder my nose."

"Don't be gone too long. I'll miss you too much," he said, looking at me in such a winsome way, my heart flopped around like a bass in an empty cooler.

The ladies' room was lushly decorated with gold fixtures and a brocade fainting couch. It smelled slightly of expensive perfume.

"Wo-o-o-o GIRL, we could get used to this," I said to my flushed face in the mirror. Then I peeked under the stalls to see if I saw any feet. The coast was clear. I had the joint to myself.

"Yip-yip-yip-yip-YA-HOO!" I half-sang, half-shouted, doing a bugaloo across the bathroom tiles. This was my third date with Ross, and each time we'd gone out, I had to steal away to the ladies' room and kick up my heels with absolute glee.

I also added one more item to my mental list of why Ross was the perfect man for me. He was genuinely interested in whatever I was yakking about, and best of all, he howled at my jokes.

I combed my bangs with my fingers as I hummed "You Make Me Feel Like a Natural Woman," a choice that reflected how elated I was to be with Ross. For the last few years, the theme song of my dates had been "Love Stinks."

It was positively head-spinning how quickly my feelings for Ross had grown. I was like a sports car that had gone from zero to sixty in three dates. Was it possible that he was actually The One? Was I finished kissing every slimy, fly-eating amphibian in the Southeast? Had I finally found my prince?

I returned to the table, and Ross gaped at me as if I were Christie Brinkley in a string bikini.

"She walks in beauty like the night," he said in a low, scintillating baritone.

I met his gaze, and for a few silent moments, we devoured each other with our eyes. My cheeks were so hot I felt as if a brush fire were blazing under my skin.

He leaned across the table and caught my hand. "What do you say we have dessert at my place?"

Three days later, I was still there, kissing him passionately in the foyer of his condominium. My lips were slightly swollen, my chin was raw from razor burn, and my hair was a bird's nest, but I was one happy girl.

"Why don't you call in sick?" he asked, coming up for a gulp of air.

"I can't," I said, working my fingers through my tangled hair. "I work for myself. Besides, I already canceled yesterday's clients. If I keep that up I'll be out of business soon."

"To hell with 'em," he said, nibbling my ear. "One day you won't need them. I have plenty of money for both of us."

Little sparks of excitement shot up and down my spine. Ross was not a man who shied away from talks about commitment. In fact, he'd been we-we-ing for the past sixty hours. "*We* will have to go to Greece together." "*We* should see the new Dustin Hoffman movie." "*We* need to learn how to tango."

But last night, he graduated from the "we" word to the "L" word. He'd laid it on me post-frolic just as we were drifting off to sleep.

Red lights flashed and sirens blared. A metallic voice warned, "Danger, Will Robinson." Suddenly it all seemed too fast, too soon.

"I hope I'm not scaring you," he'd whispered. "I just couldn't help myself."

Of course you couldn't, I thought, calming a bit, willing the sirens silent. How many times over the last couple of days had the "L" word swum around in my mind? I'd been feeling it too; I just didn't have the guts to say it.

"It's probably premature," he said. "We've only known each other a week. But we've spent every waking hour together for two days and two nights. That must be at least the equivalent of nearly a month's worth of dates."

I love the way this man thinks, I mused to myself, sirens successfully muted.

"Call me if you have some time between clients," he said as I reluctantly made my way to the door. "Call me when you have a lunch break. Or better yet, let's eat together. Hope you haven't made dinner plans."

I laughed over his unbridled enthusiasm. "What about you? Don't you have things to do?"

"My hours are very flexible," he said with a flick of his hand.

"Lucky you," I said, giving him one last kiss. Ross was somewhat cagey about what he did for a living. "Businessman" was all I'd gotten out of him so far. Whatever business he conducted served him well, because he lived in a fancy condominium and drove a big-ass, silver Mercedes.

"I almost forgot," I said with a grimace. "I have a lunch date with my friend Tammy today."

"So cancel it."

"I can't. It's been a while since we've gotten together."

"How long?" he asked, his hand slipping into the waistband of my slacks.

I pulled away. If we started down that pleasurable path, I'd miss my first appointment.

"Maybe a week or so. I don't know."

"That doesn't seem so very long." He stuck his fingers in my belt loops and tugged me toward him. "I go months without seeing some of my friends."

"That's why they say men and women are from different planets," I said, wiggling out of his grasp.

"I think you and I are both from Venus, sugar." He reached out for me, but I darted away.

"Gotta go."

"You have a powerful effect on me," he said with a sheepish smile.

The feeling is mutual, I thought. It took superhuman restraint not to drag him back to his king-size bed by his hair and have my way with him.

"Where do you usually go for lunch?"

"A Chinese buffet place in the same shopping center as the Adonis Gym."

"I'll miss you," he said, touching my chin.

"Me, more."

•

I slipped on a pair of sunglasses. "Wow! Is it bright in here or what?"

Tammy cast her gaze around the small restaurant. "What are you talking about? It's downright gloomy."

I slipped the sunglasses down my nose. "I'm talking about the *glare* coming from that sparkling new piece of joo-ry on your arm."

"Oh shit," Tammy said, touching her diamond tennis bracelet. "I forgot I was wearing it."

"Let me guess," I said with a frown. "It ain't from Bob."

Tammy sniffed. "This would cost Bob two months' salary."

"Are you at it again?" I asked. After the very first St. Paddy's Day parade, Tammy had finally come clean to the Queens about her "secret" life. The diamond earrings were a gift from her lover, who just happened to be the owner of the TV station. All those long hours Tammy claimed to be working were spent with him. Instead of getting a "promotion," Tammy was fired when his wife found out about their affair. It seemed she hadn't learned a thing since the disaster with Dr. Day.

After that debacle she'd vowed to be faithful to the clueless Bob, and for a time, she was. At least until, as a surprise for her, Bob hired a crew to remodel their sunroom and there turned out to be a too-attractive flooring installer in the bunch.

I'd pitched a fit when she told me she'd cheated again and, as usual, Tammy deflected the blame. "I was doing FINE, just going to work and then sitting my ass at home being Suzyfucking Homemaker and then goddamn BOB has to go and have TILE BOY over to the house all damn day for a month! What was I supposed to do?"

I pointed out to her that MANY people found it possible—easy, in fact—to resist the charms of all manner of persons to whom they were NOT MARRIED, Tile Boy included, but Tammy insisted that it was Bob's fault for placing her in temptation's way. Once again, though, Tammy's marriage was saved by the fact that the man du jour broke it off with her before Bob found out, and Tammy behaved herself for a time.

Recently, though, Bob had enrolled in night classes to become eligible for a principal's position. He often kept late hours at the university library, and obviously Tammy couldn't resist the opportunity to return to her old ways.

"You're not being very careful. What if you forgot to take it off before you got home?"

She unclasped the bracelet and tucked it into her purse. "I'd just tell him it was costume jewelry. He wouldn't know the difference. I might even keep that one. It's so pretty."

After her liaisons ended, she always sold the "booty." She'd amassed a modest nest egg from the proceeds.

"Have you ever thought about getting another job? And what about your singing?" I asked. Tammy was a leasing agent for temporary corporate apartments, and she met many of her "friends" through work.

"I'm not as resourceful as you, Jill, and as to the singing—well, I like to keep my evenings open."

At the word "resourceful," I had to laugh. I was working myself to a frazzle.

"Look!" Tammy said, pointing her chopsticks in the direction of the entrance. "Isn't that a *Diddy Wah Diddy* rack? I haven't seen this week's column yet."

"Neither have I. The new one came out today."

I scampered over to the rack and grabbed two copies.

"Page thirteen," I said, handing one to Tammy. Even though I'd been writing for the *Diddy* a couple of years, I still got a little thrill from seeing my byline.

It used to be that when any of the Queens were reading my work, I'd practically sit in their laps, registering every eye movement and intake of breath.

Nowadays, I was much cooler about the whole thing. Tammy let out a small "heh," and I didn't even flinch.

"*Ha! Ha!*" she laughed, holding her middle.

"What was that about?" I demanded. "Was it the bit about the fruit cake?"

"No," Tammy said. "I was reading the comic *next* to your column."

"Oh," I said with a pout.

"Just kidding," Tammy said. "It was great. I swear, you get funnier all the time. You should try to sell your columns to more papers."

I took a gulp of iced tea so sweet it made my teeth hurt. "Syndication takes too much time. My personal trainer business is growing so fast I can barely keep up with it. I'm working day and night."

"I don't know why you're killing yourself," Tammy said. "You should use some of your windfall to take a vacation. Maybe a luxury cruise or something."

"I need to save it for my retirement," I said. Recently, I'd inherited a hundred and fifty thousand dollars from my granddaddy. It was more money than I'd ever imagined having. "I'm in a tizzy trying to figure out what to do with it. I mailed off for an investment kit nearly a month ago and still haven't received any information."

"I think you're entitled to have a little blowout," Tammy said. She twirled a strand of hair around her fingers. "I'm jealous of you, Jill. The only thing missing from your life is a man, and I'm sure it's only a matter of time."

"Actually, I met someone," I said with a huge grin. "I didn't want to talk about it until now because I was afraid I'd jinx it. It's not like I've been very lucky in love in the past."

"De-tails!" Tammy demanded.

"Where do I start? Ross is a businessman and looks like a matinee idol. He seems to be very wealthy. And—"

"Say no more! I'm green. I'm literally turning into a bell pepper over here."

"He's a fantastic listener. Not to mention being funny, warm, and so very sexy."

"You've already *done* it with him! I can tell!" Tammy said, bouncing around in her seat. "You're blushing so hard you look like you have scarlet fever. What letter grade would you give him, A? B? C?"

"The best grade of all—a capital O."

"Oh?" Tammy said with a knowing smile.

"Oh, oh, oh. *If* you know what I mean." I happily sank back into the booth. "I gotta tell you, Tammy, my nether regions have never been happier."

"Where did ya meet him?"

"He came into the gym out of the blue and hired me as his trainer. Not that he needed me. He was already the proverbial brick one. He is so . . . Ohmigod," I said, pointing at the door. "He's *here*."

Tammy turned around for a quick peek. "Is he the guy in the Brooks Brothers shirt?"

I nodded and waved to Ross.

"Greek God alert!" Tammy screeched.

"Shush. Act normal."

"Hello, ladies," Ross said as he approached the table.

"Ross! What a nice surprise," I said.

"I was in the area and I'd remembered you said you were eating here." He kissed me on the cheek. "I hope I'm not intruding."

"Absolutely not." I patted the space beside me. I was tickled pink to show Ross off to Tammy, but also a wee bit disappointed he'd sought me out. Half the fun of having a wonderful new boyfriend was jabbering about him to your friends.

"This is Tammy," I said. "Tammy, meet Ross."

"It's a pleasure," she said, showing off both dimples.

The three of us shot the breeze. I couldn't think straight because Ross's thigh was pressed up against mine. The heat from his touch seemed to pulse through my entire body.

"When did you move here?" Tammy asked.

"A couple of weeks ago," Ross said. "I'm renting a condo at Governors Arms. I need to do some furniture shopping. It's practically bare."

"I handle that property, but I don't remember you. You must have come in on my day off." Tammy pointed to Ross's watch. "Oh wow, is that a Rolex Presidential?"

"Tammy," I said through clenched teeth. Sometimes her fascination with chi-chi material goods was downright aggravating.

"It is," Ross said.

"I've never seen one before," Tammy said, her eyes glittering hungrily. "Where did you get it?"

Ross removed it from his wrist and handed it to her. "A jeweler on Fifth Avenue in New York. I bought it on a whim a couple of years back."

"Gorgeous!" Tammy said, examining it from every angle. After a moment, a strange look crossed her face.

"Anything wrong?" Ross asked.

"Gosh no," Tammy said quickly, handing him back the watch. "Will you excuse me a minute? I need to visit the ladies'."

The second she left, Ross was all over me and I was panting like a collie into his ear. Out of the corner of my eye, I saw the waitress approaching the table with a tray of fortune cookies.

"Stop," I whispered. "The waitress."

We parted slowly, like pulling gum from the bottom of a shoe.

"Need anything else?" the waitress asked.

"We're good, thank you," Ross said, waving her off. As soon as she took off, Ross rushed me like a linebacker.

"Why don't you cancel your clients this afternoon?" he said.

"I have to earn a living," I said, slithering out of his embrace.

"Let me come with you? I promise I'll be very quiet."

I laughed. I'd never met a man so greedy for my company before.

"I think you'll survive without me for the next four hours or so."

He arched an eyebrow. "Are you *sure* you're going back to work? Maybe you're meeting your other lover?"

"I have them scattered all over the city," I said lightly. "Seriously, Ross. I have to go."

He lightly squeezed my kneecap. "Are you dating anyone else?"

"Absolutely not," I said, without a smidgen of coyness.

Ross let out a relieved sigh. "Good. I know we haven't talked about this, but I'd like us to have an exclusive relationship. What do you think?"

His eyes were a dizzying blue, and his succulent lips curved into a smile. Honestly, was there such a thing as a person being too good-looking?

"I can't imagine seeing anyone else but you."

"That's the best news I've heard all week," he said, locating my ear through a tangle of hair. "As soon as Tammy gets back, let's get out of here. I want to have a few private good-bye kisses in the car before you go back to work."

"Just a few," I said, holding up a finger in warning.

When he saw Tammy approach the table, he threw down a hundred-dollar bill. "It was really nice meeting you."

"I enjoyed meeting you, Ross. Jill, please call me later. We need to finish catching up."

"I'll call this evening," I promised.

"Bye now," Ross said, placing his hand on the small of my back and guiding me to the exit.

Chapter 20

It's a miracle!" Tammy said over the phone. "Jill Conner lives and breathes. I was beginning to think you were a figment of my imagination."

"I'm sorry," I said, picking the dead leaves off a plant I'd neglected. "I know I've been out of touch, but it's not like you've been that easy to track down yourself lately."

There were twenty messages on my machine when I got home, but I hadn't had time to listen to them yet.

"I've tried to call you at the gym, and I haven't been able to get you there, either."

"I've been cutting back my hours a little." I opened the refrigerator and was hit in the face by the stench of rot.

"I'm just glad I got you on the phone," Tammy said. "There's a lot of stuff going on. Have you heard about Patsy?"

"No. What's up?"

"Jack is having an affair with his secretary."

"SHIT! That's terrible. How's Patsy doing?"

"Me and Mary Bennett have been trying to comfort her, but she's a wreck. I suspect Mary Bennett isn't in the greatest shape herself."

"Why do you say that?"

"Brian married the actress who plays his wife on that sitcom he stars in. It's been in all the papers."

"Does she seem upset?"

"You know Mary Bennett. She pretends it doesn't bother her, but suddenly she's dating up a storm, just like she did when they first broke up."

The Queens had never discovered the real reason behind their breakup, but we always suspected it wasn't Brian's fault.

"The main reason I called is Mary Bennett thinks it's high time for a Queen get-together. She's been nominated for an Emmy and wants to fly us all out to L.A. for the awards show in two weeks."

"*All* the Queens?" I asked. "Did she ask Gerald?"

Gerald and Mary Bennett had continued to be on very shaky ground since their Parade Day blowup several years back.

"She asked Gerald, of course. But he said he was busy."

I sighed. "What's he doing now? Last week, you know, he chained himself to the door of a pharmaceutical rep's car—protesting the marketing program for the company's HIV drugs. It took them all day to get him loose. He had a terrible sunburn—and an even worse case of diaper rash from sitting in a wet Depends all day. Apparently, his *Activism for Dummies* manual didn't mention that possibility in the 'How to Stage a Successful Sit-in' section."

After his emotional breakdown at Hal & Mal's, the Queens convinced Gerald to get an AIDS test. To everyone's relief, his results came back negative. Shortly afterward, he started attending regular meetings for P.A.B.A. (Persons Affected by AIDS) and at first, he seemed better. He learned the truth about HIV and he quit acting so weird about being touched. But soon, he became an activist, and he became more and more militant by the day. Though P.A.B.A. was a gentle support group, the loving, compassionate atmosphere somehow riled him up and our sweet, easygoing Gerald had turned into a wild-eyed zealot.

His every waking thought seemed devoted to thinking up all manner of social action groups, from the mild-mannered and well-meaning G.A.G. (Gay and Great), helping people come out as homosexual, to the well-meaning but nonetheless caustic-sounding group designed to introduce the uneducated straight population to their gay neighbors, I.A.M.G.A.Y. (Ignorant Assholes Meeting Gay American Youth) to the proposed dial-up service for the education of mainstream heterosexuals about HIV, C.H.I.A. (Crisis Hotline for Ignorant Assholes).

We tried to tell him he might have more luck recruiting members if he toned down the names a bit. Who wants a T-shirt with IGNORANT ASSHOLES on it?

"Oh, Lord, I hadn't heard about the car-door incident," Tammy said. "But I swear, every time I talk to him, it seems like he's thought up a new and angrier group. I wonder if his friends in that P.A.B.A. group have any idea how furious he is, or if he ever even mentions his 'social action group' ideas to them. But anyway, he just said he had some kind of family deal to go to and begged off—though I know he's just avoiding Mary Bennett. God, I wish they would patch things up."

"Well, hell," I said. "We all do, but I think they're both dealing with bigger stuff than we really know about, and nothing's gonna get better 'til it's all out in the open."

"There's nothing we can do in the meantime, though, so you'll go with me to California, won't you?" Tammy pleaded.

"Of course I will," I said. I felt a slight pang about leaving Ross behind, but what the hell, it was only for a couple of days. I'd survive, and our reunion would be worth the trip.

"What's been going on with you? I assume you've been hanging out with that Ross guy a lot."

"We're inseparable," I said happily. "Forgive me for being such a crummy friend lately."

"Ross is definitely a looker." She paused for moment. "There's something that's been bothering me since I saw you at the Chinese restaurant. I don't know if it's important, but—"

There was a knock at the door. "Hang on, Tammy. Someone's here.

"Ross?" I said, motioning him inside.

"I'm missing you," he said sadly. I'd been gone only a few hours.

"Ross, I told you I needed to get some things done here and I just—"

"Who are you talking to?" he said, pointing at the phone in my hand.

"Tammy. She just called and . . . Hold on a minute. Tammy, Ross just got here and—"

"Let me have it," Ross said, holding out his hand.

"Why? I just—"

When I didn't immediately surrender the phone, he took it out of my hand and said, "Hey there, Tammy. What's shaking? Listen, I hate to hustle you off the phone, but Jill and I are going to be late. I'm whisking her off to the Bahamas for a surprise getaway."

"What?" I said, still stunned that Ross had snatched the phone from me.

"You take care, too, gorgeous. I'm sure Jill will tell you *all* about it when she gets back. Bye now."

"The Bahamas? Ross, what are you—?"

He wagged a couple of plane tickets in my face. "Ready for a little R and R?"

"I can't go! I have clients to see. I'm not packed. There's a million things—"

"I did a little shopping and I have your bag packed and ready in the car. It's stuffed with all kinds of goodies."

"I just—"

"Come on, baby. Live a little! What kind of person turns down a trip to the Bahamas?"

"It's so sudden," I said, but I felt myself weakening. There was something very appealing about dropping everything and taking off to the tropics. Why was I resisting?

"All right," I said with a smile. "I'll go."

"Come on then," Ross said, tugging on my arm.

"My bills!" I said, looking at the pile of mail on the table. "I'm behind."

Ross scooped them up and tucked them under his arm. "I'll take care of 'em."

"What? I can't let you pay those."

"Why not?" Ross said with a laugh. "You think your piddling little rent and power bills will make the slightest dent in my bank account? I won't even notice."

"That doesn't seem right to me. I've always—"

"You're a piece of work," Ross said, shaking his finger and smiling indulgently. "You don't want a trip to the Bahamas. You balk when the man who loves you wants to help out a little with a few bills."

"But I don't need help. I make enough money to—"

"I know that, baby," he said, holding my face. "Just let me do something nice for you, okay?"

I have to say, it was nearly impossible for me to refuse him anything when he held my face and looked me in the eye. Every time his fingertips made contact with my skin, I turned into a quivering mound of Jill Jell-O.

"Okay. Just this once," I said weakly.

•

Before I knew it, we were in first class heading toward the Bahamas. Ross, who drank a Scotch and water before takeoff, was snoozing softly beside me. His face was a collection of perfectly defined curves and peaks.

The stewardess fawned all over him and couldn't resist sneaking looks as she passed by. When she finally noticed me, her eyes widened with bewilderment. If she had a thought bubble over her head, it'd say, "What is Robert Redford doing with Big Foot?"

I flipped open my compact mirror. Well, maybe not Big Foot, but my collection of genes wasn't near as flawless as Ross's. Now that we were on the way, I'd finally begun to unwind. I had perked up at the thought of a little partying in the flashy Bahamian casinos and nightclubs and little seaside lolling. Since we met, Ross and I had been as isolated as two bears in a cave.

•

"To the docks," Ross said to the cabdriver after we'd collected our luggage in the baggage area.

"Is our hotel on the water?" I asked, shading my eyes against the bright Bahamian sun. I'd forgotten to bring sunglasses, but imagined the hotel gift shop sold them.

"We're taking a boat to our final destination."

"What?" I said, gazing out the window as we passed rows of pastel buildings thronged by palm trees. "Call me crazy, but isn't *this* the Bahamas?"

"This is Nassau, but they ought to call it Nas-ty, because it's touristy, crowded, and commercialized. We're going to a secluded out-island called Spanish Wells. We might go days without seeing another soul."

My heart dropped at the word "secluded."

"What's wrong, sweetie?" Ross asked, draping his well-muscled arm over my shoulders. "You look upset."

"What is the deal, Ross? Are you ashamed of me or something? Why do we always have to be off by ourselves?"

"Jill. Baby." He tightened his grip around me. "Course I'm not."

"I know I'm no Heather Locklear."

"You're breathtaking! Don't you ever look in the mirror? I thought you knew why we hardly go out in public."

"Why?" I asked in a small voice.

"Because I don't want to share you with anyone."

•

"Isn't this the most gorgeous sunset you've ever seen in your life?" Ross said. We were lounging on the porch of our villa, which had a panoramic view of the spectacular aquamarine Atlantic. Our room was mere footsteps from the ocean, separated by only a narrow strip of sugary white sand. Soon the sunset would give way to a sky studded with more stars than I'd ever seen in my entire life.

"And to think I was worried about missing *Wheel of Fortune,*" I said, taking a long draw on my piña colada.

I'd become completely taken in by the tranquillity of our little paradise. Sadly, real life was fixin' to rear its ugly head.

"I gotta write a column," I said with a groan, rising to go inside. I wore a flowered sarong Ross had packed for me. "Don't leave me," Ross said, tugging on the hem of my skirt. "It's so beautiful right now. Whatever they pay you for that column, I'll quadruple it."

"You can't quadruple it, Mr. Money Bags," I said, swatting him away. "I write the column for free."

"You're kidding," he said, frowning. "Why are you selling yourself short like that?" He encircled my waist with his arms, and pulled me onto his lap. "No column writing tonight."

I tried to squirm away from him but he held fast. "Come on, Ross. I have a deadline. And I *like* writing it."

"More than you like being with me?" he whispered in my ear.

"One thing doesn't have anything to do with the other."

"This is our last night together here and you want to spend it writing a column you don't even get paid for. Can't you put it off until we get back?"

He looked so pitiful. I relented.

"All right," I said. "I'll write it on the plane on the way home. I don't feel like doing it right now anyway."

"You seem to have enjoyed relaxing in the sun," he said, covering my hand with his.

"Hunny, I'm *the* queen of not-doing-jack-shit. The only thing I want to interrupt my lolling is meals, naps in the shade, and romps in the bedroom, and not necessarily in that order."

He laughed. "Stick with me, baby, and you'll have plenty of opportunity for all those things."

"You *do* seem to have a lot of free time," I said with a grin. "I'm dying to know what kind of business allows for so much goofing off. I'd love to get in on the ground floor of that deal."

He sighed. "I knew this conversation was coming. I've been trying to avoid it. The truth is, I have good reasons for being vague about what I do."

A drug dealer. I knew it! He's come to the Bahamas to make a buy.

"I'm ashamed to say what it is I really do," he said awkwardly.

Shit! Pornography!

"My father's estate was huge. I'm the only heir. Basically, I manage money."

"That's all?" I said, trying to conceal my relief. "What's to be ashamed of?"

"It's not a *real* job," he said with a shy smile. "Makes me appear lazy. Actually, it takes a lot of effort to manage large sums of money. I'm very good at what I do. I've doubled the estate in two years."

"Damn, hunny." I leaned back in the lounge chair I was now sitting in, trying to absorb the news. I'd suspected Ross was wealthy, but I had no idea we were talking so many zeros.

He planted a soft kiss on my cheek. "Now I just need someone to help me spend it."

•

"Jill! Thank God I ran into you," Tammy said, steering her buggy into the produce section of the Piggly Wiggly. "I've been worried sick. I called your house and the machine never picks up, and the gym says you haven't been in for over two weeks."

"I'm sorry for not calling, but I haven't been home in days. So much has happened! I moved in with Ross."

She didn't jump up and down and holler like I'd hoped. Instead, concern crossed her face.

"So soon? Y'all barely know each other."

"First of all, have you forgotten how much shit I know about YOU? I can't believe I'm getting this from the Queen of Fuck First Ask Questions Later—but you would not believe how wonderful Ross is," I said, placing a bunch of bananas into the cart.

"He brings fresh-squeezed orange juice and hot coffee to me in bed every morning. He gives me foot massages galore. I've never been so spoiled in my life."

"But what about your work? Why haven't you been to the gym?"

"Before I met Ross I was putting in seventy-hour weeks. That's just not healthy. You yourself said I deserved time off. And again, let me say, I can't believe I'm getting this crap from you—I would've expected pointers from you, not questions and certainly not disapproval. What is this about?"

"What happened to your column in the *Diddy*? I noticed it was missing this week."

I picked up a cantaloupe and gave it a squeeze and sniff. "I decided I can't spare the time to write a column for free."

"But you *love* that column," Tammy said, shaking her head in disbelief.

"Paging Jill Conner," said a voice over the PA system. "Please come to the courtesy desk. Jill Conner."

I swung my cart and rushed over; Tammy followed on my heels. Ross was the only person who knew I was at the grocery store.

"I'm Jill Conner," I said breathlessly to the clerk behind the counter and she handed me the phone.

"What's taking you so long, baby?" Ross asked.

"I was just about to go through checkout," I said. "I'll be home in just a few minutes."

"Good!" he said. "You know what a worrier I am. I miss you."

"I miss you, too," I said, hanging up the phone.

Tammy stared at me, green eyes narrowing. "That was Ross, wasn't it? What in the world did *he* want? I haven't been able to talk to you for five minutes without being interrupted by him."

"He's just overprotective," I said. "Listen, I'll call you when I get home."

"That's what you said last time. We're supposed to go to California. Remember the Emmys? That's one of the reasons I've been trying to reach you. We're leaving on Saturday."

"Count me in," I said, a little nervous about how Ross would react to the news. He hated for me to be out of his sight for a couple of hours, much less a couple of days. "I gotta go. I'll call you later, and we'll discuss the plans."

"You promise?" she shouted after me. "There's something I need to talk to you about. Today!"

"Yes!" I called back, hustling to the checkout line.

•

Later, after dinner, while Ross relaxed in his easy chair with a book and some iced tea, I brought up the trip to L.A.

"I haven't discussed the Queens with you much, but they're like family to me."

"I don't want you to go." He tucked me under the chin. "I have something very special planned for us this weekend."

"You do?" I said. "Can't we put it off?"

"I suppose we could, but I really don't want to."

"I'm sorry, Ross. As much as I'll miss you, I *have* to go. This is a huge night in Mary Bennett's life, and I just cannot miss it."

"Didn't you say two other Queens were going? Let the others cheer her on."

"That's not the issue. I can't just send my proxy to something like this. I want and need to be there—we all need to be there. We've always been there for each other in the past."

He pointed a finger at me. "The key word is 'past.' The Queens are your past. *I'm* your future."

"Course you are, but I've been ignoring my friends and I need to fix that. This trip is really important to them and to me."

He gave me his now-familiar pathetic puppy dog look. "More important than me? You know I hate to be left alone."

"It will just be for two nights," I said, refusing to meet his eye for fear I'd weaken. "I'm going to California. It has nothing to do with you."

He slowly lifted his drink to his lips. "So that's your final say on the subject?"

"Yes," I said, proud I hadn't caved in.

His drink came flying at me so fast I didn't have time to duck—it hit me square on the jaw.

"You're so goddam ungrateful!" he said, his handsome face warped by anger. "I do *everything* for you, and all I ask of you is one simple thing."

I touched my jaw and slowly backed away from him.

His hateful expression immediately fell away. "Oh my God, Jill. What have I done? I didn't mean to. That was a mistake. I—"

I didn't stick around to hear another word, but instead turned tail and tore out of the house to my car. Ross followed me, but tripped on his front step.

I was halfway down the drive when I saw him waving and running in my rearview mirror. I roared down the street, sobbing hysterically. It wasn't until I was several miles away that I realized I had nowhere to go.

I drove past Tammy and Bob's house, but all the windows were dark. Bob was probably at night school, and God only knew where Tammy was.

How could I have been so foolish as to move in with someone I hardly knew? All of my furniture was in storage, and everything else I owned was at Ross's. The only thing I had was my purse and the clothes on my back.

I stopped by the drugstore to buy toothpaste and a toothbrush, and checked into the Best Western. As soon as I was in my room, I called Mary Bennett, Gerald, and Patsy. All I got was three answering machines. I'd never felt so alone in my life.

I switched on the TV and stared at it mindlessly through a torrent of tears. An hour later the phone rang.

"Jill, it's Ross. Don't hang up."

I sat straight up in bed. "How did you find me?"

"I drove around to all the hotels until I saw your car. I'm in the lobby. Thank God you're okay."

"I don't want to talk to you," I said coldly, but couldn't bring myself to hang up.

"Sweetie," he said in ragged whisper. "I didn't mean to hit you with that glass. I swear I didn't. It was an accident, but I never should have lost my temper and thrown it in the first place."

Was it possible he hadn't meant to hit me? It had happened so fast I couldn't be sure.

"I love you, Jill," he said, choking out the words.

My grip loosened on the receiver. I could feel something shifting in my chest.

"We're so good together. You *know* we are. Don't let one isolated incident ruin everything."

Anger slowly drained from my body. I stared at my reflection in the mirror. It was only a plastic stadium cup so it really hadn't hurt all that much. It was almost as if nothing had happened.

"Meet me down in the lobby, and let's go home. I *need* you." His voice dropped to a husky whisper. "And I know you need me."

It was true. Despite the horrible thing that happened between us, my whole body ached for him.

"I'll be right down," I said.

We barely got into the door of Ross's house, and we definitely didn't make it to the bedroom. As we tore away each other's clothes, our hands shook as if we couldn't wait to get our fix.

Ross kept whispering "I'm so sorry" and kissed my jaw over and over. We made love until our bodies were limp and spent. Afterward, Ross pulled open the drawer of his nightstand and withdrew a small velvet box.

"This was the reason I didn't want you to go to California this weekend," he said, handing it to me. He got down on one knee beside the bed. "Will you marry me, Jill?"

•

Two days after he'd proposed and I accepted, Ross sat at his desk doing some paperwork. I brought him a Coke.

"So you *do* work after all?" I said, looking over his shoulder.

He sighed. "That's one of the burdens of having a lot of money—constantly having to figure out what to do with it. Luckily, I've gotten a tip that gold and silver are going to go through the roof. I'm investing half a million, and I'll probably double that before the month is up."

"Isn't that risky?"

"Not really," Ross said. "Precious metals never lose value, long-term anyway." He grinned up at me. "And besides, I have a lavish wedding and honeymoon to pay for."

"It just so happens I've been looking for some investment opportunities myself," I said. "Maybe I should buy some silver and gold."

"Baby," Ross said, flipping through his papers. "You'd need at least ten thousand dollars to make it worth your while."

"I've got a hundred and fifty thousand," I said softly.

Ross swung around in his chair. "You're kidding! I would never have guessed you had that kind of money. Where is it invested?"

"Nowhere, yet," I said. "It's just sitting in the bank."

"Jill!" Ross shook his head sternly. "We gotta do something about that. Right away."

"I know, I know," I said. "I sent off for a free investment kit but I haven't gotten it yet."

"That's good. There are all kinds of scams out there. Do you want me to take care of this for you? I'll find you some safe investments."

"Would you?" I asked. "I hate to—"

He rested his hands on my hand. "Sweetie, that's what husbands do. Besides, this is my area of expertise. We'll go by the bank Monday to sign a signature card so I can get access to your account."

I hesitated. "You need access?"

"Of course." He chuckled. "What's wrong? Don't trust me?"

"No, it's not that," I said, feeling somewhat foolish. "I just didn't know how it worked."

"Any transactions concerning your account would require both of our signatures. I'd first clear any decisions with you, but if you don't feel comfortable—"

"No, no, no. I do!" I said. "We'll go first thing Monday."

•

The next morning, I started to read the Sunday paper but the text blurred. I'd gotten only four hours' sleep. Ross, who never required more than five, couldn't stand to be up by himself.

I tuned the TV to CNN. The anchorwoman was reporting on Hollywood.

"Dreams will come true in the Shrine Auditorium tonight in Los Angeles," she said.

I was so startled I immediately turned it off.

The Emmys are tonight? I'd completely forgotten! I'd been so wrapped up with Ross I'd never called Tammy back. The Queens would be worried sick. I was torn between wanting to get on the phone—or a plane—to them immediately, and wanting to crawl in a guilt-filled hole for being a shitty friend. I was paralyzed by my inner turmoil.

•

Ross and I were eating French toast for breakfast when the phone rang. I jumped.

"Did you give anyone this number?" he asked.

"No. Was I not supposed to?"

He didn't answer but instead picked up the phone.

"Yes?" he said in an abrupt voice. His face grew stony as he listened to whoever was on the line. After a moment, he hung up without ever saying a word.

"I have to leave," he said. His voice was unusually cold. "There's something I need to deal with right away."

"Can I come?" I asked, following after him. We hadn't been apart in days. The idea of being left alone was unsettling.

"No," he said, opening the front door, not even looking back. "Just stay here. I'll call you later."

"Where are you going?" I shouted, but he didn't reply, just headed determinedly to his Mercedes. "Ross, please tell me. You're scaring me," I said.

He ignored my pleas. And before I knew it, he was gone.

I stood in the yard for a couple of minutes, befuddled. What the hell was going on?

I went back inside and started picking up the dirty dishes from the table. The doorbell chimed, nearly scaring the crap out of me. Ross never had any visitors.

"Jill, are you in there?" yelled a voice from outside.

Was that Gerald?

"Jill! Open the door!"

It was Patsy's voice. No mistaking it.

I cracked the door, and both Gerald and Patsy stood on my porch.

"Thank God," Gerald said, grabbing me and hugging me tight.

"What are y'all doing here?"

"No time to talk," Patsy said. "We've got to go to Tammy's house. One of the Queens is in deep trouble."

"Who?" I said, cocking my head in confusion.

"We'll explain everything when we get there," Gerald said. "There's not much time."

"All right, I'm coming," I said, caught up in their urgency. As soon as I took a step outside I froze. "Wait a minute. I can't go. Ross had to leave suddenly, and he'll pitch a fit if he comes home and I'm not here."

"Call him from Tammy's," Gerald said, putting an arm around my waist and gently pushing me toward the car.

"You don't understand. Ross is very protective of me. I just can't—"

"Jill!" Patsy shouted. Her eyes were blurry with tears. "We need you! This is a matter of life and death."

I'd never heard Patsy raise her voice before. Her outburst stunned me into compliance. They led me to Gerald's car parked in our circular drive.

"What the hell's going on?" I said, my heart booming in my ears. I was terrified about what might be wrong and equally upset about Ross's likely reaction to my being gone.

"We're almost there!" Gerald said from the front seat. "Hang tight for a minute."

A dozen horrible scenarios flashed in my mind. Who was in trouble, Mary Bennett or Tammy? I thought of Tammy's suicide attempt. Had she tried again?

Gerald lurched into Tammy's driveway, and as soon as the car came to a stop, we all rushed inside the house. Mary Bennett was standing in the kitchen, talking to a tall, dark-haired woman I didn't recognize. Obviously, the trouble was with Tammy—Bob must've finally caught her in the act. She was nowhere in sight.

"There's Jill. Hey, hunny," she said very calmly, as she gave me a hug. "Jill, I want you to meet someone," she said, indicating the brunette.

"What's happened to Tammy?" I demanded, ignoring her.

"Nothing's happened to Tammy," Mary Bennett said. "She's perfectly fine."

"Where is she? What's the big emergency then?" I glanced at Patsy and Gerald. "I thought you said Tammy was in trouble."

"I said *one* of the Queens is in terrible trouble," Gerald said. "I didn't say it was Tammy."

Just then Tammy strode into the kitchen from the back of the house. She looked completely normal, not a hair out of place.

"There she is," she said with a relieved sigh. "Have you told her yet?"

"Told me what?" I asked. "What the fuck's going on?!"

An almost imperceptible exchange went on between the four Queens.

"Haven't you guessed?" Mary Bennett said. "It's you. You're the one in trouble."

"Are all of you fuckin' crazy? There's nothing wrong with me!" I turned to the phone on the wall. "I need to call Ross, then one of you assholes needs to take me back home."

"Don't worry about him right now," Mary Bennett said. "He won't be coming back home anytime soon."

"You were the one who just called?" I said, feeling queasy.

Mary Bennett nodded. The Queens were all staring at me in

an extremely peculiar way. "Take me home now! You don't understand Ross. He's—"

"I understand him very well, Jill," said the brunette. "I was engaged to him myself just a few months ago."

"What?" I said, sinking into a kitchen chair. "Who the hell are you?"

"My name's Hillary Gray. I'm from New Orleans. Your friends asked me to come up. They were afraid for you. And with good reason."

"Why? What the hell are y'all talkin' about?!" I demanded, giving the Queens an incredulous look. "Everything's perfect. I've never been happier." I waved my hand in front of them. "Look! I'm engaged."

No one seemed at all happy with my news.

Hillary surveyed me with calm brown eyes. "I understand you haven't been going to work, and that you no longer write a column that you truly enjoyed. Whose idea was that, yours or Ross's?"

"Mine," I said in a defensive voice. "Ross was naturally concerned that I was putting in so many hours, but he—"

"Did he discourage you from seeing your friends?" Hillary asked. "Did he isolate you from other people?"

"It's perfectly natural for two people to cocoon at the beginning of a relationship," I said, directing my comment to the Queens. "Good God, when Tammy and Bob first got married, they didn't come up for air for weeks, and Patsy—"

Hillary didn't blink. "Has he ever lost his temper with you? Grabbed you? Hit you?" she asked.

The air in the room seemed to get thinner. The Queens tensed at the questions. Everyone's eyes were trained on me.

"He threw a drink at me," I said, involuntarily touching my jaw. "It was an accident, and it didn't even hurt."

"Good God! I can't believe what I'm hearing," Mary Bennett said with a wince.

"It's nothing," I said. "People lose their tempers all the time. He apologized his head off and promised he'd never do it again. I believe him."

"Will you fuckin' listen to yourself, Jill?" Tammy said in a firm voice.

"It *was* an accident, I tell you," I said.

"What in the hell has happened to you?" Tammy said, shaking her head in disbelief. "First you practically drop off the face of the earth. You stop working. You ignore your nearest and dearest, and now you're defending this asshole who tried to hurt you. I feel like I'm talking to a stranger."

"There's something y'all don't understand," Hillary interrupted. "Jill *isn't* herself. She's been in the nonstop company of a master manipulator for several weeks. Ross occasionally loses his temper, when he doesn't immediately get what he wants, but that's not his biggest problem. I just hope we aren't too late."

"What do you mean?" I said, searching her face. "Will you *pleeeze* just tell me what's going on?"

Hillary took a deep breath. "Has Ross offered to help you manage your money yet?"

"What? How did you—?"

"Does he have any access to your bank accounts?" she asked, in a strident voice.

"No," I said, desperately trying to make sense of what was going on. "But what would be so terrible about that? That's what he does. He's—"

"Oh, Jill," Gerald said softly.

"Y'all've got it all wrong!" I said. "Ross didn't offer. I asked him! He didn't even know I *had* any."

"Yes, Jill, he did," Hillary said. "He's known from the beginning. That's why he picked *you* to prey on."

"Excuse me?"

"You filled out a request card for an investment kit, didn't you?" Hillary asked. "Those cards go to Ross's P.O. box."

My head felt as if it could float away from my neck, except there was no air in the room. "This doesn't make sense," I said. "Ross has so much money of his own."

Hillary crouched down so her face was level with mine. "I'm sure he told you he inherited millions, but that's a lie. The only money he has is what's he bilked from women like us."

"But his car—"

"Leased," she said.

"My ring?" I said, protectively rubbing the oversized diamond.

"Cubic zirconium."

"His Rolex Presidential?"

"It's a fake," Tammy said. "That's how I knew he was lying. I know my tickers. The minute hand was jerky instead of smooth."

"He took me to the Bahamas!" I said.

"Ross took me there, too," Hillary said. "He considers the trip an investment. He makes many grand gestures to gain your trust. It's also a way for him to insinuate himself into your life without anyone around. *Everything* he does is just a step to get closer to your money."

"I can't believe this . . . ," I said.

"He'll stop at *nothing* to make a woman fall in love with him. I'm sure you know *exactly* what I'm talking about."

I thought of Ross's expert moves in the bedroom. "I think I'm gonna puke."

"When you filled out that card, it asked how much money

you wanted to invest," Hillary continued. "That's how Ross decides if you're worth his while. He visits women at their jobs to see if he's interested in them, as marks. After three intense weeks of dating, he proposes. By then he's done his job so well that when the time comes to steal her money, the woman is practically begging him to take it."

The room was deadly silent.

"Oh my God," I finally said in a whisper. "That's exactly what he did to me."

"Ross took me for two hundred thousand dollars," Hillary said, standing. "You're very lucky. You have wonderful friends who recognized early that you were in trouble. I wish I'd been so blessed."

I glanced up at the Queens. I'd never seen them look so serious before.

"How did y'all know?" I asked.

"When Tammy told me about the Rolex and how you'd practically given up your life for this guy, I didn't like the sound of it one bit," Mary Bennett said. "I hired a private dick to check things out. He led me to Hillary, who at first didn't want to say anything about Ross."

"I was humiliated," Hillary admitted. "I didn't want anyone to know what he did to me. I never even went to the police."

"I could tell she was hiding something, so I played the fame card. I said this is Mary Bennett Manning and you better damn well tell me what's wrong with Ross or I'll open up a big ol' can of whoop-ass on you."

"I'm a huge fan of *Eagle's Cove,*" Hillary said with a slight smile. "When Electra Frostman tells you to do something, you just do it! Plus, when I learned Ross was involved with a new woman, I knew I had to stop him from cheating someone else."

"So, I brought her up here," Mary Bennett said, stirring cream into her coffee. "Tammy found Ross's address and phone number at the leasing company, and we planned our little intervention."

"How did you get Ross out of the house?" I asked.

"I told him Hillary was finally sending the cops after him. I'll bet he took off outta there like a spotted-ass ape," Mary Bennett said.

"I've never felt so fuckin' stupid in my life," I said. "To think y'all had to go to such lengths—" Then I remembered. "The Emmys! They were tonight! You're not supposed to be here," I said, covering my face with my hands. "You were nominated for best actress. You're missing out because of me."

"Don't sweat it," Mary Bennett said, drawing me into a hug. "Who needs the excitement and drama of the Emmys when I can get more than that right here at home?"

Chapter 21

"Could we go somewhere for a tall one?" Tammy said. She was trying to play it cool, but I could tell she was as agitated as a shook-up soda can. She had shown up unexpectedly at the gym just as I'd showered and changed into my street clothes.

"Sounds like a plan," I said. I'd been so busy putting my life back in order after my run-in with Ross, I'd scarcely seen Tammy for the last couple of weeks.

We went to a dark, dingy sports bar—Tammy's choice—and sat in a back booth pulling on frosty mugs of Bud draft and listening to the steady click of balls from a pool game a few feet away.

"You know how much I love you and the Queens," Tammy said, quaffing her third beer. "I'd do anything for y'all."

"You definitely saved *my* ass."

"And I'd never do anything to hurt you."

Whatever it was that Tammy had stuck in her craw, she'd been skirting around it for the last hour. At this rate, I'd be shit-faced before she finally came out with it.

"Go ahead and say what's on your mind," I said. "I promise not to bite."

Even in the gloom of the bar, Tammy's face was easier to read than a mood ring. She may as well have had "guilty as sin" stamped on her forehead.

She took a big breath. "I'm finally leaving Bob."

"I take that back," I said, plunking my mug down on the table. "Maybe I will bite you after all."

"I haven't been happy for a long time," Tammy said. "I tried, but it's not working. This isn't a snap decision."

"Who is he?" I said, bracing myself for the whole catastrophe. On some level I'd expected this breakup for a very long time—I just always expected it would come from Bob—but I still wasn't quite prepared for it to be happening.

"You're not going to believe it," Tammy said, excitement washing away the guilt on her face. "His name is James and he's a lord. He has his *own* manor house in England. Do you know what that means? He's real live *royalty*, just like Princess Diana."

All of the Queens were bewitched by the Princess Diana frenzy (we'd stayed up all night to watch the wedding) and we were downright covetous of her genuine tiaras. However, leaving your darling husband to have a dalliance with a B-list Prince Charles was taking it too bloody far.

"*Have* a liaison with Lord Lover Boy if you must," I said. "But that's no reason to break up your marriage."

Tammy shook her head. "James wants me to come to England and live with him. I'm leaving tomorrow."

"What?" I said, banging my head against the back of the

booth. "Are you out of your fuckin' mind? You don't even have a passport."

Tammy slid a small blue book across the table. "All set. Remember when Bob and I went to Paris?"

I'd forgotten. Bob scrimped and saved for months to surprise Tammy with that trip for their fifth anniversary.

"How long have you been planning this?"

Tammy stared into her empty mug, then held it up for the barkeep to see. "Since just before you met Ross. James gave me the diamond tennis bracelet you caught me wearing."

"Why haven't you told me?"

"I couldn't. You weren't around or available. Besides, I was afraid you'd *do* something."

"Like stage an intervention with the rest of the Queens the way y'all did me?"

"Something like that," she said, stuffing the passport back into her purse.

"I *do* want to stop you. I think you're making the worst mistake of your life."

"Come on, Jill," Tammy said. "He's a *lord*! His money is so old, it dates back to before the earth cooled. Not like these North Jackson bitches, with their tacky new money."

"Like Marcy Stevens?"

"Yes, like her. Imagine if James and I got married; I'd be Lady Tammy. People like Marcy Stevens Whatever-the-fuck's-her-last-name-now would have to curtsy to me."

I shot her an appalled look. "Marcyfucking Stevens—Tammy, good God, hunny—will you EVER let that go? You are gonna fuck up your life on the off chance that it might give you some kind of warped upper hand with some bitch from HIGH SCHOOL? What is it gonna take for you to get over that bullshit?"

"I'm also madly, deeply in love with James," she added quickly, obviously realizing how shallow she sounded but ignoring my rant.

"And you've known him *how* long?"

"Long enough. He was here visiting a cousin for a month. We went out almost every night while Bob studied at the library. He's back in England waiting for me to come." She happily hugged herself. "He's sent me a love letter every day since he got back."

"Didn't you learn one thing from my mistakes? *Never* rush into things with a man."

"I'm not that gullible! Oh, I'm sorry. I didn't mean to say *you* were gullible. I just meant—"

"The savviest woman in the world can be gullible if she thinks only with her heart instead of her head. I learned that the hard way." I paused. "But it sounds to me like you're thinking with your pocketbook and your fucked-up inner Social Register."

"Not true. I'm crazy about James. It's just a happy coincidence he's loaded."

"When did ya tell Bob?"

Tammy twisted her beer mug back and forth. "I haven't. I'm leaving him a note."

"Un-fuckin'-believable! Very classy."

"I know it's chickenshit . . . but I can't bear to see his face," she said. "He's a wonderful man. He's just not the one for me."

Bob would be completely devastated. At that very moment, he was working himself to a nub for his supervision degree just to be a better provider for Tammy.

I took a deep breath. "Tammy, I love you, but you're doing a horrendous thing and for fucked-up reasons. How many times are you gonna do this? There is no 'society' for you to 'arrive' in—people are just PEOPLE, no matter where you go. If you won't learn from MY mistakes, at least learn from your OWN! I wish to God you'd give this more thought."

"Believe me, Jill, this is the best thing that ever happened to me." Tammy chugged the rest of her beer. "You'll see. One day, all the Queens can come visit me in my castle. Don't you think for once in my life I deserve to be happy?"

PART SIX

1989

Chapter 22

"It had to be the cabana boy," said a buxom blonde who was sitting at the juice bar sipping on a cup of green tea. "She was *so* hateful to him after she ended their affair."

"I think it was her cousin, Felicity," said her companion, a sharp-nosed woman with a shiny black bob. "The one she had the huge catfight with."

"Who in the world are y'all talking about?" I asked, swiveling my stool in their direction. The two women worked out regularly at the Adonis Gym.

"You haven't heard?" said the blonde. "It's all over the news. Everyone wants to know who electrocuted Electra."

"Electra's been electrocuted?" I hadn't watched *Eagle's Cove* the night before because my cable went out. "What happened? Did she survive?"

"Someone dropped a hair dryer in her Jacuzzi!" the blonde continued. "And no, she's dead as a boot. The paramedics couldn't find a pulse."

"It doesn't mean she's *really* dead," said her friend. "Remember Bobby Ewing on *Dallas*? And how Pam dreamt his death for an entire season? You can *never* be sure with soaps."

"Did you know Mary Bennett Manning is originally from Jackson?" the blonde said to her friend. "It's hard to believe the producers of the show would kill off Electra. She's the biggest thing since Madonna."

Over the last couple of years Mary Bennett, a.k.a. Electra, had become a huge phenomenon. There were dolls, a clothing line, perfume, playing cards, and even dartboards. Whenever Mary Bennett came home, she'd have to dress in disguise or fans would mob her. You'd think such great fame would give her a big head, but not our Mary Bennett. She was utterly dismissive of her Electra persona.

"It's a fuckin' soap opera, for God's sake," she'd say if anyone got too gushy on her.

Mary Bennett was her same ol' self, especially with the Queens, and she didn't like to talk about her public life. She said that she wasn't like other stars. She didn't snort cocaine ("I was always taught not to stick anything smaller than a finger up my nose," she'd said) and she didn't have an eating disorder. She'd had a very long, public series of torrid affairs after she and Brian broke up, but they were extremely short-lived. In fact, as far as anyone knew, she hadn't had a serious relationship since Brian.

"You're the most boring superstar I've ever met," I often said to her with mock disappointment. And she'd counter with, "I'm the ONLY superstar you've ever met."

Patsy barreled into the juice bar, wearing a painter's smock. "Did you hear?"

"Let's go outside," I said, slipping off the stool. I didn't want to talk about Mary Bennett in front of the two other women.

Patsy followed me out the glass front doors of the gym and we settled on the stone bench under a large water oak.

"Has Mary Bennett said anything about this to you?" Patsy asked. Six months ago Patsy and her son Mack had moved in with her mother in Jackson. Jack had turned out to be a serial cheater and she'd finally divorced his sorry ass.

"Nope. Not a word," I said.

"Sometimes the writers kill off actors and don't even let them know," Patsy said, pushing a strand of hair back behind her ear with a paint-stained hand. She commissioned portraits, and gave art lessons out of her studio.

"I guess we'll get the full scoop tomorrow night."

The Queens were getting together to celebrate our all-singles' Valentine's Day.

"You hear anything from Tammy?" Patsy asked. Tammy, unfortunately, would be the only Queen not there. Gerald, to my surprise, had agreed to come even though it conflicted with a Persons Affected by AIDS meeting.

"Not for a couple of months." When she'd first moved to the UK, Tammy wrote frequently on stationery embossed with a fancy coat of arms. She sent photos of her and James standing in front of their seventeenth-century manor house. "It's been so bloody rainy here in the Cotswolds that James and I spend most of our days watching the telly," she wrote, showing off her Britishisms. "We may be off to Cannes soon. Cheers!"

But lately, her correspondence had been spotty, at best.

"I ran into Bob at that new Italian restaurant the other night," Patsy said. "He looked so happy."

After Tammy left, Bob, as predicted, had fallen into a deep, dark funk. He dropped out of grad school and took a leave of absence from his job. I helped him pack up and store all the clothes and personal items Tammy left behind. I visited him several times, but eventually he asked me to stop coming by because it was too painful for him.

Six months later, he perked up and started dating again. After a year, he was granted a divorce on the grounds of desertion.

"He was with Katy and Hannah," Patsy said.

"I'll bet she's as cute as a bug's ear." A year ago Bob sent me his and Katy's wedding announcement, and nine months after that, a baby announcement.

"Hannah is our honeymoon baby," the proud papa had written inside the card.

I've always liked Bob, so I was thrilled to death at how his life was turning out. He claimed he regularly read my columns, which now appeared weekly in Jackson's daily paper *The Clarion-Ledger.*

"Does Tammy ever ask about him?" Patsy asked.

"No," I said with a sigh. "And I don't volunteer anything. I don't think she has a clue about Katy and Hannah."

Patsy bent forward and rested her chin in her hands. "I miss her. It's been over two years. Tomorrow won't be the same without her."

Chapter 23

Beer belly, nine o'clock," I called out to Patsy, and we both eagerly marked our cards.

Patsy's gaze searched the room. "I spy . . . a mullet."

"Where?" I said, trying to follow her line of vision.

"The guy next to the cigarette machine. Oh, and a double bonus, he's got on white socks. Bingo!" Patsy said, holding up her card.

"Shit!" I said. "All I needed was a pair of Sansabelt pants."

A short man wearing a turban and sunglasses approached our table.

"Hello, beautiful. May I buy you a drink?" he said in a thick foreign accent.

"Sorry, buster," Patsy said, holding her hand slightly above his swaddled head. "You gotta be at least this tall to ride."

"How very rude of you," the man said with a frown. "Perhaps your friend will be more agreeable.

"Save your breath," I said. "You'll need it to inflate your date."

Patsy and I shared a grin—we were getting good at keeping the weirdos at bay.

"If I cannot buy you ladies a drink, what about a small, Middle Eastern country?" the man persisted.

"Didn't you hear what I said, cat toy?" I asked.

"Take a powder, purse hook!" Patsy said with a sneer.

The stranger lowered his sunglasses, and I saw a familiar pair of gray eyes peeking over the top.

"You bitches are a couple of tough customers."

"Mary Bennett!" Erika said.

"Shhh!" Mary Bennett said, holding a finger to her lips. "Don't say that too loud. We don't want a stampede."

"We heard about Electra," I said in a low voice. "Is she really, truly dead?"

"Deader than disco, darlin'," Mary Bennett said, taking a seat at our table.

"Why?" Patsy asked.

"I'll tell you all about it once I get a drink." She picked up my bingo card. "What's this?"

"Bad Bubba Bingo," I said. "Patsy and I amuse ourselves with it when we go out."

"And what's that?" Mary Bennett said, pointing to our martini glasses.

"Try some," Patsy said, offering her a drink. "Jeff, the bartender here, he made it up. It's a Revirginator—in our honor."

Mary Bennett raised an eyebrow. "Hmmm, very tasty. I'll get one after y'all explain."

"It's been a while since our last booty call," I said.

"A looooong while," Patsy said, taking a sip of her drink.

"Because it's been forever since our forests have been trod upon, so to speak, we figured we've reverted back to being virgins. This drink is symbolic of the return to our unsullied state."

"Like a virgin," Patsy sang, running her fingers up and down the buttons of her dress, "touched for the very first time."

"Hmmm," Mary Bennett said. "I'm sensin' a smidgen of hostility toward the opposite sex?"

"It's far more than hostility. It's a healthy-size and burgeoning loathing," I said.

"Men suck," Patsy said, happily. "I only need BOB."

"Who's Bob?" Mary Bennett asked.

"BOB stands for Battery Operated Boyfriend," Patsy said, nearly knocking over her drink.

"Known also as PIG. Plug-in guy," I added, and both Patsy and I went into a fit of hysterics.

"Stop," Patsy said, trying to control her laughter. "I gotta go to the ladies', I'm about to PIMP."

While she hurried to the restroom, Mary Bennett turned to me. "Pimp?" I explained it was shorthand for Pee In My Pants. "Well, our little Swiss Miss is acting more like Sloshed Miss, and you're hardly Miss Clean and Sober yourself. How long have you two been at it?"

"On Valentine's Day, I prefer to start at sunrise, but actually not that long today. We're really just getting cranked up, we ain't drunk—just a little bit silly," I said with a hiccup.

"Seems our little Yankee has joined your she-woman man-haters club."

"Why not? Every worthy man I know is either married, gay, or dead. And believe me, it doesn't take us long to fill up these bingo cards around here."

"I hear ya, hunny. But I'm just not sure this is the healthiest tack for you or Patsy to take."

"Who died and made you Dear Abby?" I asked.

"Ooooh," Mary Bennett said, drawing back. "Was there some Tabasco in your drink?"

"Sorry. That *was* a little testy. But you don't know how many Big Bad Bubbas there are in this town."

"Hunny, I live in Hollywood, the dickwad capital of the world. If you think garden-variety jerks are bad, wait until you meet some rich-and-famous ones."

"Point taken," I said. "It's just been a rough couple of years. When I finally got the nerve to get back on the bike, all I got was flat tires and rusty chains. When you're creeping toward your forties, there is *nothing* out there."

Mary Bennett nodded. "You're preaching to the choir."

"The irony is everything in my life is going *great*, except my love life. I can't get it all together."

"Getting everything to go well at once is like trying to stuff an octopus under the bed. One leg's always flopping out."

"Speaking of love life, do you ever hear anything from Brian?"

Mary Bennett jutted out her lower lip. "Just from reading *People*. Supposedly he's still happily married to his co-star."

"That was a relief," Patsy said, as she wandered back to the table.

"Glad everything came out all right, Swiss Miss," Mary Bennett said. She squinted in the direction of the door. "Here he is. Our very own HueyAnn Lewis."

Gerald strode to us, dressed immaculately and sporting a lapel pin with the pink feline logo of the one social action group he finally succeed in organizing: the Pink Panthers, dedicated to the furtherance of any and all gay causes everywhere, all the time. He had no trouble recruiting members—Gerald was cute, the pins were cute, and the meetings provided ample opportunity for dressing up cute and bitching. Gerald was still seething most of the time, but his constituency didn't seem to notice or care.

"Hi everybody," he said as he sat down. He noticed Mary Bennett in her turban and glasses and said, "I'm sorry. We haven't met."

Mary Bennett looked over her glasses, winked, and said, "It's me, Geraldine. Incognito."

"Well, it's certainly an effective disguise." He wrinkled his nose at our Revirginators. "Barbaric women." Looking up at the waitress, he said, "A Kir Royale, please."

"Good lord, Jill," Patsy said, listing slightly to the left, "do you think there is a faggier drink on the planet than a Kir Royale?" I allowed as how I doubted it seriously. Our attempts at levity fell on the deaf ears of the two we were trying to levi-tate.

"It's been a while, Gerald," Mary Bennett said with forced politeness after she gave her order to the waitress. "How are you?"

"Tired," Gerald said, brusquely. "I'm trying to coordinate a fund-raiser for the AIDS hospice, and all the Pink Panthers want to do is have a big drag show so they can prance around like big ol' girls. I spend most of my time trying to shout them down, and you can't even IMAGINE what THAT'S like."

"Sounds like that new group of yours is a pretty fun deal, in spite of the leadership—a vast improvement over that whole Ignorant Asshole concept you had going earlier," Mary Bennett said, lighting a cigarette.

"I read the morning's paper," Gerald said, ignoring her comment. "Your picture was on the front page." The waitress set a drink in front of him. "Thank you," he said.

Patsy and I swapped a look. Now Mary Bennett was ignoring HIS comment—they were both talking, but neither one was answering or listening to the other. We watched in morbid fascination, but without much hope for a pleasant outcome.

"Have you quit the show?" Gerald asked. "Not that I watch it—it comes on during my P.A.B.A. meeting. You'll be happy to know that ALL the Pink Panthers watch it religiously, although mostly for the fashion tips, I expect. I understand your character is a complete and total BITCH—however DID you get that part?"

"Well, Geraldine, you'll be glad to know that Electra Frostman is no more. I'm back to being plain ol' Mary Bennett Manning."

"Why?" I asked. "You were the most reviled TV star in America. People loved to loathe you."

"Yes. As much as I relished people yelling 'bitch' at me when I walked down the street—oops, sorry Gerald—it was time to get out," Mary Bennett said. "Plus, there was something else." She paused, toying with a straw on the table. "It's my daddy. He's dying. I came back home to take care of him."

"Oh, no! I hadn't heard that he was sick—I am so sorry. Is there anything we can do?" I said. Patsy and Gerald murmured similar sympathies. Gerald squirmed uncomfortably in his chair. "I didn't think y'all were speaking." Mary Bennett never stayed with her father when she came to Jackson—not since he'd cut her off financially for dating Brian.

"We've talked a time or two over the years," she said. "We're far from close. Still, he doesn't have anyone else, and even a son-of-a-bitch like him shouldn't have to die alone."

"What's wrong with him?" Patsy asked.

"Brain tumor," Mary Bennett said. "He has some lucid days but barely recognized me when I stopped by tonight. There's a full-time nurse looking after him. She'll take care of his physical needs. I'll just be there as family."

"I'm thrilled you're back, even if it is under such shitty circumstances," I said.

"I might be here indefinitely," Mary Bennett said. "I don't have anything on my plate for a long time."

"I'm glad you're gon' be here for a while," I said. "It's just a little over a month until St. Paddy's Day."

"I'll come for the parade, but not to Hal and Mal's after," Gerald said, mopping up a wet spot on the table with his napkin.

"Why not?" I asked. Gerald had become more disapproving of the parade festivities as it had gotten larger and rowdier over the last two years—"useless frivolity," he called it. "I promise, no one will puke green beer on your shoes like last year."

"It's not that," Gerald said. "I have to leave right after the parade to attend a seminar," he said, pulling out a brochure from the pocket of his sports jacket and handing it to me.

"Gay Guerrilla Warfare," it said. I guess our expressions said it all. Gerald said he wanted to learn new political and civil disobedience tactics in hopes of inspiring the Pink Panthers to become more aggressive.

"Sounds pretty grim," Patsy said with a shrug.

"You aren't seriously going to go through with this?" I said, dropping the brochure on the table as if it were nasty or burning.

Gerald swiftly picked it up and tucked it back into his jacket with a flash of his now-chronic anger. "I certainly am. I can't go on living like this—flitting through life as if there isn't oppression and death all around me. I've got to DO something about it. I've got to . . ."

"Gerald," I said, gently. "It probably won't even work. I don't think your Pink Panthers are gonna want to chain themselves to anything that doesn't involve Judy Garland. They don't strike me as the angry mob type."

"And why would you want them to be?" Patsy said. "Why do YOU want to be? We thought you were perfect before . . ." She stopped short of saying what we were all thinking: "before William died." Mary Bennett kept her mouth shut, but she looked just as concerned as Patsy and me.

"How can you say that?" Gerald said, his chin shaking. "I taught silly kids stupid shit they didn't need to know—nothing that mattered, nothing that made a difference in the world."

"We're not trying to be contrary," I said. "We love you and we're proud of your achievements and your teaching—you were, too, back then. We're worried about you right now. You're really mad—a lot—and we don't understand it. We think the Pink Panthers CAN do a lot of good, and make a real difference, but this gay guerrilla thing is gonna be bad for them."

"Very bad," Patsy said with a nod of her head. The serious nature of our conversation had sobered her up completely.

"Being gay is what's bad for me!" he said, blowing his nose into a tissue. "It's ruined my whole life." He sprang from his chair. "Excuse me a minute."

"Can somebody explain to me what the hell is happening here? Why's Gerald so mad? Why does he want the Pink Panthers to be gorillas—it's *way* too hot here for gorilla suits and I really don't think his crowd will go for 'em. And now he doesn't even want to be GAY anymore? Can you QUIT?" Patsy was indeed nonplussed, as were me and Mary Bennett—completely nonplussed, not a plus among us to be had.

"I'm fresh out of ideas," I said, my drink suddenly tasting sour in my mouth. "I guess we can't always fix things in each other's lives. God knows I've tried. I certainly couldn't convince Tammy not to move to England."

"Maybe you weren't meant to," Mary Bennett said. "Bob is

remarried and happy as a clam. Tammy's running around with blue bloods, just like she always wanted."

"I guess so," I said. "She never invites us to visit. It's weird. I think she doesn't want anything to do with us anymore. Tammy's over *there* and Gerald's lost his mind—the Queens are falling apart before my very eyes."

Chapter 24

"Damn, woman, that was one hell of a workout," Mary Bennett said, rubbing her biceps. "You're almost as tough as Fredrick, my trainer in Hollywood. What a sadist! He'd drag me kicking and screaming out of bed every morning at five. Threw medicine balls at me. Made me lift weights until my eyeballs bugged out."

"No pain, no gain," I said, tying my running shoe as I sat on the weight bench. At ten a.m. Adonis Gym was nearly empty.

"Fredrick wasn't into pain. He was into torture," Mary Bennett said, rummaging in her purse. Out came a MoonPie, which she unwrapped and wolfed down in two seconds flat.

"I can't believe you just did that," I said, my mouth hanging open.

"Excuse my manners." She licked her fingers. "I should have offered you a bite."

"That move, missy, just canceled out your entire workout."

"I can't help it. I've been depri-i-ived living in California. Just try to find you a decent blue-plate lunch out there—they ain't got a collard nor a grit to their name. All they got is 'nouvelle cuisine'—which means 'just enough food to really piss you off.'"

"Do you really think you might stay in Jackson for good?"

"The South's in my blood. I've missed *everything* about it! Big wraparound porches. People saying 'hey' or 'mornin'' when you pass by. And magnolia trees! I'd trade twenty of those scrawny, narrow-ass palm trees for the cool, delicious scent of one big, fat magnolia."

"Which reminds me. We need to cool down." I grabbed the back of my calves and started stretching.

"Just pour a bottle of Evian on me and I will be plenty cool," Mary Bennett said, not budging from her mat on the floor.

I tugged on her arm. "No wonder Fredrick had to be a sadist."

Joey Monroe, another personal trainer, paused on the way to the locker room.

"Jill, your delts are looking good."

"I've been working on 'em. That exercise you showed me did the trick. I see *you're* making progress on your biceps—quite a set of guns you got there."

"Gittin' there." He then noticed Mary Bennett, who was still sprawled stubbornly on the floor. "Sorry. I didn't mean to interrupt your session."

"I think this one is over," I said, scowling at Mary Bennett. "My client is being remarkably disobedient."

Joey laughed. "That's why I always carry a cattle prod. Works every time."

I introduced him to Mary Bennett, who finally rose off her duff to shake his hand.

"A couple of us are meeting in the juice bar around five," Joey said. "You game?"

"Not today." I waggled my hands at him. "I'm getting a manicure after work."

"Another time. Nice to meet you, Mary Bennett."

"Who was that sack'a diamonds?" Mary Bennett said after he departed. "He could trap my zoids any day of the week. And why the hell would you give up a rendezvous with him for a freakin' manicure?"

"I've neglected my cuticles."

"I think there's *other* parts of your body you've neglected. And the way ol' studmuffin was looking at you, there's no doubt that he'd be *de-lighted* to attend to 'em."

"Not interested," I said, twisting my torso back and forth. Just because Mary Bennett wasn't cooling down didn't mean I couldn't.

"And pray tell, why the fuck NOT? He's a cutie pie."

"There's no chemistry."

"Hunny, if there's no chemistry with that, your Bunsen burner's busted."

I stepped forward into a lunge position. "Joey doesn't do it for me."

"Supposing it was Richard Gere who wanted to meet you for juice. Would you turn *him* down?"

"He's not my type," I said, reaching my arms skyward. "Too much of a pretty boy."

Mary Bennett grasped my elbow. "Jill, hunny, I think you better stop cooling down. You're already an iceberg."

"If you like Joey so much, *you* go after him," I said, pointing in the direction of the showers.

"Maybe I will."

I noticed a piece of paper on the floor near the weight bench, and knelt to pick it up. "What's this?"

It was a page from *People* magazine: "Big Trouble on the Set of *Yours and Mine.*" I started reading. "'Sit-com cutie Stacy Williams gets quickie Dominican divorce and leaves co-star and hubby Brian Landers in a lurch.'"

"That's mine," Mary Bennett said, snatching it out of my hand. "It musta fell outta my purse when I got out that damn MoonPie."

"It's about *your* Brian."

"He ain't *my* Brian—he hasn't been that for a long, long time."

"How interesting! He's free. You're free. Maybe after all this—"

"You read too many romance novels. I don't even know why I tore that stupid thing out." Mary Bennett balled the article up and threw it into the trash. "Come on, I want a drink."

We went into the juice bar and climbed up on stainless steel stools. Mary Bennett planted both elbows on the counter. "Barkeep. Pour me your strongest."

"That would be our wheatgrass shake," said Randy, a babyface kid right out of high school.

"I'd rather eat dirt—at least it'd be chewy," Mary Bennett said with a scowl.

"How about a glass of guava juice?" he stuttered.

"We'll both have spring water." I ushered Mary Bennett to a table. "Don't worry," I whispered to her. "I have a flask of Jack in my gym bag. In case of emergencies."

Mary Bennett gave me a weak smile. "That's one of the several million things I like about you. Always prepared."

"This is a full-service operation."

Our water arrived and I poured a few fingers of bourbon into Mary Bennett's glass.

"Daddy's losing ground every day," she said after drawing on her drink. "Sometimes he thinks I'm some old girlfriend of his named Toots. You should hear him sweet-talk me. 'Toots! You're the only woman I've ever loved!' The old fart still won't stop flirting. Women and wine, that's all he ever cared about."

"I know it's been hard between the two of you over the years," I said.

"It ain't any easier now," she continued. "On his good days, the man's a slave driver. For breakfast, his eggs must be soft-boiled and served over toast points. Every afternoon he wants the entire *Wall Street Journal* read to him. Thank God, he falls asleep before page two. The only reason I'm running myself ragged is out of respect for my mama's memory. She loved him, even though I never saw him shed a tear when she died."

"Is there anything the Queens can do?"

"Nah. I've got hot-and-cold running nurses. But thanks for asking. His doctor says he doesn't have much longer. I am actually meeting with the funeral director tomorrow. No more about Daddy Dearest. Anything new?"

"I'm still fretting over Tammy. I sent her three letters recently, and I haven't heard a peep from her."

"She ignores my letters, too, the hussy," Mary Bennett said with a frown. "Hey! Why don't we call her right now? Is there an office we can use? I have a calling card."

"I've tried, but no one ever answers."

"No harm in trying again."

We went into the assistant manager's office, and I looked up the number in my address book and dialed.

"It's ringing," I said, the phone pressed against my ear. Foreign phone rings always sounded so tinny.

"You've reached an out-of-order line," said a recorded voice in a crisp English accent. "Try your connection again."

"No good," I hung up. "The phone is on the blink."

Mary Bennett tsked. "We can't phone Tammy. She doesn't answer our letters. Short of flying our asses over there, I don't know what else we can do."

•

"I'm feeling lucky tonight," I said, rubbing my hands together as I tossed Patsy a bingo card. "I've added another category. Men with comb-overs." I scanned the crowded pub for candidates. "Check out the guy leaning on the jukebox."

Patsy shook her head. "I don't really feel like playing tonight."

"No wonder," I said, pointing to her drink. "You haven't touched your Revirginator."

"I don't feel like drinking, either," Patsy said, pushing the glass away. Her cheeks were flushed, and I noticed she'd taken special pains with her makeup. "Something happened today."

"What's up?"

"Remember that guy I told you about who's commissioned portraits for practically every member of his family, including his great-aunt Gertrude? Well, today he told me he was only doing it as an excuse to get to know *me* better."

"Typical Guy Shit!" I cried out. "That's TGS for ya'. Sneaking around, not letting women know what he's really up to." I took a big gulp of my drink. "I hope you told him to go to hell!"

"Not really," Patsy said, squirming in her chair. "I . . . I . . . I actually thought it was kind of sweet. And I was wondering if you'd mind if I left early so I could meet him at the Sizzler. His name's Earl."

I swiped at my face with a napkin. "You have a *date?*"

"Sort of," Patsy said with a shrug.

"What about Jack and the way he stomped on your heart?" I demanded. "You were a mess for months. Are you *really* willing to put yourself out there again at the risk of having your fingers slammed in the car door of lu-u-uv?"

"We're just going to have supper."

"Go ahead," I said, waving her off. "But you're going to miss one hell of a bingo game. I just spotted a guy with butt cleavage sitting at the bar."

"I'll call you later." She got up to leave, but I pretended to be too busy with my bingo card to say good-bye.

I ended up playing a little longer, but it wasn't much fun by myself. Eventually I paid my tab, and on my way out, tossed the bingo cards in the trash. A tall Tom Selleck look-alike stood by the exit.

"Leavin' so soon?" he said with disappointment.

"You must be a psychic." My voice dripped with sarcasm.

He chuckled. "Aren't you feisty? Don't suppose I could talk you out of leaving? I'd like to buy you a drink."

I hesitated. His manner was sweet, and he was definitely easy on the eyes.

"No thanks," I said, finally deciding I wasn't in the mood for boy-girl games.

"Too bad. What do you want to bet we have something in common?"

"Sorry," I said, pushing open the door. "I'm not the gambling type."

Chapter 25

I wore a Santa Claus hat and stood in front of the Piggly Wiggly, ringing my bell. People averted their eyes as they neared. "Tightwads!" I shouted, and rang my bell even harder.

My eyes flew open and I discovered I was not at the grocery store but tangled up in the covers of my bed. The digital clock blazed red with the godforsaken time of three a.m., and the phone on my bedside table was ringing so loudly that it jarred loose my remaining brain cells. I fought my way out of the sheets, knocked over a glass of water, and grabbed the phone.

"Did I wake you?" Mary Bennett said.

"It's okay—had to get up to answer the phone anyway." I searched for the lamp switch and in the process, turned over everything. The lamp broke into what sounded like a hundred different pieces. Mary Bennett didn't even comment.

"Daddy's gone. Would you mind coming over?"

"Oh, hunny—I'll be right there."

•

Mary Bennett's house blazed with light when I pulled up into the drive. As I stood on the porch waiting for her to answer the door, I noticed my pajama top was misbuttoned and I was wearing an aerobics shoe on one foot and a running shoe on the other. I hadn't bothered to brush my hair, so my shadow looked like Medusa's. The only thing I'd done before leaving my house was squirt toothpaste on my finger, and I used it as a toothbrush while driving over.

"Hey," Mary Bennett said, surveying me as she opened the door. "I hope you didn't get all gussied up just for me."

Mary Bennett's hair was pulled back into a sleek ponytail, her khakis were sharply creased, and her face shone as if she'd taken a scrubbing brush to it.

"I don't know why I called," Mary Bennett said, motioning me inside. "Everything's taken care of. The funeral home picked him up a couple of hours ago. The maid washed and changed his sheets. I knew this was coming, so everything's been done."

I followed her into the kitchen, where Patsy and Gerald were slumped over cups of coffee. A puffy-eyed Patsy grunted a greeting. Gerald, his cheeks prickled with whiskers, acknowledged me by pushing out the chair beside him with his foot. Suffice to say, except for Mary Bennett, the Queens weren't morning people.

The table held a huge tray filled with an assortment of pastries and croissants. I poured a cup of black coffee to yank myself out of my predawn fog.

"When a person dies, you're supposed to call *somebody* besides the coroner," Mary Bennett said, leaning against the kitchen counter.

"You did the right thing calling us—we're family. We want to be with you for this," Patsy said. The coffee was already working its magic. She was sitting upright in her chair, and the pillows underneath her eyes were beginning to flatten out.

"That's just it," Mary Bennett said. "I'm not upset. I was such a Daddy's girl when I was real little, but I didn't have much of a relationship with him after Mama died—he was just absent, whether he was here or away. We *were* closer at the end, but that wasn't the Daddy I remembered. That was just the shell of him after the tumor took its toll."

"Maybe we could help call relatives or friends," Patsy offered in a drowsy voice.

"There's nobody really," Mary Bennett said. "Just a string of women who likely wished him dead over the years. Daddy didn't have any friends, just acquaintances and business associates, and I'm sure they'll come out in droves once they read the obituary. Nothing brings out Southerners like a funeral."

"There has to be something we can do to help," I said, warming my hands around the coffee cup.

"No. But there's something I want to share with y'all." She left the kitchen.

"I'm glad to see you came, Gerald," I said with a smile.

"Mary Bennett asked me to be here," he said with a shrug. "I don't know why. My presence is completely unnecessary."

"Why do you say that?"

"Mary Bennett said it herself," Gerald said derisively. "Everything's under control. She doesn't need us. Her daddy's death hasn't affected her the least bit. It's always 'easy come, easy go' with Mary Bennett. I don't think she has a sentimental bone in her body."

"You're not being fair," Patsy said. "She wasn't close to her father."

"She's not close to anyone," Gerald said with a snort. "It's all on the surface with her. You don't know her like I do. She has about as much depth and sensitivity as Formica."

"You keep saying that, Gerald, like you know something about Mary Bennett that we don't," I said. "It's fuckin' time to clear the air. I think you're wrong about Mary Bennett. She has plenty of feelings. She just keeps things locked up inside her—" I clammed up when I heard Mary Bennett's feet on the stairs.

She came back into the kitchen carrying a bulging shoe box.

"Y'all, I have to tell you, the most amazing thing happened with Daddy—this morning—right at the end. I thought at first he was having a flashback, but then I realized he was totally lucid for the first time in days. I had fallen asleep in my chair with my head on the side of the bed. I was dreaming that I was a little girl—and Daddy had come in to wake me up from my nap. He called me Monkey. That was his nickname for me when I was little. I hadn't heard the name in years, but I'd never forgotten it. He was stroking my face, saying, 'Wake up, Monkey—your Daddy loves you so.' And I woke up—and he was stroking my face and saying those words and he was looking at me as clear-eyed as he ever did in this life and I looked right back at him and said, 'Oh, Daddy, your Monkey loves you so!' And he squeezed my hand and was gone. I don't know—somehow it just *fixed* something in my heart."

After the group sob subsided a bit, somebody asked her about the shoe box.

"I found these in the attic," she said. "There are dozens of them filled with letters." Mary Bennett opened the box and withdrew a letter. "Here," she said, handing it to me. "This one says it best, I think."

"Dear Toots," I started to read aloud. "Another year without you, and the pain doesn't get a bit easier, no matter how many drinks I take or how many women I sleep with. Monkey can't understand why I act the way I do, or why I can't bear to be around her. She's a young lady now and she reminds me too much of you. I'm a weak man. Forgive me my failings." I folded the letter and gave it back to her. "Your daddy wrote this?"

"Yes." Mary Bennett nodded. "Hundreds of them. A few within the last few months. All to my mother after she died. He never got over her. Toots was his nickname for her. I didn't even know that."

"Did you have any idea how much he grieved for her?" Patsy asked.

"Not a clue. He never talked about her," Mary Bennett. "The way he behaved with all those women, I just assumed he didn't miss her."

"Why did you want us to read that letter?" I said gently.

She fixed her eyes on Gerald. "You're the main reason. When I read all those letters to my mama, I realized that I'm more like my daddy than I ever wanted to admit. They were a real eye opener."

"Go on," Gerald said.

"I know you don't think I missed Brian. My way of showing I 'miss' someone is just like my daddy's. It started in high school when I chased after every boy in sight just to forget that my daddy never paid any attention to me and to hide how much it hurt."

"You missed Brian?" Gerald said. His tone was extremely skeptical.

She bit her lower lip so hard it drew a spot of blood. "Very much."

"Quit acting, Mary Bennett," he said coldly. "This isn't a fuckin' TV show. Jill said we should finally clear the air, and I agree."

Mary Bennett winced. "I have no idea what you're talking about."

"If you won't tell them, I will," he said coldly. "Mary Bennett lo-o-o-oved Brian *so MUCH* that she gave him up for her career."

"What?" Mary Bennett said, drawing back.

"Oh, please. Don't play innocent," Gerald said. "Brian *called* me. It was the night before Valentine's Day, about two in the morning, before our first St. Paddy's parade. Brian said that you were up for a huge part. He said you'd have to choose, him or the role, because the studio didn't want their star to be married to anybody—not as much fodder for the tabloids, they like to have the press following their stars around, speculating on who's doing what with whom. They might have been amenable to a big-deal real estate tycoon or a famous plastic surgeon, but they really saw no media value in her being married to a down-and-out actor (which Brian was at the time). 'What will she do?' he asked me. I said, 'I *know* Mary Bennett, she'll choose you.'" He shook his head. "Boy, was *I* ever wrong. Next thing I heard, you were cast as Electra and Brian was history."

"No!" Mary Bennett cried. Her complexion was completely drained of color. "This is the first I've heard of this."

"What do you mean?" Gerald asked.

Mary Bennett's face was twisted with distress. She took a moment to compose herself. "The night before Valentine's Day, Brian and I were invited to a party at a director's house. I knew I was in the running for the part of Electra, and I assumed the party was a way to check me out one last time. In the middle of the party Brian started drinking heavily, and he continued after we got home. I ended up going to bed without him. The next morning, Brian told me he didn't love me anymore and he wanted me to move out. I begged him for an explanation but he refused. He never said one word about the studio."

"What?" Gerald said, not looking nearly so sure of himself.

"Brian's phone call to Gerald doesn't make any sense. If I was ever offered a choice between getting the part of Electra and being with Brian, there'd be no contest," Mary Bennett said with vehemence. "I loved Brian more than anyone in this world. Much more than any stupid part."

A thought occurred to me. "Was Brian ever alone with your director that night?"

"Sure," Mary Bennett said. "He took him on a tour of the grounds. Why?"

"That's your answer," I said.

"Wait a second. Do you mean to say—?"

"Yeah. I think your director told Brian he was standing in the way of your getting the part," I said. "You never knew about the choice, because Brian decided for you."

"Oh my God," Mary Bennett said, her shoulders heaving. "Oh my God! I can't believe . . . all these years . . . I never guessed." Her eyes welled up, and she collapsed into tears. It was the first time any of us had ever seen Mary Bennett cry.

"Mary Bennett." Gerald's face crumpled with shame. "Can you ever forgive me?"

Her answer was to throw her arms around him and weep loudly into his chest. Patsy and I hung back. Gerald and Mary Bennett were locked in an embrace for a very long time, well after she'd stopped crying. They were making up for seven years.

•

Mary Bennett's dining room table groaned with so many casseroles it threatened to turn into a pile of splinters.

"I swear, is there anything better than funeral food?" I said, scarfing my fifth deviled egg.

"Nope," Gerald said as he put away his second hunk of Miss Mildred's famous banana upside-down cake. "Miss Mildred has outdone herself this time—this cake is KILLIN' ME."

"Too bad someone actually has to die for us to get it. Miss Mildred only bakes for funerals these days," Patsy said. There was a smidgen of chicken salad on her upper lip.

"We should open a place called the Rest in Peace Restaurant and only serve funeral food," I said. "We'd make a fortune, is all I'm saying."

"We'd be waddling all the way to the bank," Gerald said, filling his plate yet again. "In a bit, let's lounge by the fire and plan the menu for the Rest in Peace, and the outfits for the wait-staff—perfect relaxation exercise, talkin' 'bout clothes and food."

"Thank y'all for coming! Keep in touch!" Mary Bennett was at the front door, seeing off the last guests from the funeral.

Her pumps clip-clopped on the glossy hardwood as she entered the dining room. She wore a black wool dress and gold earrings, looking every bit as chic as Jackie Kennedy.

Earlier, Mary Bennett had delivered such a beautiful eulogy, everyone in the church thought Charles Manning had been the most doting father in the history of the world, living or dead. She'd seemed at peace with herself afterward, and looked ten years younger. Who knew forgiveness could be just as flattering to a woman's face as having a little work done?

During a rare quiet moment before the funeral, I asked her what, if anything, she was planning to do about Brian. She said she didn't know yet. Between her daddy's death and healing her rift with Gerald, she was trying to corral her thoughts and emotions.

"I hope there's some goddamn fried chicken left," Mary Bennett said, and I knew all was mostly right with the world.

"Lord's name in vain?!" Gerald cried, covering his ears.

"Sor-ry," Mary Bennett said. "I hope there's some fucking fried chicken left."

Both Patsy and I were so glad to see Mary Bennett and Gerald acting like their old selves, we smiled until our faces hurt.

"You know what's missing?" I said.

"I sure as hell do," Mary Bennett said. "Red Jell-O with those tiny, mini marshmallows. It's not a proper funeral spread without it."

"I was thinking of Tammy," I said. "All the Queens are living back in Jackson except for her."

"I have been studying on that very thing," Mary Bennett said, snapping a napkin open. "Do you know how long it's been since the Queens have been out of pocket?"

I'd almost forgotten that expression. Back in high school, whenever we went on a road trip in the Tammymobile, we'd called it being "out of pocket."

"It's high time for us to take a vacation," Mary Bennett said. "We could go to England and pay Tammy a surprise visit."

"Sounds great." I grimaced. "Too bad I gotta earn a livin'."

"I'm not sure this is a good time for me to be away from the Pink Panthers—those bitches are plotting something behind my back. I just know it's some kind of big drag show," Gerald said, twitching his nose. "Here I'm trying to make a serious impact on the AIDS crisis in Mississippi and if I left for five minutes, I'd come back to find all of them prancing around in ball gowns, boas, and tiaras."

"I'm way behind on my work," Patsy said. "I could never get away."

"None of y'all are so fucking busy that you can't spare a week to go on a free vacation to Great Britain!" Mary Bennett said, waving her fork. "Think of this! Four-star hotels and meals.

Gorgeous scenery! Fabulous nightlife. And best of all, I did say 'free,' right? This is my gift to you. I am footing the en-tire bill."

"Well, if you put it that way," I said. "I *suppose* I *could* do a little rearranging of my schedule."

"Have y'all forgotten my fund-raiser?" Gerald asked.

"Of course we haven't," Mary Bennett said. "We'll be back in plenty of time. This trip will give us some excellent rebonding time. Knowing your proclivity for groups with acronym names, I am proposing that we form a group in our own honor, and this trip to reclaim Tammy as our own, Q.U.E.E.R.—Queens United for the Evolution of Everlasting Relationships," she said with a flourish. "I've already had the T-shirts made. Give it up—you're going."

Gerald's face lit up at the mention of the T-shirts—the man clearly loved an acronym. "Well, I suppose an inaugural out-of-pocket trip is in order for the charter members of Q.U.E.E.R. I *love* it!"

"I'd have to find a babysitter for Mack, and I'd be too far behind in work when I got back," Patsy said. "Besides, I'm seeing this guy named Earl, and he and I—"

"Don't make me play the dead daddy card, Swiss Miss," Mary Bennett said, pointing a chicken wing at her.

"Well, I've always dreamed of going to London," Patsy said, knowing it was pointless to argue further. "And of course, I'd love to see Tammy again."

"It's settled then," Mary Bennett said. "I'll just give my travel agent a 'ringy-dingy,' or whatever it is that they say over there."

•

Two days later we were at thirty-five thousand feet on a 747 bound for London.

"Do you see Big Ben yet?" Patsy asked, a few minutes after

our pilot announced our descent into Heathrow. This was also my first trip to London.

"I can't see a thing," I said, my nose smooshed against the window. The city below looked intricate and unusual, like the inside of a transistor radio. As the jet descended, things became intelligible. A series of tiny colorful squares became a full parking lot. A moving red blip turned into a double-decker bus.

The cabin came alive with the rustles and stirrings of the passengers in anticipation of landing.

"We're here!" Mary Bennett said as we jounced along the runway. I glanced out the window. This particular view of England didn't look altogether jolly. It seemed pretty wet and mostly gray.

Once we cleared customs, we picked up our rental car. Gerald had spent a little time in London so he volunteered to drive.

"Land's sakes alive," Patsy said, opening the door to a blue Peugeot. "Someone has goofed up big time at the auto factory. This car is defective."

Gerald chuckled. "That's not a mistake. In London they drive on the left side of the road, so the steering wheel is on the right."

"That's four-plus crazy," Patsy said, shaking her head. "I thought the only difference between England and America is England is run by a queen."

"Which we approve of mightily," added Mary Bennett.

"There's more differences than you would expect," Gerald said. He opened the trunk and started tossing our suitcases inside. "The trunk is called a boot, and the hood is a bonnet. The British call gas petrol and they sell it by the liter, not the gallon."

"What are these called?" Mary Bennett said, pointing to the wheels.

"Tires," Gerald said, wiping his hands together. "Not everything's different."

We arrived at our hotel just as the dining room closed for lunch.

"There's a pub 'round the corner, if you're feeling peckish," the desk clerk said.

"We ain't peckish," Patsy said. "We're starvin'."

After we'd settled in our rooms and freshened up, we all met in the lobby and strolled to a pub called The Frisky Friar.

"I heard the weather in London was gloomy," I said, shivering as we stood in the entryway of the cozy building, "but I'm frozen. I can't feel my toes."

A waiter, holding aloft a tray of gold-hued ales, smiled at me. "Keep your pecker up," he said brightly. "This beastly weather is supposed to take a turn for the better."

Mary Bennett made a face and I shrugged.

We settled in a comfortable booth near a crackling fire and were offered menus.

"You know," Patsy said, as she perused hers, "when I was looking at guidebooks, there was not a single mention of the English's obvious obsession with penises. First someone asks if we're peckish, then the waiter tells us to keep our peckers up, and now they're serving spotted dick on the menu." She tossed it aside. "I do believe I am losing my appetite."

"What in the world's a toad in the hole?" I said with a frown. "I have a powerful hankering for a big wad of bacon, but I don't see it here."

"Bacon is called rashers and French fries are called chips," Gerald said with amusement. He almost seemed like his old self.

"I don't understand why these Brits don't speak American English," Patsy said, shaking her head. "We whupped their butts in the war, after all."

"Try to keep that keen observation to yourself," Mary Bennett said drily as the waitress returned with pints for everybody.

•

"So what's the plan of action?" I asked.

"I'd like to stay in London for a couple of days, then drive to the Cotswolds to Belmont Manor and pop in on Tammy," Mary Bennett said.

"I hope to hell she and James aren't off jet-setting somewhere," I said. "It would suck not to see her."

"She *has* to be around," Patsy said. "We've come all this way."

The next two days we toured London. We visited Harrods and found it to be far grander than Macy's ever thought about being. We took in a Mary Cassatt exhibit at the National Gallery, and saw the crown jewels at the Tower of London. While Gerald gathered info on the local gay activist groups, the girls had high tea at our hotel, where we discovered that the tea was Earl Grey instead of Luzianne and the biscuits definitely weren't the kind you served with flour gravy. Buckingham Palace wasn't open to the public because it was winter (we were hoping for a glimpse of Di or, at the very least, Fergie), but we did walk around Kensington Gardens.

On the third day, with Gerald at the wheel, we made our way to the Cotswolds region.

"It's like a postcard around here," I mused, as we passed through scores of tiny villages filled with stone cottages, cobbled courtyards, and tidy gardens.

"We're looking for a town called Upper Slaughter," Gerald said to Mary Bennett, who had the map unfolded on her lap.

"Better Upper Slaughter than lower, I suppose," Mary Bennett said with a smirk.

We took a wrong turn, so Gerald stopped at a petrol station to find our bearings. I spotted a telephone and said, "I'm going to try Tammy one more time. Maybe we'll have better luck now that we're in her neck of the woods."

I got out of the car and slipped some coins into the phone. After a few rings, there was a click, and to my delight, Tammy answered.

"Tammy!" I said, excitedly. "This is Jill. It's so good to hear your voice."

"Jill? Oh my goodness! It's been so long. I know I haven't been very good about writing lately. I'm been so incredibly busy."

"I've tried calling, too. This is the first time I've been able to get through to you."

"Yes," Tammy said with a sigh. "We're in a very small village, and the phones aren't always reliable."

"You aren't going to believe this! The Queens and I are HERE—we've been in London and right this minute, we're only about an hour away from you. We hadn't heard from you in so long, we decided to just track your ass down and surprise you!"

There was a long silence on the other end, and I wondered if I'd lost the connection.

"Tammy, are you there?"

"I'm here," she said in a faint voice. "I'm afraid you've picked a dreadfully inconvenient time to come. James and I were just on our way out the door to visit Lord and Lady Amherst in Derbyshire. They're having several couples in. We've planned it for weeks."

My heart sank. "We've flown all this way just to see you. Couldn't you put off your trip for a couple of hours?"

"I can't. James would be in a snit, and we're supposed to ride with friends because our Bentley is on the blink," Tammy said, with a little bit of an English accent.

I was so stunned and so deeply disappointed I could scarcely speak.

"Have a good time," I managed to choke out. "We really have to keep in better contact. All of the Queens miss you so much."

"I'm terribly sorry, Jill," she said, curtly. "But I really have to ring off now."

I hung up the phone and trudged back to the car, where the Queens had the map spread out, plotting their route to Upper Slaughter.

"Might as well forget the whole thing. Tammy won't be there," I said as I got back into the car.

"What's going on?" Mary Bennett said, craning her neck from the front seat.

"She's flitting off to some party with a bunch of lords and ladies. She didn't seem the least bit pleased we were here," I said. "The only reason she hasn't been answering our letters is because she's been too busy social climbing. I was worrying for nothin'."

"Are you sure?" Patsy said, practically in tears. "I can't believe she wouldn't want to see us."

"Tammy always wanted to be one of the beautiful people," I said, pierced through the heart by her dismissal of us. "Now that she's finally gotten it, she doesn't need us anymore."

I tucked the gift I'd brought her under the front seat so I didn't have to look at it. It was a photograph album filled with the pictures of the Queens I'd collected over the years.

"I'm with Swiss Miss on this one," Mary Bennett said. "That just doesn't sound like Tammy. Maybe we pissed her off."

I didn't want to believe it either. I'd spent more time with Tammy than any of the other Queens. I'd saved her life when she'd taken sleeping pills, and she'd stopped me from losing all my money to Ross. I'd ridden out all her affairs over the years. I'd assumed the bond between us was invincible, but apparently I was wrong.

"She was so cold on the phone, I'm surprised the receiver didn't sprout icicles," I said. "We might as well head back to London."

"We don't have reservations in London," Gerald said in a dejected voice. "Why don't we stay the night in Upper Slaughter like we planned? We'll just have a nice time without Tammy. It's supposed to be a quaint village."

"Whatever," I said, staring out the window and wiping away tears. What I really wanted to do was to head straight back to Jackson.

The drive was quiet. All the Queens were brooding about Tammy. I alternated between fury and despair.

As soon as we got to Upper Slaughter, a bit of sunlight peeped through my pall of darkness. I couldn't help but smile at the string of honey-colored, ivy-patched cottages, and the sleepy stream that wound its way through the village like a silver ribbon. It was as if we'd been transported to a fairy-tale land. I half expected it to be populated with elves, gnomes, and hobbits.

The other Queens seemed similarly enchanted. They tumbled out of the car as soon as it stopped at our hotel. We were staying at the Horse and Hound Inn, a homey structure with a slate roof and dormer windows.

My eyes eagerly cataloged the details around me. A man on an ancient creaking bicycle clattered across the cobblestones, his red wool scarf trailing in the wind. A woolly sheep ba-a-ahed from behind a hedgerow.

"This *really* feels like England!" I said. London, as different as it was from Jackson, still had many familiar aspects of a city. Upper Slaughter, on the other hand, was like stepping into a completely different universe.

We checked in and then settled into the restaurant for a late lunch of Scottish eggs and some beer.

Afterward, Patsy and Gerald opted for a nap underneath their feather-bed duvets, and Mary Bennett and I bundled up in down coats and mittens and took a hike around the village.

"Now I understand why people love to travel," Mary Bennett said, as we paused to study some crumbling remains of a medieval castle. "New sights and smells wash your mind clean for a while. Lifts you from the old ruts."

I had to agree. In the car I'd been twisted up with thoughts of Tammy, but for these moments I felt completely removed from her.

"It's happening with Gerald," Mary Bennett said. "He's letting go of some of his rage. He seemed almost happy when he came in from that last gay-guy meeting. I've been wanting to have a talk with him, and I think the time may finally be right."

"What do you want to talk to him about?"

"I'm thinking differently, too," Mary Bennett said, ignoring my question. "I just called Brian and left a message on his machine. I told him he could reach me tonight in the Cotswolds, or tomorrow night in London."

"What did you say?"

"Just that I had been thinking about him." She paused for a minute. "I also might have thrown in a little something about how I never stopped loving him."

"I hope he calls you back," I said.

"Me, too," Mary Bennett said. "I've never been so nervous about anything in my life."

We crossed a footbridge and passed a ruddy-cheeked Englishman. He tipped his herringbone touring cap to reveal a wavy head of glossy dark hair.

"God save the queen," Mary Bennett whispered after he passed. "I wouldn't toss him out of bed for eating kippers."

"He looked shifty-eyed to me," I said, wrinkling my nose.

"Some ruts, on the other hand, are deeper than others," Mary Bennett said, giving me a sideways glance.

"I'm not in a rut," I said quickly. "I'm being particular."

•

The next morning was drab and gray, tempting me to linger in my cozy nest of linens. But thoughts of a steaming mug of hot coffee coaxed me out of bed. I dressed quickly, planning to shower later. The Queens were supposed to meet for breakfast in an hour to plan our next excursion. There was no point staying on in Upper Slaughter if Tammy wasn't around.

I left my room and headed for the café. I heard the squeak of wheels behind me and a voice—a voice I knew as well as my own—calling out, "Miss, do you need any more towels?"

I abruptly turned around and there behind me, garbed in a peasant blouse and black skirt, was Tammy—wheeling a maid's cart down the hall. When she recognized me, her body tensed and I expected her to bolt. I could almost see the gears of her mind turning, struggling to come up with an explanation. Her shoulders drooped in surrender when she realized the jig was up.

I, on the other hand, was so delighted to see her familiar pert nose, green eyes, and abundant red locks, I let out a whoop that was likely heard all the way over in Lower Slaughter.

"Tammy!" I said, tears pouring from my eyes as I opened my arms to her. "I've missed you so much."

Over two years of carefully constructed artifice fell from her face.

"Oh Jill," she said, receiving my embrace. "Thank God you're here. Take me home, please."

•

The Queens couldn't stop talking or eating. We were tearing through a huge English breakfast of deviled kidneys, honey pancakes, kedgeree, coiled wild boar sausage, black pudding, farm-smoked bacon, bread rounds, freshly churned butter, fruit preserves, eggs, baked beans, sautéed field mushrooms, and grilled tomatoes. We didn't know what half the stuff was, but we ate it with a vengeance anyway.

"I cried all night last night after we spoke," Tammy said,

wedged between Patsy and Gerald in a booth at the hotel's restaurant. Gerald kept patting her hair and stroking her cheek as if he couldn't believe she was real.

"I wanted so badly to see y'all, but somehow I couldn't bring myself to admit the truth about my life."

The truth, as Tammy spilled it out in one long, tearful confession, was that everything had gone wrong since she'd set foot in Great Britain.

Although James was indeed a lord, he was nearly penniless. What money he did have was squandered on gambling and drinking. She didn't actually live in Belmont Manor (it had been turned into a hotel twenty years ago, when James's family fell on hard times) but instead resided in a drafty and crumbling gatehouse adjacent to the property. Phone service came and went because James frequently drank away the bill money.

"When the heat got turned off, and we practically froze the first winter, I decided to get a job at the Horse and Hound," Tammy said.

James, with his nasty habits and surly attitude, was shunned by the British peerage and rarely invited anywhere. All the hobnobbing with royals Tammy had written about in her letters was pure fiction. People assumed she was as lowdown as James and as a consequence, she had few friends.

"I was never going to be Lady Tammy," she said. "The only title I've ever had was 'the wench who shags James.'"

"I don't understand," Mary Bennett said. "Why did you keep quiet about this? Why didn't you tell us?"

"I wanted to, many times, but I'd already lied so much! I wasn't sure you'd want to associate with me after all my bullshit," Tammy said, her chin drooping to her chest. "I also felt like I *deserved* what I got. I'd left a wonderful man and the best friends anybody ever had in the world. For what? Selfishness, pure and simple. And the idea of being 'somebody.' She gazed across the table at me, her eyes shiny with tears. "But then I ran into Jill in the hall . . . and when she saw me, she seemed so *glad* to see me—just plain old ME. Just one look from her, and I knew it was possible that she might forgive everything. And I knew for the first time in my life that if I'm with y'all, that's the best 'somebody' I could ever hope to be. I can't believe y'all came all this way to find me—thank God you did!"

"That's what you do for the people you care about," I said softly. "You love 'em no matter how badly they screw up."

"I'm afraid to ask," Tammy said, stirring her coffee with a teaspoon, "but I have to know. What's happened with Bob?"

"Are you sure you want to know this now?" Gerald said, stroking her back.

"Yes," she said. "I really want to hear."

"He's married to a very sweet lady," I said quietly. "He also has a baby girl, Hannah."

Tammy didn't speak for a moment, just nodded her head absorbing the news. "Good," she said, after a moment. "I'm glad he's happy."

A tall woman in a maid's uniform with braids crisscrossed atop her head approached the table. "What do you think you're doing, love? This isn't break time. Are you looking to get sacked?"

"I'm having a spot of breakfast with my family," Tammy said with her faux English accent. "And no, I'm not looking to get sacked, because I quit. I am a Queen, and the Queen is returning to her Court!"

•

After breakfast, we drove to Tammy's cottage and helped her pack up her meager belongings. A bloated and snoring James was passed out cold on a couch in the living room and didn't stir once while we were there. Tammy scribbled a brief note saying she was leaving him and never coming back. She stuck it in the fridge near his beer so he wouldn't miss it.

"If I never have another steak-and-kidney pie, I will die happy," Tammy said in the car on the way back to London. "Soon as I saw that mess on a menu I shoulda known I'd fucked up."

"It's all about the food for you, isn't it, Tammy?" Gerald said, smiling so wide his cheeks looked like twin cherry tomatoes.

"She ain't the only one," Mary Bennett said. "Hollywood was bad enough. Never again will I live anywhere with no grits and gravy."

"One more night in London and we'll be on our way back to God's Country," I said. "We need to have a kick-ass celebration tonight before we leave."

"Well, I was going to go to a rally for a gay political candidate, but I suppose I could skip it," Gerald mused.

"Did I hear correctly? Is our little gay guerrilla mellowing a bit?" Mary Bennett asked, smiling her signature shit-eating grin.

"Well, maybe," Gerald said. "This will be the first full meeting of Q.U.E.E.R. I really shouldn't miss that."

"Okay, Gerald—it's now or never for this. Now that we're all together, I've got something to say to you. None of us has understood why you have been so pissed off since . . ."

"You know I don't want to talk about that, Mary Bennett." Gerald's face once again flushed with that all-too-familiar fury.

"Well, we're GOING to talk about it, so just shut the fuck up," Mary Bennett commanded. "We couldn't understand why William's death has made you so . . . so MAD. And so I did a little digging."

Mary Bennett found out that back in San Francisco, Gerald and William had been in a car wreck. Gerald was essentially unscathed, but William was nearly killed. He had to have a blood transfusion, and that's how he contracted HIV.

"I believe that you felt guilty that he was hurt and you weren't—he got AIDS and you didn't, he died and you're still here and you don't think you deserve it—and it's gotten all twisted up inside you and you're just fucking pissed off at the world because of it. That's what I think. Am I wrong?"

The tears flowed freely from all our eyes as we reached out to Gerald, who had begun leaking tears at the first mention of William's name and was now heaving with great sobs.

"It's time to let yourself grieve, hunny—and to be happy you're alive," Mary Bennett said with loving firmness. "We thank God every day we've still got you. And I believe there's a way to do something positive—to make a difference in the world—without cutting off everybody's heads and shittin' down their neckholes!"

"Have I really been that bad?" Gerald asked, snuffling.

"WORSE!" we all shouted.

"All those hateful group names you make up—all that gay go-rilla stuff—you're so mean to the Pink Panthers, I can't believe they keep coming back," Patsy said. "Pretty fucking scary shit, hunny."

His grief finally allowed to vent, Gerald thanked Mary Bennett and all of us for loving him in spite of it all.

After all the tears were dried, the mood in the car was as sparkling as champagne. It felt grand to have all the mysteries solved and, more important, to finally have us all back together again. We were, in fact, Queens United for the Evolution of Everlasting Relationships.

Chapter 26

I can't believe I had four Revirginators." Gerald moaned, holding his head.

"It's a good thing we were all together—after three of 'em, one tends to DE-virginate," I said.

"The barf bag's tucked in the seat in front of you if you need it," Patsy said. "After last night, the city of London won't be forgetting the Sweet Potato Queens anytime soon. I think Mary Bennett is the only one whose head isn't throbbing today."

Mary Bennett didn't respond. She had her face pressed up against the plane window, but the only thing that could be seen at this altitude was the blank whiteness of the sky. She'd been mighty quiet the whole flight. Brian hadn't returned her phone call.

"Who knows?" I said, in an attempt to cheer her. "You might have a message waiting for you at home."

"I know Brian," she said without turning to look at me. "If he was going to call, he'd do it right away."

"Maybe he's out of town and he didn't get—"

"If he was out of town he would have called to get his messages. His sitcom was canceled, so he's back to being an unemployed actor. His phone is his lifeline."

There didn't seem to be anything else I could say to mollify her, so I plumped up my puny little airplane pillow, hoping to saw a few logs before landing.

It seemed like only moments until the pilot announced our descent into Atlanta. The long flight and the over-the-top boozing and bingeing the night before had pretty much waxed our asses. We sleepwalked our way off the plane and stumbled through customs.

We boarded our flight to Jackson, and a short time later we were back on our home turf.

As we approached the baggage claim, there were several people holding hand-lettered cardboard signs. They were an alert bunch compared to the sluggish passengers they were meeting. One sign caught my eye, and I elbowed Mary Bennett, who was walking beside me.

"Get a load of that," I said. "Some yay-hoo's holding a sign that says 'true love.' I wonder who he's meeting?"

Mary Bennett's bleary eyes followed my pointing finger. Her mouth dropped open, and she immediately dropped her carry-on bag and coat and sprinted away. My glance traveled down from the sign to its holder.

It was Brian. When he spotted Mary Bennett flying toward him, I saw a look I'd never seen on a man's face before. It was the purest, sweetest, most uncomplicated expression of love I'd ever witnessed. His expression completely matched the message on his sign.

The two embraced, and I was so choked up I found myself trying to catch my breath. The other passengers must have sensed this was no ordinary reunion, because several of them broke out in spontaneous applause. All the other Queens were crying. As I watched Mary Bennett and Brian hugging the life out of each other, I felt a flutter in my chest. The shell I'd built around myself over the last couple of years developed a hairline crack. Maybe there was something to this true-love stuff after all.

Chapter 27

"We're going to need waaaay more padding in the boobs and butt, Clyde," I said as I studied one of the emerald green Sweet Potato Queen costumes he'd constructed. "I want people to see us coming from a loooong way off, and I want 'em to remember us coming and going."

"More stuffing coming up, sugar lump," said Clyde as he plucked a straight pin from his mouth. "You'll be so dazzling, the masses will simply be struck dumb by the sight of you."

"The more attention, the better," I said, holding up a costume next to my body as I looked in a mirror.

I'd finally gotten over my lifetime aversion to the color green. I was light-years away from being the Jolly Green Giant. In my to-die-for Queen costume, I would be the Glittering and Gorgeous Green Giant.

"I almost forgot," I said. "This year we're having a special consort to the Queens. He'll ride on the float with us."

"Who's the lucky boy?" Clyde asked, carefully hanging up one of the Queens' costumes on a long rack in the back of his shop.

"Brian. He's Mary Bennett's fiancé. They're getting married in a few months. She told me she's coming to see you later on this week to talk about designs for her wedding gown."

After Brian met Mary Bennett at the airport, they immediately took up where they'd left off. He moved into Mary Bennett's house, and the two of them were as giddy as goats in clover.

"What's your vision for the Queens' consort?" Clyde asked. He was impeccably turned out in a pair of Italian leather pants and a tight silk shirt that showed off his whippet-thin physique.

I pressed my fingers to my temples. "I see a gold lamé smoking jacket with a green hankie poking out of the pocket. Nothing too swishy. Brian's a man's man. Oh! I almost forgot. Gerald's coming over in a few minutes to be measured for his costume."

"Right. You want him in a vest in the same fabric as the Queens' and a green cummerbund. What do you think about a matching green top hat to complete the ensemble?"

"You're a genius!" I said, pecking his cheek. "Thanks to you, the Queens will be more titillating than ever before."

"Thank you, sweetie, but frankly you Queens are so fabulous you'd look darling in flour sacks," Clyde said, which, of course, was the main reason I'd hired him to make our costumes. Besides being a genius with fabric and a Singer, he instinctively knew there was no such thing as too much sucking up.

The bell above Clyde's door jingled, and Gerald strode in with a book under his arm. His mop of frizz had been trimmed and moussed within an inch of itself, and he was tan and happy and mighty handsome.

"Hi, Gerald!" I said. "Come on to the back."

"Hi, hunny. Hope I'm not too late. I was two doors down at the salon and—" He stopped talking as soon he as spotted Clyde.

"Gerald, this is Clyde," I said. "He's making the costumes this year."

"Are you reading *The Road Less Traveled*?" Clyde asked, pointing to Gerald's book.

"Yes. I usually have to wait in the salon and all they have is hairstyling magazines, so I thought—"

"'Life is difficult. This is a great truth, one of the greatest truths,'" recited Clyde, hand pressed against his heart. "When I read those first lines in the book I nearly swooned. I said to myself, 'Scott Peck gets it and he *gets* me!'"

"I had the exact same feeling," Gerald said, eyes filled with wonderment. "It was as if he was speaking directly to me."

"Have you read *Way of the Peaceful Warrior*?" Clyde asked, exhilarated.

"Not yet, but I heard it's worthwhile," Gerald said.

"Omigod! If you think Peck's on the money, then you *have* to read Millman. Your life will be transformed!"

"I'll get it today," Gerald said softly. "May I ask a personal question?"

"PLEASE!"

"Are you a friend of Dorothy?"

"Guilty." Clyde stared at Gerald as if transfixed.

Pheromones were flying in the shop like Roman candles on the Fourth of July. It was time for me to beat feet on outta there.

"I guess I'll be moseying along, then," I said. "Clyde, I'll drop by in a couple of days for the final look-see. Y'all have fun." I might as well have been elevator music for as much attention as they paid me.

•

"I can't get over how big it's gotten," Tammy said, marveling at the crowds of people buzzing around our float, which now sported a fourteen-foot papier-mâché sweet potato wearing a green-and-pink-polka-dot bikini and a giant silver crown.

"Everyone wants to be a Queen," I said. "They come from miles away. They beg, bribe, and bawl their eyes out, wanting to be one of us."

"I'm so grateful you didn't give away my spot," Tammy said.

"A few Wannabes were working overtime for it, but I knew in my gut you were coming back to us."

Tammy donned her rhinestone sunglasses. "I don't know why I chased across the fucking ocean trying to get a title when I've been royalty in Jackson all along."

"A Sweet Potato Queen is the best kind of queen to be," I said, checking my coat of Revlon's Love That Pink lipstick in a compact mirror. "You get all the glory and none of the bullshit."

A woman wearing a leather jacket and skirt strode by, menacingly wielding a loaf of French bread.

"SPQ Security," I said. "Wait until you see the crowds. We have so many fans now we need protection."

"Queens! Gather 'round for a final costume check!" called out Clyde from a small temporary tent that had been put up exclusively for our use. Over the years we'd become the runaway stars of the St. Paddy's Day parade.

Tammy and I went inside. Clyde was making a final adjustment to Gerald's tie. Gerald was giddy and positively beaming. I knew there was something going on between them, but Gerald hadn't said boo. I figured he'd tell us when he was ready.

"Look at my dashing man," Mary Bennett said as she entered with Brian, who was fairly stunning in his gold lamé jacket.

Patsy followed behind, saying, "My tits are just about to leap out of my dress."

"Come here, kitten," Clyde said. "I have some double-side tape that will reign those babies back. Turn, everyone! Let me have a look at you."

"I was talking to a group of Wannabes who came all the way from Maryland just for the parade," Mary Bennett said. "They started their own Queen group called the 'Crab Queens,' and there's a group from Plano, Texas, calling themselves the 'White Trash Lingerie Coconut Queens'; the 'Raspberry Queens' are from about six states; the 'Reel Divas'—their motto is 'Whip me, strip me, tie me, fly me,' they all like to fly-fish, get it? And have you seen NuClia Waste? Hunny—you cannot miss HER, she's on STILTS, pulling an inflatable alligator, 'Gaytor,' in a wagon!"

"That is fuckin' amazing," Tammy gushed. "Jill, you really oughta write a book about the Queens and this parade."

"A book? Get real—just 'cause I managed to get a few columns published doesn't make me Jackie fuckin' Collins," I said.

"That mealymouthed bullshit won't fly anymore, Jill," Mary Bennett said. "We all know damn well that you can do anything you set your mind to."

"That's for sure," Patsy chimed in. Gerald was too busy being turned into a MoonPie by Clyde to comment.

I threw up my hands. "It's such a helluva burden being Boss Queen. Plan the parade. Design the costumes. Write a book. Will it never end?" But while I was ranting, I was also thinking a book wasn't such a half-bad idea after all. Didn't the whole world deserve to hear about the Queens?

"You look *de-vine*!" Clyde said. "Time for places!"

The Queens and our swashbuckling consort all marched out of the tent (except for Gerald, who was likely lingering for a last-minute smooch) and made our way toward the float.

"Queens!" A very stout blond woman waved and waddled over to where we were standing.

"Can I help you?" I asked.

"I've been hearing many outrageous things about y'all," the big woman said. "You're the talk of the town."

"Yes," I said with a haughty little yawn. "I suppose."

"I was wondering how *I* could become a member. I just think y'all are precious."

"Join the Queens?" I said, clutching at my chest. "That's impossible."

"You have to be born a Sweet Potato Queen," Tammy explained. "The only way a position opens up is if one of us dies. And then you'd have to be a Wannabe first, and bow and scrape your way in."

"Couldn't I skip the Wannabe part?" the woman said, chins a-jiggling. "I'm Marcy Highsmith. My husband's quite prominent in Jackson."

We were so dumbfounded we nearly toppled over like bowling pins.

"Well," I said stroking my chin. "I knew a Marcy in high school. Did we happen to be in the same class?" It seemed as if Marcy wanted us to believe that she didn't remember the Queens from high school.

"It's possible," Marcy said. "I went to Peebles High School and graduated in 1969."

"Oh, well, that makes a *huge* difference," I said.

"Goody! I'm so glad to hear it," Marcy said. "I *was* popular in high school."

"Well, hunny, I just BET you've heard that ol' sayin'—you know the one about THAT was THEN and THIS is NOW," I said, bearing down on her short, squatty self. "The Marcy Stevens

I knew in high school was the most black-hearted, name-calling, snoot-ass skank who ever trod the earth."

"That was eons ago," Marcy said with a flippant wave of her hand. "Surely after all these years—"

"After all these years, you ain't any more popular on THIS float than you were way back then," I said. "Where's Patsy? Patsy!"

"The Boss Queen has spoken!" Tammy said with a flawless hair toss.

"Why not let bygones be bygones?" Marcy continued. "I'll even start off as a Wannabe, if you insist."

"Security!" Mary Bennett shouted. A phalanx of woman carrying loofahs, Nerf bats, and bread sticks immediately charged in our direction. I pointed my scepter at Marcy a.k.a the Heifer from Hell.

"My husband will help pay for the costumes!" Marcy said, just before she was swallowed up by the leather-suited SPQ Security squadron—but not before Patsy appeared on the scene.

"Patsy!" I exclaimed gleefully. "You remember Marcy Stevens, don't you?"

The evil gleam in Patsy's eyes answered in the affirmative as she said, "Why, hello, MARCY!" She turned to assume launch position, and suddenly Tammy hunkered beside her. "I've waited my whole life for this, Marcy Stevens! Here's what I think of you and your whole fucking KEY CLUB!"

Marcy was last seen fleeing the scene with her hair and ears slicked back from the blast. Howling and high-fiving broke out on the float at the spectacular return of Queen Poot—and the Final Revenge of Tammy—and all truly seemed right in the Queendom this day.

"I've got pictures! I've got pictures!" Danged if it wasn't Darla Hopkins, who had captured our first assault on Homecoming Bitch Marcy back in high school. Darla was in full

Queenly regalia, including a sequined camera bag. We dubbed her PhotoQueen and named her O-fficial Photog to the Sweet Potato Queens—for life.

"Come, Queens!" I said when we finally quit laughing. "Our subjects await."

A couple of Spud Studs were standing by to help us onto the float. As the others climbed up, a grinning Gerald emerged from our tent and joined us.

"Nice hair," I said sarcastically.

"Oops," he said with a blush as he attempted to rein in his tousled mop. "I suppose you've guessed by now that there's something going on between me and Clyde."

"I had my suspicions," I said.

He smiled shyly. "I think I might be in love again."

"Oh, darlin', I'm so happy, I could just squeeze your guts out," I said, drawing him into a hug.

"After William died I didn't think I'd ever be able to laugh again, let alone love again. But I was wrong." He paused. "Guess what else?"

"What?"

"I've decided to let the Pink Panthers have their drag show. It was Clyde's idea—to honor William, who did love the occasional dress-up, as you know! It's gonna be a PAGEANT—we're calling it 'The Night of the Hundred Gowns.' Contestants will pay an entry fee and we'll sell ads in the full-color program. The winner will be crowned Empress for the entire YEAR—she'll win a gorgeous crown—and all the money will go to the Grace House AIDS Ministry."

The best part of this deal was that they wanted the Sweet Potato Queens to be the judges. We both squealed in delight and did a major happy dance, causing the float to pitch and roll alarmingly—getting the attention of the other Queens, who then, of course, joined in the squealing happy dance so that we were nearly thrown from the float by the force of our own exuberance. Perfect.

"Gerald, hunny, go get Clyde—we need all our sistahs with us on this float today," I said.

"Really?" Gerald said, eyes lighting up.

"Hey, y'all!" Mary Bennett hollered. "We need to practice our routine!"

"Go get Clyde and join the others," I told him. "I have a little sumpen to take care of."

I motioned over a Spud Stud named Steve and whispered in his ear.

"I'm not sure if there's enough time for that," he said. "The parade's going to start in a few minutes, and—"

I pulled him closer and whispered a little something else.

Steve's face took on an almost ethereal glow.

"Right away," he said, taking off to do my bidding, leaving Ked marks in his wake.

I took my place in the center of the float as Boss Queen and my court flanked me on either side. It felt grand to have all the Queens back together again. We were bebopping around like a bunch of June bugs from the sheer thrill of it.

A few minutes later, a winded Steve appeared at the float. He handed me a cassette tape and a cold bottle of Dom Perignon. "I hope I got what you wanted. I flew to the record store so fast it felt like my Chevy was on fire. I nearly ran over a guy in the liquor store parking lot. Is there anything else I can do? You can just name it and claim it, baby!"

"Thank you, sweetie," I said, tossing him a wink. "But I think everything's under control now."

Mary Bennett, who'd been observing the whole interaction, sidled over to me. "What's up with the slave boy?"

"I had an errand for him to run. He dragged his feet at first, but then I made him a little *promise*."

Mary Bennett hooted. "The Promise! I had forgotten about it. I don't think I've used it since high school."

"Me either," I said with a wicked grin. "Figured it was high time to dust it off. Turns out it's as potent as ever—I guess blow jobs never go out of style."

"Time to roll," yelled out the driver of our truck.

"I made a little last-minute change in the music," I announced to the Queens, slipping the cassette into the player. "Hope you don't mind."

"No 'Tiny Bubbles'?" Tammy said with a pout.

"It'll come later. This is a little somethin' special for this occasion. First, a quick toast—this is truly OUR day, Queens," I said as they all put a hand on the bottle and joined me. "HERE'S to US!" we shouted with unbridled joy. "And FUCK *everybody else*!" And we really did mean it as we passed the Dom bottle around the float.

The unmistakable whiskey voice of Delbert McClinton boomed out of the speakers: "GIVIN' IT UP FO' YO' LOVE—EVERY DAY—I'M GIVIN' IT UP FO' YO' LOVE RIGHT NOW!"

Mary Bennett grabbed Brian around the waist and said, "Hunny, they're playing our song!"

"It's for ALL of us!" I shouted as the float once again rocked and rolled with ecstatically dancing Queens.

"Perfect choice," Tammy whispered, and then she added her own clear, strong voice to Delbert's, and I thought, "Uh-huh—and that's our NEXT Queenly project: getting your happy ass back on a stage with a microphone, little Missy."

I looked out into the mass of spectators, who seemed positively stupefied by our newly enhanced costumes. Was it possible that somewhere among all those worshipful onlookers there was a man for me?

My entire life I'd been looking for Prince Charming and taking home toads.

Obviously, I'd been setting my sights too low. Toads—and even Princes—just weren't going to cut the mustard anymore. They were too weak-willed and wet behind the ears. I needed a MAN. One strong enough to appreciate and celebrate the Queen I'd finally grown up to be. Until that man came, I was going to keep on living and loving my own life and I wasn't going to settle for anyone else, no matter how scared, tired, or needy I happened to be.

Some day my king will come, I thought to myself. For the very first time, I thought I might be willing to let it happen.

Recipes from the Rest in Peace

I simply cannot offer you a book from which you cannot expect to gain ten or fifteen pounds—it just wouldn't be right. So here you go, Queenies!

If me and the Queens were to open our ideal restaurant, we would call it the REST IN PEACE, and we would only serve food that you might (and would certainly hope to) find at the home visitation after any decent Southern funeral. I know that you (like us) get tired of sitting around WAITING for somebody to die just so you can get something wonderful to eat. At the Rest in Peace, our customers will be able, at any time, to drop by for some Southern comfort whether anybody's died or not.

The Queens occasionally like to gather 'round with this kind of food and contemplate all the folks we sometimes WISH would die—I expect you will enjoy this innocent pastime as well. COME AND GIT IT! (That's y'allbonics for *bon appétit.*)

WHO CROAKED? CROCK-POT PORK

If you've got a big enough Crock-Pot, you can double up on this, and if there's a morsel left, it freezes great. It's yummy over rice (especially if you cook the rice in chicken broth instead of water), and it's supposedly got only about 8 grams of fat per serving, not that we give a shit.

Into the Crock-Pot dump: one 16-ounce can whole-berry cranberry sauce; 1 medium onion, chopped; one 5.5-ounce can apricot nectar; ½ cup Splenda; ½ cup chopped dried apricots; 2 teaspoons white vinegar; 1 teaspoon dry mustard; 1 teaspoon salt; and ¼ to ½ teaspoon crushed red pepper (I like it spicy, but that's just me). Stir all that up pretty good and then put about a 2½-pound boneless pork loin roast in there and spoon the sauce over it. It's even better if you put it all in the fridge overnight to marinate, but it's sufficiently wonderful without that step. Cover and cook on low for 6 to 8 hours. It will be literally falling apart and you will be bathing in the sauce. It is so gratifying to put this on to cook in the morning and then to come in and see what the Crock-Pot hath wrought in your absence.

PROMISED LAND PASTA SALAD

Okay—me and my precious neighbors, Laura and Angie, made this up. Well, we didn't make up the WHOLE thing, but the part we did make up sure does make it even MORE fabulous than it is in its original state and we are taking total credit for the transformation and that's just that.

The basic foundation for the Promised Land is this: 4 cups (or so) cooked pasta—rotini or something else fairly substantial—we like to CHEW; one 4-ounce jar pimientos, drained; one 2-ounce can sliced black olives (also drained); ½ cup (or so) chopped onion; ¾ cup Splenda; ½ cup white vinegar; ¼ cup Enova oil (you can use canola, but this is so much healthier, so why not?); and ½ teaspoon crushed red pepper. So, you just stir all that stuff up together—the good thing about Splenda is that it dissolves instantly in cold stuff, so you don't have to fool with heating it—and then stir it all into the pasta. It needs to sit a spell in the fridge and then you'll need to stir it all up again real good before you eat it. I know it sounds awful, but trust me—it ain't. BUT THEN, what WE do is this: same thing pretty much except omit the chopped raw onion. Now, chop up a bunch of asparagus and 1 or 2 Vidalia onions and the best tomatoes you can find (cherry or grape will do if tomatoes aren't in season) and toss 'em with a little oil and throw 'em in a grill basket and grill 'em up. Obviously, the asparagus and onion will need a little while, so hold off on putting the tomatoes in there till the last few minutes. When you add the tomatoes, also add some pre-grilled chicken breasts, chopped up in bite-size chunks. You just need the tomatoes and chicken to get hot—they won't take long. Then sling all that into the bowl of pasta with the other stuff and stir it up. This is TOO GOOD to serve to most people you know, so be VERY particular about who's invited over.

TINY BUT POWERFUL GRIEF-RELIEVING MEAT LOAVES

Not only is this the best meat loaf EVER—and by the way, as far as I'm concerned, the ONLY reason to make meat loaf is for meat loaf SAMMICHES, which will make me feel better no matter what—but you can also have these meat loaves IN YOUR BELLY in a little over 30 minutes. Now, I call that downright miraculous and a boon to all mankind.

Mix an egg with a little bit of milk. Chop up about 1½ stalks celery, half a bell pepper, and an onion. Mix all that with 1 cup bread crumbs, the egg and milk, and about 1½ pounds ground sirloin. I like to put some salt in it, too, but that's just me—I'm a salter.

In another bowl, stir up 1 cup barbecue sauce, ½ cup salsa, 1½ tablespoons Worcestershire sauce, and ¼ teaspoon ground red pepper (and a leetle bit of salt). Take half of that mixture and stir it into your meat stuff.

Put about ½ cup meat mixture per hole in a big muffin pan (mini meat loaves!) and paint the tops with the rest of the sauce. Bake 'em at 450°F for, like, 18 to 20 minutes. How great is THAT?! Meat loaf usually takes forfuckingEVER. These little buggers will freeze great, too, given the opportunity.

BOYS 'R' US BEANS

We call 'em that 'cause a friend of ours who's got a husband and about a hundred little boy-type chirren gave us the recipe. Everybody—even little boys—will gobble up these beans, and you can use canned ones, which is so easy and who cares if they're not as good FOR you—we're only interested in taking care of our DISPOSITIONS here.

Melt together 1 stick butter (always a good start), ¾ cup dark brown sugar (you can use the brown Splenda—can you tell I just LOOOOVE Splenda?), 1 tablespoon soy sauce, and about a teaspoon or so of chopped garlic. Mix all that up and stir in 2 drained cans green beans. Put a whole bunch of nice crispy crumbled-up bacon on top and cover the dish with foil and bake it at 300°F for about 45 minutes. You won't even care that this actually IS a green vegetable.

JEWISH BARBECUE

Queen Susan got this recipe from a wonderful woman named Phyllis, who, during Susan's particularly rancorous divorce proceedings, declared herself to be Susan's much-needed Jewish Mother and brought her this "barbecue" to soothe her ravaged soul. Blessings on the House of Phyllis.

You just need one slab of brisket—NOT corned beef! And you put it in the Crock-Pot with a jar of Heinz chili sauce and a can of whole-berry cranberry sauce and let it sweat on low for 6 to 8 hours. We would follow Phyllis in the desert for close to forty years for this.

CHICKEN SHIT

Queen Jeanne of Pascagoula, Mississippi, shared this with me with her profuse apologies for the name. It seems that Jeanne had a girlfriend who would occasionally, after an evening of plentiful libations, crash on Jeanne's couch and, before taking her leave the following morning, scarf down whatever happened to be in Jeanne's refrigerator. Upon sampling it, she was quite taken with one of the fridge's occupants and left a note demanding the recipe for "that chicken shit." And the name just stuck—as is wont to happen. I told her I wouldn't DREAM of changing the name.

Mix together 3 or so cups cooked chicken, 1 can condensed cream of chicken soup (what is funeral food without Cream of Something?), ¾ cup sour cream, ½ teaspoon black pepper, and

¼ cup milk. Dump it all into a greased casserole dish and top with a couple of cups Ritz cracker crumbs and dab on some little hunks of butter. Bake for 30 minutes at 350°F. We find that Chicken Shit goes real nice with rice.

CAN'T DIE WITHOUT DEVILED EGGS

Can't live without 'em, either, in my opinion. Queen Nancy told me that once when they had a death in her family, her mom's best friend, Lucy, came over to field the phone calls from far-flung family and friends regarding the services and all. When Nancy's mom came in that afternoon, Lucy reported on who all had called and that, when asked, she had advised them all to bring deviled eggs to the visitation—all *of them—she told ALL of them to bring deviled eggs—because Lucy, like myownself, JUST LOOOOVES deviled eggs and she wanted to make sure they got some. They got about fifty dozen, which, in my opinion, is just about enough. I want Lucy on the job for the next funeral I'm involved with—unless it's my own, in which case I don't reckon I'll care too much what y'all have to eat.*

These are your basic deviled eggs and I don't care what you do to 'em, I'll EAT 'em—but I don't think they'll be any BETTER.

Hard-boil a dozen eggs. When they cool off enough, get the yolks out and mash up the yolks with 2 tablespoons sweet pickle relish, 2 to 3 tablespoons of Hellmann's mayo, and 2 teaspoons yellow mustard. Fill the whites with this goo and git outta my way.

MAKETH ME TO LIE DOWN IN MAC 'N' CHEESE

Queen Cherie H. just knows that nothing is more comforting than cheese . . . and pasta . . . and potatoes. It's just all too rare that we find all these elements in combination, and while we are perfectly capable of procuring and consuming them all separately, it's just so danged convenient to have 'em all corralled in one easy, yummy pile.

Cook a 12-ounce package of some kind of pasta—shells or rotini—something that will hold sauce well. And about that sauce—melt 1 stick butter and add ¼ cup flour, stirring briskly. Add 2 cups hot milk and 1 teaspoon seasoned salt and ½ teaspoon black pepper, stirring all the while, until it starts to thicken. Then add 1 cup (a great, big, overflowing one) shredded Cheddar and heat until the cheese is melted.

Fry at least 12 strips of bacon until crispy, then crumble. In at least some of the bacon grease, fry a chopped onion and 1 cup sliced mushrooms.

In a greased 13 by 9 by 2-inch pan, mix the pasta, the onion and mushrooms, the cheese sauce, and the bacon, and to that, add about a pound of shredded Cheddar or Monterey Jack and stir that up. And on top of ALL THAT, put as many frozen Tater Tots as will fit on there in a single layer! And sprinkle THAT with a fair amount of grated Parmesan cheese and then bake it at 375°F for around an hour or until it's bubbly and the Tots are crispy. Or, in a panic situation, you can bake it for about 40 minutes and then run it under the broiler for a bit to brown the Tots faster. This will serve about as many people as you can bring yourself to share it with—mine's a pretty short list.

Damon Lee's Divine Intervention

If we could hope to attain heaven on this earth, one of our key personnel would be chef Damon Lee Fowler. Damon Lee has an assortment of gorgeous cookbooks available all over the place and I hope you will avail yourself of them all—Damon Lee has his own plastic surgery fund to contend with, after all. But because of his great love for me and all Queens, Damon Lee has bestowed upon me some of his MOST Queenly recipes and is allowing me to share them here with you now. He has further agreed that, at such time in the future, we should actually OPEN the Rest in Peace Funeral Food Restaurant, he will come and be THE Chief Cook—we'll all be his Bottle Washers. Heaven truly sent him from above.

PASSION FOR PIMIENTO

Damon Lee believes, as do I, that pimiento cheese is PERFECT just the way it is, and we don't neither one of us take kindly to folks messing with it, in the name of "gourmet" or anything else. Damon Lee exhorts us to use the sharpest Cheddar we can find—and if we live outside of Wisconsin, we're pretty much screwed, but do the best you can. (You can add a little bit of REAL Parmesan—which will NOT come in a green container.) He says we should use orange Cheddar because it looks better. It's a natural vegetable dye and it's been in cheese for about two hundred years, so just get over it. Use real mayo. And don't put anything else in there—no matter what—except for maybe a little cayenne.

You'll need about 2 cups grated extra-sharp Cheddar, ½ cup grated Parmigiano-Reggiano, 5 to 6 heaping tablespoons mayonnaise, cayenne pepper to taste, and one 4-ounce jar diced pimientos, drained—but save the juice. Now, Damon wants us to mix this by hand—and by that he means WITH YOUR ACTUAL HANDS—a food processor will make paste, and a spoon won't moosh it together good enough—so wash up and dive in (think of the glorious licking to follow). Moosh away and add pimiento juice if needed for consistency—this is a personal judgment call.

BLESSED BACON BISCUITS

Damon Lee knows of our deep and abiding love for all things bacon and he concocted these morsels in tribute to Sweet Potato Queens everywhere. We love him almost as much as we love bacon.

Preheat your oven to 450°F and sift together 2 cups of soft-wheat flour (like White Lily, if you're in the South; perhaps cake flour will work if you're not—good luck is all we can say), 1 teaspoon baking powder, and 1 teaspoon salt. Cut in 6 tablespoons chilled bacon drippings (yum) until you've got pea-size lumps of dough. Make a well in the middle and pour in ½ cup milk. Mix it as LITTLE as possible—just until the dough pulls away from the sides of the bowl and is no longer crumbly. Use a tad more milk if needed.

Turn the dough out onto a floured board and pat out 'til it's ½ inch thick. Grind black pepper over the dough and fold it in half. Pat it flat again and pepper it again. Then pat and fold it two more times—but don't pepper it any more unless you're really into pepper.

Re-flour your board and roll or pat out the dough until it's about ¼ inch thick. Cut into a dozen or so biscuits and bake on an ungreased cookie sheet 'til brown—about 8 to 10 minutes.

I am thinking that a hot one would be pretty tasty with some of that 'minner cheese on it!

POTATO SALAD—REINCARNATED

Damon Lee is THE smartest man in the world, I swear. You know how when somebody dies, about a thousand people will bring some version of potato salad and although you love it more than air, there IS a limit, after all, and you end up with assorted wads of rotting potato salad in the refrigerator but you can't bring yourself to throw it out until it truly is totally rotten because (a) it was a gift and (b) it's potato salad? WELL! Damon Lee has GOT the answer—to this and so many of the world's problems—seriously, go buy his cookbooks! This is, like, a whole new WORLD of potato salad—and no matter how much potato salad you've eaten over the course of the visitation, you'll be ready for more when it's reincarnated.

Just take any and all leftover potato salad (BEFORE it rots) and dump it into a 13 by 9 by 2-inch pan. Melt ½ stick butter and then stir in 1 cup bread crumbs or Ritz cracker crumbs—or even potato chip crumbs (just omit the butter for these). Put the crumbs on top of the potato salad and BAKE it at 400°F for about 25 to 30 minutes and serve it hot. It's so good, you will just DIE!

Here's another little Damon Lee decadent delight: Make *real* popcorn—as in *not* microwaved. Put the hot popcorn in a paper sack and drizzle in a few spoonfuls of HOT BACON GREASE and shake it 'til your arms fall off. Then salt it a whole lot and eat it up. We do so love Damon Lee.

BEULAH LAND BOO-BOO PIE

Queen Jeanne got this recipe from a Queen in western Kentucky and it was called Boo-Boo Pie because the Queen who made it first apparently screwed up the original recipe (now lost to the ages and who cares?) and this is what she ended up with and it is mighty fine. I added the Beulah Land to it in honor of my daddy and his buddy Brooks Jones from Nashville. They loved ol'-timey gospel music and used to do a helluva rendition of "Beulah Land," with Brooks bellowing out the chorus, which went something like "I've FOUND the land of CORN and WINE and ALL I see is SHIRLEY mine," to the everlasting delight of me and my seester, Judy. We don't know any other words to that song—but we learned those real good.

Mix together one 7-ounce bag sweetened flaked coconut and one 14.5-ounce can sweetened condensed milk and set it aside—don't eat it, no matter how BAD you want to. Melt together 1 stick butter and 3 ounces (3 squares) unsweetened chocolate—you can nuke it for a few minutes, no big deal, just don't burn it. Then stir in ¾ cup sugar, ½ cup flour, 3 eggs, and 1 running-over teaspoon vanilla. Put all that into a greased 9-inch pie pan. Spread the coconut stuff over the top—but leave about a ½-inch border uncovered all around the edge, because when you bake it, the chocolate stuff on the bottom will come up and form a kind of crispy crusty thing for you—yum! Bake it for about 25 minutes at 325°F. And die happy.

COSMIC CLIMAX COOKIE CAKE

Courtesy of Queen Melissa—a crowd-pleaser for sure, if you give 'em any, that is.

Crush an entire 12-ounce box of Nilla Wafers and set 'em aside for a minute. Cream together 2 sticks butter, 2 cups sugar, and

6 eggs. Then slowly add, alternately, the mashed Nillas and ½ cup milk. Then add one 7-ounce bag sweetened flaked coconut and 1 cup chopped pecans. Bake it in a greased, floured tube pan at 275°F for 1½ hours. You'll be too fat but certainly happy enough to ascend directly unto heaven.

HEAVEN IS A PLACE CALLED HICKORY PIT

In Jackson, Mississippi, you can go to this little barbecue place and get some very fine sweet tea and all manner of excellent barbecue, BUT when you say the name of it, Hickory Pit, what EVERYBODY immediately thinks of—and craves—is their Hershey Bar Pie. It is truly To Die For and definitely From, if you overindulge.

Make an Oreo crust in a 9-inch pie pan with enough butter to hold the mashed Oreos together. Heat ½ cup milk and 15 large marshmallows in a double boiler until melted. Add 6 Hershey bars with almonds and stir until that's all melted together. Let cool and stir in ½ cup Cool Whip. Pour into the Oreo crust and chill overnight. Before serving, top with the rest of the Cool Whip and sprinkle with Oreo crumbs and either hide with it or expect to share a whole lot more than you'd like.

DELICIOUS DEATH DUMP CAKE

Lord, we do love a dump cake down here. There are umpteen variations on this theme and all of 'em are fabulous—poison, but fabulous. By poison, I mean that if you eat these cakes—and any other recipe you got from me—all the time, you will die. And you will die with a HUGE ass. However, that being said, it's all very good for your disposition and I like to think of that as my contribution to World Peace. So here, courtesy of Queen Trish, is one more dump cake.

Dump (hence the name) one box butter pecan cake mix into an 11 by 8-inch Pyrex dish. Dump a couple of 15-ounce cans crushed pineapple, juice and all, on top of that. Cut a stick of butter into little chunks and put 'em all over the top of that pile. Bake it at 350°F for about 30 minutes or however long it takes it to get kinda bubbly and crispy on top. And if you die from it, don't come whining to me about it: I warned you—it's poison.

As Queens, we make no bones about it, we KNOW HOW TO EAT. We love to eat, and whenever we can get away with it, we eat the most fattening crap we can get our paws on. We are not too proud to eat stuff made with Cool Whip and cream of mushroom soup—if somebody's mama made it and it's really yummy. If it tastes good, we'll eat it. We offer no excuses for our plebian selves. Queen Cherie G. from Pueblo, Colorado, wrote to tell me that her sister Diane is always nagging her about eating healthy—and Cherie staunchly resists. She claims she has eaten so many preservatives over the course of her life, she will most likely never die and, in fact, will remain ageless. However, should she be proven wrong and, in fact, die, Cherie G. good-naturedly suggests that her loved ones have her chemical-laden remains cremated out in the open—where she is likely to burn brightly with many varicolored flames, like that fancy stuff you can throw in a fire to create that effect. Truly heartwarming.